PRASE FOR HELENA

"Perfect for fans of Helen Hoang's . . . [a] snappy love story with high stakes and ple[nty] . . ."

—*Kirkus Reviews* on *Meet Cute*

"Bestselling Hunting's latest humorous and heartfelt love story . . . is another smartly plotted and perfectly executed rom-com with a spot-on sense of snarky wit and a generous helping of smoldering sexual chemistry."

—*Booklist* on *Meet Cute*

"Entertaining, funny, and emotional."

—*Harlequin Junkie* on *Meet Cute*

"Hunting is quickly making her way as one of the top voices in romance!"

—RT Book Reviews

"Sexy. Funny. Emotional. Steamy and tender and so much more than just a book. *Hooking Up* reminds me why I love reading romance."

—*USA Today* bestselling author L. J. Shen

"Heartfelt, hilarious, hot, and so much sexiness!"

—*New York Times* bestselling author Tijan on *Shacking Up*

"Helena writes irresistible men. I loved this sexy, funny, and deliciously naughty story!"

—*USA Today* bestselling author Liv Morris on *Shacking Up*

"Fun, sexy, and full of heart . . . a laugh-out-loud love story with explosive chemistry and lovable characters. Helena Hunting has done it again!"

—*USA Today* bestselling author Melanie Harlow on *Shacking Up*

"With that perfect Helena Hunting flair, *Shacking Up* is the perfect combination of sexy, sweet, and hilarious. A feel-good beach read you won't want to miss!"

—*New York Times* bestselling author K. Bromberg

"A look into the world of tattoos and piercings, a dash of humor, and a feel-good ending will delight fans and new readers alike."

—*Publishers Weekly* on *Inked Armor*

"A unique, deliciously hot, endearingly sweet, laugh-out-loud, fantastically good-time romance! . . . I loved every single page!!"

—*New York Times* bestselling author Emma Chase on *Pucked*

"Sigh-inducing swoony and fanning-myself sexy. All the stars!"

—*USA Today* bestselling author Daisy Prescott on the Pucked series

"A hot roller coaster of a ride!"

—*New York Times* and *USA Today* bestselling author Julia Kent on *Pucked Over*

"*Pucked Over* is Helena Hunting's funniest and sexiest book yet. *Scorching hot* with *pee-inducing laughs*. All hail the Beaver Queen."

—*USA Today* bestselling author T. M. Frazier

"Characters that will touch your heart and a romance that will leave you breathless."

—*New York Times* bestselling author Tara Sue Me

"Gut wrenching, sexy, twisted, dark, incredibly erotic, and a love story like no other. On my all-time favorites list."

—*New York Times* bestselling author of *Wallbanger* and the Redhead series Alice Clayton on *Clipped Wings*

A LIE FOR A LIE

OTHER TITLES BY HELENA HUNTING

PUCKED SERIES

CLIPPED WINGS SERIES

SHACKING UP SERIES

Shacking Up
Getting Down
Hooking Up
I Flipping Love You
Making Up
Handle with Care

STAND-ALONE NOVELS

The Librarian Principle
The Good Luck Charm
Meet Cute

A LIE FOR A LIE

HELENA HUNTING

Montlake
Romance

Text copyright © 2019 by Helena Hunting/Ink & Cupcakes Inc. All rights reserved.

Published by Montlake Romance, Seattle

www.apub.com

Amazon, the Amazon logo, and Montlake Romance are trademarks of Amazon.com, Inc., or its affiliates.

ISBN-13: 9781542015356
ISBN-10: 1542015359

Cover design by Eileen Carey

Cover photography by Regina Wamba of MaeIDesign.com

Printed in the United States of America

This one's for the Den. You put a smile on my face every single day. Thank you for your relentless passion for reading and your incredible sense of community.

CHAPTER 1

BIRTHDAY BLUES

Rook

"What are the chances there will be booze at a birthday party for a pair of three-year-olds?"

"Uhhhh . . . slim to none?" My sister's voice crackles through the car speakers on a scoff. "Why are you going to a birthday party for toddlers anyway? Is this some kind of new dating strategy? Like you'll pick up more women if they see you interacting with small children? Oh! Is this like when we went to visit Kyle, and we took Max to the zoo, and, like, five women slipped you their numbers?"

She's referring to an incident that happened when I was visiting our older brother, Kyle, in LA earlier this summer. Our nephew is like catnip for women. "No, Stevie, it's not like that. The party is for my teammate's kids, and his brother-in-law used to be the team captain, so it's a good idea for me to make an appearance."

"Right. Okay. Well, that makes it a lot less exciting."

"Not everything about my life is exciting. What about you? Any plans this afternoon?" I need to move the conversation away from dating, because my little sister always has an opinion on my lackluster love life.

"I have a date tonight, so I need to try on half my wardrobe before I decide nothing is good enough, and then I'll need to run out and buy something new."

"A date? Who is he? How'd you meet him?"

"Listen to you, sounding like Dad." Even though she laughs, there's sadness in her voice. We lost our dad three years ago to complications from diabetes. We're a pretty tight family, even with me living in Chicago, my brother being on the West Coast, and my sister and mother having relocated from New York to LA. My sister went out there for school, and my mom decided it was time to retire, so she sold the house and farm and moved out west at the end of last summer, right after Max was born.

"He's in my program, we have a couple of classes together, and his name is Joseph."

"How many times have you been out with him?"

"It's our second date. Speaking of dates, when was the last time you went on one?"

I grip the steering wheel, hating that we're back to this. "I don't know. A while. I've been busy."

"Busy pining over Alaska girl."

It irritates me that she continues to use that nickname for the woman I spent the better part of last summer with in Alaska. "Don't call her that."

"It's been a year, RJ. Don't you think—"

I pull into the parking lot of the aquarium. "I'm at the party. I have to go. I'll talk to you later." I end the call. I'd like to say this isn't a conversation we have often, but I'd be lying. Between Stevie and Kyle, someone brings her up at least once a month. Her name was Lainey. *Is* Lainey. Provided she's still out there somewhere.

I park next to the massive blue pickup truck that manages to stand out in this parking lot full of silver and black SUVs. It belongs to my teammate Randy Ballistic, who's currently leaning against the tailgate, thumb typing on his phone.

I cut the engine and get out of the car. Randy falls into step with me, pocketing his phone as we cross the lot. "I'm a little surprised to see you here." He eyes the gifts tucked under my arm, covered in rocket wrapping paper.

"I haven't seen most of the guys since playoffs, so I figured it'd be good to stop by."

He nods in understanding. "Yeah, I tried to get out of it, but Lily insisted we come. She came early to help set up." Randy and Lily have been together for as long as I've been on the team, and while they don't have kids, they have a dog, which is like training for a baby.

Inside the aquarium, one of my teammates' kids runs by holding a giant inflatable shark, screaming at the top of his lungs. I like kids, and kids generally like me. But I prefer my current role as an uncle to my nephew, Max. I can be the uncle who gives awesome presents, and when Max starts crying, I can pass him back to my brother or sister-in-law and walk away.

"This is like an advertisement for birth control right here," I mutter as a little redheaded toddler comes wobbling over, face covered in chocolate and a doughnut in his hand. The kid—who definitely belongs to my redheaded Scottish teammate, Lance Romero—reaches for Randy's leg with his doughnut-filled hand but misses by about six inches, which causes the kid to trip over his own feet.

I swoop in and catch him before he can do a face-plant. He startles and loses his hold on the doughnut, so he bursts into tears.

"Hey, buddy, you're all right."

"Mah doughnut!" he screams and lunges for it.

"Five-second rule." Randy shrugs.

"Quinn! Don't pick food up off the ground," Poppy, the kid's mother and Romero's wife, calls from across the room.

I crouch down in front of him. "Why don't we toss that one in the garbage and get you a new one?"

"I want dat one!" he screams in my face, then proceeds to throw himself on the floor and have an epic meltdown.

Romero stalks over. "What're you two doing to my kid?"

Randy raises both hands in the air. "He tripped and dropped his doughnut."

Romero looks to me. He's a nice guy, and I like him, but sometimes he has a short fuse, and I prefer not to be the one to set him off. "I told him we should get a new one. He didn't like that idea much."

Romero picks his kid up off the floor and cringes when he sees his face. "Quinn, my man, yer never gonna get the ladies like this. Let's wash yer face and get ya a new doughnut, aye?"

"Want dat doughnut!" He points to the floor.

Romero steps on the doughnut in question. "What doughnut?"

"Da-eee! Mah doughnut!"

Romero gives us both a look. "I gotta take care of this. After the party wraps up, we're headin' to the pub. You two in?"

"With or without the kids?" Randy quirks a brow at Quinn, who's fighting his dad's hold and smearing his chocolate-covered face all over his dad's arm.

Romero rolls his eyes. "Without. What the hell would be the point otherwise?" He lifts the kid over his head and makes airplane noises all the way to the bathroom.

"I should've brought a flask," Randy mutters as he fills a plastic cup with soda.

I opt for a bottle of water. We make small talk with our teammates while I keep an eye out for Alex Waters. He went into sportscasting as soon as he retired from the ice. The camera loves him, but he's got the background and the temperament to coach a team, and I want to find out if the rumors are true that he's thinking about making the switch in the next couple of years.

"Hey! Rookie! How's it goin'? Glad you made it back from Alaska in time for the party." Alex claps me on the back. I have to brace myself so I don't stumble forward with the impact. Alex is a big guy, and just because he's not on the ice anymore doesn't mean he's lost any of his size.

I accept a man hug and back pat. "Me too. Things are good. Just getting settled in—you know how it goes. Looking forward to preseason training."

"Team's looking good this year. You wanna talk strategy at all, just give me a call."

Before I can segue, his wife appears. "There you are! Can you please take Robbie to the bathroom? Every time we go into a women's bathroom, he tries to climb up on the sink and pee in there." Violet gives us a slightly strained smile. "Hey, guys, sorry to interrupt, but getting kicked out of the aquarium for letting my kid use a sink as a toilet isn't on my to-do list today."

She points at another child, who I think is one of Miller Butterson's four kids. I can't keep their names straight, and I'm pretty sure the one I'm looking at is one of their twins, which makes it even more difficult. "I'm just waiting for that one to pee in one of the fake potted plants. This summer Miller thought the best way to potty train Liam and Lane was to let them wander around with their doodle hanging out so they could pee whenever and wherever. Now Liam keeps trying to take his pants off, and he thinks if it's a plant, he's allowed to pee on it."

"That's actually awesome," Randy says with a snort.

Violet grins. "I know, right? Liam has been the best thing to ever happen to me."

Alex clears his throat, and Violet rolls her eyes. "I mean in terms of offsetting my own humiliating moments. Last weekend we had a barbecue, and Liam got into the greenhouse. Let's just say there's a lot of contaminated science experiments in there now."

"Daddy, can we play yer-nal hockey now?" Robbie tugs on Alex's sleeve while cupping his junk through his pants with the other hand.

"Sure, kiddo." He nods to us. "I'll be back."

Violet watches them disappear into the men's bathroom. "Robbie likes to aim for the salt pucks. He thinks it's like playing hockey with his wiener."

Randy nods. "Pretty much, actually."

Five minutes later all the kids go rushing over to the dolphin exhibit. Apparently there's some kind of guided tour. Since neither of us has kids, Randy and I hang back near the food table. I grab a chicken wrap and another water, wondering how much longer this will go on before we can head over to the pub. I'm guessing—since they haven't done cake yet—it's going to be a while.

Screaming comes from the gaggle of kids. "What the hell is going on over there?"

"Your guess is as good as mine. I'm gonna go check it out—maybe you should go have a chat with some of those girls." He inclines his head in the direction of a group of female aquarium staff who are standing in a gaggle, whispering and gawking. We're not especially low key today, since we're all wearing team hats and shirts.

"Uh, I'm good. They're probably all in high school." I follow him toward the dolphin exhibit, curious about the shrieks and screams and what sounds a lot like someone crying.

"Everyone stay calm! It's perfectly natural during mating season for something like this to happen!" The shrill, panicked voice is familiar. Maybe one of the wives?

"Oh shit," Randy mumbles. He has a little extra height on my six-foot-two frame, so I'm guessing he can see something I can't.

I make my way around the edge of the group; some of the moms have their kids' faces buried against their stomachs, and one kid is yelling about someone being stabbed.

But the commotion barely registers, because across the sea of screaming, laughing, and crying kids is a very familiar woman wearing an aquarium-issued beige button-down.

Lainey.

Alaska girl.

CHAPTER 2

ALL THE CRAZY BUNNIES

Rook
Fourteen months earlier

"Oh my God! *Oh my Gooooood!*"

My eardrum is probably broken, based on the sheer volume of the scream and the sudden ringing in my ear.

Once upon a time it would have been reasonable to assume I was eliciting this reaction because of my amazing stick-handling skills—not the on-ice kind either. However, I'm currently seated on an airplane heading for Seattle, waiting for the rest of the passengers to load. And while I've engaged in public sex, I usually kept it confined to places with doors, like bathrooms. But I don't do that anymore. I'm a reformed public-bathroom fucker.

I cringe as the screamer drops into the seat beside me, still yelling in my ear. "Rook, I haven't seen you in forever! How crazy is this? I can't believe we're on the same plane!"

"Totally crazy?" I've managed to stay under the radar without being recognized . . . until now. "Is this your seat?" *Please say no.*

"No." She pouts for a second, before a wide grin breaks across her face. "But I'm right behind you! Last-minute upgrade. Are you flying alone? What are you doing in Seattle?"

"I'm meeting my brother." That's not exactly true; my brother and I are meeting in Anchorage, but she doesn't need to know that. *How the hell do I know this chick?* I rack my brain for a name, something, anything. She's familiar—and not in a good way.

"In Seattle?"

I nod.

"So you *are* flying alone! Me too! I bet we can get the person sitting here to switch spots."

"Oh, you don't need to do that."

"Of course I do, silly!" She hugs my arm. "Then we can catch up!"

I'm still trying to place her, but that's not always easy. I'm embarrassed to admit that in the time I've been playing professional hockey in Chicago, there were a couple of years where I did a lot of fucking around. Literally. I screwed pretty much any bunny who dropped into my lap. Until the shit hit the fan.

I took a break from the bunnies after I mistook a case of jock itch for crabs—which resulted in the nickname Crabby for the better part of that season, thanks to my asshole teammates. But every once in a while, I run into one of the women I slept with during my partying days. It's always awkward. There were a lot of women in a very short span of time. Sometimes more than one at a time. It was bad. I'm not proud.

And then there was that fake pregnancy blackmail—

Oh hell no. Now I remember exactly who this woman is. She's the blackmailer. It was literally the weirdest thing I've ever experienced. She took plaster casts of her sister's growing baby belly every couple of weeks and then stuck them under her shirt and posted pictures online, tagging me in every single one. Until my lawyer got involved. The jock itch incident happened right around that time too. Thus ending my puck-bunny days for good.

"How've you been? What're you up to? You look great! What are you doing in Seattle? Wait, I already asked that last question!"

There is no way I'm going to be able to sit next to her for five hours and stay sober.

When the woman who's supposed to be beside me finally boards the plane, my extra enthusiastic companion takes control of the seat situation. She hugs my arm and presses her cheek against my shoulder, her extra wide smile matching her extra wide eyes. I think she's going for innocent, but she really just looks bent.

"Hiiiii!" she says to the middle-aged woman. "So I hope you don't mind, but my boyfriend booked our seats, and he couldn't get ones beside each other. We're celebrating our one-year anniversary, and it's the first time we've flown first class." She crinkles her nose. It makes her look odd. She's also disturbingly convincing in her lie. "Would you mind trading seats with me so we can be together?" She bats her lashes.

I try to make eye contact with the woman, but she's too focused on the blackmailer to notice my panicked expression. "Aw. Aren't you two sweet? Of course I can trade seats with you."

"Thank youuuuu! I'm seat 3C."

The lady moves to the row behind us. Awesome. Now I have no escape.

Sissy—whose name I finally remembered—doesn't stop talking all through takeoff. Once we're in the air, I order scotch on the rocks and make it a double. I'm going to need a lot of alcohol to survive this.

About a half hour after takeoff, she leans in, her mouth at my ear and her hand on my leg. She's way too close to my junk to be appropriate. I try to move her hand, but she digs her nails in. "I need to use the bathroom. Wanna meet me in there?"

"Uh, I hardly fit in there on my own, let alone with another person."

"Maybe I should ask for blankets instead." She gives me an exaggerated wink.

I drop my voice to a whisper. "You do remember how you pretended to be pregnant and said it was mine. All over social media."

She throws her head back and laughs loudly. "Oh my God! Rook, you are sooooo funny! That was just a joke!"

This chick is legit out there. "You posted about it for two months."

"Well, you stopped answering my messages, and for like a month I thought I might actually be pregnant."

"We used a condom."

"Yeah, but there's this drink my sister had, and I tried it too." She waves her hand around. "Anyway. It didn't work for me like it did for her, which is too bad because I think we'd make pretty babies together." She nuzzles my biceps again. "We could try again if you're staying in Seattle for a while."

"Yeah, I don't think that's a good idea."

"Why not?"

Because you're certifiable. "I'm in a relationship," I lie.

"Oh." She stops hugging my arm. "Really? I haven't seen you with anyone, and I follow all your social media accounts. I had to set up all new ones after you blocked me." She seems annoyed by this.

"It's pretty new."

"We're in another time zone, so it technically wouldn't be cheating, right? Or you could just come in a cup for me if you think it's a big deal. They can last a couple of days, as long as they don't dry out."

I spend the next several hours fighting off her advances. As far as flights go, this is the worst. I'd take turbulence and a crying infant over Sissy. The torture is prolonged when the pilot says we have to circle the airfield for another hour before landing.

Sissy rushes along beside me when we finally get off the plane. She's still trying to persuade me that being in another time zone would make cheating okay. She follows me all the way to the gate and then wraps herself around me like an octopus.

Eventually security steps in, and she's forced to let go of me. The whole situation reinforces my pledge to never sleep with another bunny, no matter how hot she is.

CHAPTER 3

SAFETY CUDDLES

Rook

I manage to make my connecting flight to Anchorage despite our delayed landing. I'm grateful that the person next to me is a suit this time. I settle into my seat—it's an aisle instead of a window, which isn't my preference, but I'll survive as long as I don't have a crazy bunny next to me.

I stuff my earbuds in and cue up a movie on my entertainment console. After the last flight, I deserve three hours of brain candy.

Just as I settle on an action flick, a body lands in my lap. At first, I think I'm being accosted—yet again. It's not unusual for women to literally throw themselves at me. Typically I'm not on a plane, though, but considering my last flight I shouldn't be surprised by anything right now. "What the—"

"I'm so sorry!" says the voice attached to the body in my lap. She scrambles to right herself but jerks back, gagging, her tidal wave of silky, dark hair slapping me in the face. It smells like mint and cucumber, which would be nice if it weren't in my mouth.

She grabs my shirt with one hand and catches my earbuds, yanking them free. The other hand curls under the fabric wrapped tightly around her throat. She's sprawled across my lap, legs hanging over the armrest, face level with mine. She's totally blocking the aisle, making it impossible for anyone to get by and creating quite the spectacle. "My scarf is caught," she rasps. "Oh my God. I'm choking myself. I'm so sorry. This is so embarrassing." The more she struggles, the more the scarf tightens, which in turn causes her to flail.

I slide a supporting arm behind her. "Stay still for a sec."

She freezes, still gripping my shirt, eyes wide with panic. I turn my head to the side and lean forward. Her lips connect with my cheek.

"Oh!" She tries to turn away, but she really is stuck, so her nose ends up in my ear and her lips are still pressed against my jaw.

"Just give me a few more seconds, and you'll be free." She exhales heavily against my jaw, warm breath making my skin prickle. I lift her carry-on and use my foot to pull the scarf free from the wheel.

She loosens the fabric around her throat, dragging in a long, deep breath. "Thank you. So much. Choking to death on an attractive man's lap really isn't the way I wanted to go." She squeezes her eyes shut and pushes to a stand. "I'm so sorry."

She keeps her gaze averted as she gathers up the scarf that never seems to end. It gives me time to check her out. Well, shit. This woman is hot. Like *pour a gallon of gasoline on me and light me on fire* hot. She has long dark hair, a shade of brown so deep it's nearly black. Her eyes are the color of coffee or chocolate—something with caffeine in it. Something that would amp me up. And her face . . . daaaaamn. High cheekbones, full lips, a dainty nose, arched brows, thick lashes.

I take in the rest of the package, which gives me pause because her outfit is just . . . out there. She's wearing a full-on parka, hiding her figure, but based on her legs I'm thinking she's probably slender. That's a guess, though, with all the layers she has going on. And that scarf has to be a mile long with how many times she winds it around her neck, hence the near strangulation.

Her little wardrobe malfunction has resulted in a line of people waiting to board, so she rushes down the aisle, throwing another "So sorry" over her shoulder as she disappears into coach.

I'm almost disappointed. Almost, but not quite. I plug my earbuds back in and veg out to movies for the next three hours.

Once I land in Anchorage, I call my brother. He's meeting me here so we can get on the putt-putt plane to Kodiak Island. It's been a family ritual since I was a teenager. Even though our dad died two years ago, Kyle and I still carry on this tradition where we spend a few weeks fishing in Alaska. It is my favorite part of off-season and the thing I look forward to the most every year, even without my dad.

"RJ, hey, bro, I've been trying to get in touch with you for hours." He sounds off—worried, maybe.

"I didn't bother connecting to Wi-Fi on the plane. Where are you? Is everything okay?"

"It's Joy." He coughs, like he's trying to hold back emotions.

I drop into the closest chair. "Is she okay?" Joy is his pregnant wife. I'm aware that there's no way Kyle is coming with me for three weeks to hang out in Alaska next year. Not with a new kid. He might get a long weekend, but this is the last trip we're supposed to take together for a few years, especially if one kid leads to more.

"She's been diagnosed with gestational diabetes. The doctors have put her on bed rest."

That explains the waver in his voice. I sit up straighter, a tight feeling in the pit of my stomach, since we lost our dad to complications from diabetes. "What does that mean? Is she going to be okay? Is the baby all right?"

"It's fine. She's fine. The baby's fine." He sounds like he's trying to reassure himself, not me. "She just needs to be monitored. The doctor said it's not uncommon. It's not like what Dad had—it's a lot different."

I relax a little. "Okay, that's good. Do you want me to come to LA?"

"No. You don't need to do that. We're okay. Mom and Stevie are talking about bringing Stevie's stuff out here now instead of later in the summer." Our younger sister is working on her master's and decided out west is where she wanted to be, away from the cold winters.

"Mom and Stevie are coming? Are you sure I shouldn't too?"

"Positive. You know how Mom is—as soon as she heard bed rest, she was already packing. It sounds a lot more serious than it is, but I can't come to Alaska. I don't want to leave Joy right now, and being that far from her really isn't an option. I'm sorry, RJ, I know how much you were looking forward to this." He sounds torn, which I don't want, not when Joy is experiencing complications.

I conceal my disappointment. "You don't have to apologize. I get it. Joy and the baby are priority number one."

"If you don't want to go on your own, you can come here."

I consider the offer. I love my brother. We're pretty close, even though we live thousands of miles apart, but I need this vacation. I need this time away from the media and the constant demands, time when there aren't any expectations placed on me. I need to be in the one place I feel close to my dad. More than anything else, I crave the peace and solitude I find in Alaska and the escape from the circus my life has become. Last year our team captain retired, and I stepped into the role. He was well loved by the team and a legend in the sport, so I've had big shoes to fill.

"Thanks, Kyle, but I'm gonna catch some salmon, grow a massive beard, and avoid showering for four days at a time."

He laughs. "I figured you'd say that. If I can come out later in the month, I'll call. Well, I'll call anyway. Touch base every few days so I can make sure you haven't been eaten by a bear—and I'll keep you updated on things here."

The reception can be pretty spotty where we stay, and I like it that way. I want the time to disconnect and just be a human, not an NHL team captain. "Don't worry about me. I can handle the bears—you just take care of your family. I'll send pictures."

We say our goodbyes, and I drop my head against the wall. It sucks that my brother can't be here, but I still want the time at the cabin, even if I have to do it on my own.

Half an hour later, I carry my bag out to the Cessna. The first time I ever flew on a plane that small, I tossed my cookies, so I've learned to refrain from drinking on the flight from Seattle to Anchorage.

I'm last in line on this tiny eight-seater, which is fine. It's a short flight, and almost every seat has a spectacular window view. Except the ones at the back—they're a little tight for space.

I have to duck and turn sideways to get on the plane. It comes with being over six feet and more than two hundred pounds. It's a full flight, and there's only one seat left . . . at the very back of the plane. I shimmy down the narrow aisle. Tucked into the corner, clutching a purse, is the same dark-haired woman who fell into my lap on the previous flight. Well, now, this should be interesting.

She glances away from the window, her nervous smile falling as her eyes go wide. Her cheeks flush, and she lifts a hand to cover her mouth. "Oh no."

I grin and fight a chuckle as I take the seat beside her. It's actually like one of those bench seats you'd find on a school bus, with about as much room.

She slides closer to the window, trying to make more space for me. She drops her hand. "I'm so sorry I fell on you."

I flash her a grin and a wink. "That was the most exciting part of this trip so far, so don't worry about it."

"I didn't mean to kiss you. I mean your cheek." Hers grow redder. "Oh my God, Lainey, just shut up and leave the poor man alone," she mutters and ducks her head.

"It's really okay. Shit happens, right?"

She peeks back up at me, a tiny smile pulling up the right side of her mouth.

I hold out a hand. "I'm RJ."

I don't know why I give her that name. My dad called me that, and my brother and sister still do, but that's it. Everyone else calls me Rook or Rookie. Maybe because she doesn't seem to know who I am, and I don't want her to find out? Oh well, too late now.

She slips her mitten-covered hand into mine, then makes a face. Pulling off her mitt, she tries again. Her hand is warm and a little damp—and much smaller than mine—but her grip is firm. She gives me a solid shake. "I'm Lainey."

"Hi, Lainey."

"Hi, RJ." Her eyes stay locked on mine for a few seconds. Still no hint of recognition, which is fantastic.

"So what brings you to Alaska?" I ask, buckling myself in.

Her eyes light up. "Well, I'm currently working on my master's thesis, and my focus is aquatic animals. I'm fascinated by dolphins and whales, so I'm spending six weeks out here to study them."

"A master's thesis, huh? You must be pretty smart."

She shrugs. "I just like learning a lot. This is my third master's."

"Your third? How old are you?" She doesn't look old enough to be pursuing a first master's, let alone a third. Although her outfit might be to blame for that.

"Twenty-five."

"And this is your *third* thesis?"

She bites her bottom lip and nods. "Mm-hmm. I love learning new things, and I keep getting full scholarships, so here I am. I have a master's in sex therapy and another one in geology. This one is going to be in marine biology. Specifically, ocean mammals. I thought it would be interesting to study the mating patterns of dolphins versus whales."

"How do those go together?"

She shrugs. "They don't, really. I just have a lot of different interests. For instance, did you know dolphins mate not just for reproduction but also pleasure, like humans?"

"Huh. I didn't know that." But now I'm thinking about sex and how I haven't had it in a long time.

"Oh yes, they're *very* sexually active. And some people think they mate for life, like lobsters, but they don't. They take several partners. Just like some humans do too, although in Western society we're sociologically conditioned to choose one mate and stick with them, unlike dolphins. They just like to get it on because it's fun."

She bites the tip of her finger. "I'm sorry, I get carried away. I've been doing a lot of reading in preparation for this trip, and my brain is full of so many facts, sometimes they just come out of my mouth. I can stop talking if you'd like." She motions to the phone in my hands with the earbuds wrapped around it.

I slip it into my pocket. "Nah, you're more interesting than anything I could listen to on there."

Her smile widens, and then she ducks her head again, blushing. God, I miss shy women. The kind who don't throw themselves at me looking to fuck a star.

"What about you? Why are you coming to Kodiak Island?" She looks me over in an assessing way, as if she's trying to figure me out.

I'm dressed casually in a pair of jeans, a T-shirt, and a hoodie. "I come out here every summer to fish with my brother, but he can't make it this year, so I'm on my own."

"Oh. That's too bad."

I shrug. "I'm okay with it. Sometimes it's nice to get away from all the crazy and be at peace with nature, you know?"

"I definitely do. I went to school in Seattle for a year. Well, more like a month. It was a lot." She shudders and shakes her head. "I'm not from the city. Our town had less than two thousand people, so it was a big change. Cities can be exciting—but scary. Are you from Seattle?"

"I grew up in New York."

"I've always wanted to go there, but it looks so . . . overwhelming."

"Well, to be fair, I grew up in Upstate New York, which is nothing like the city. It's pretty rural in some areas."

"Oh yes, I read that somewhere."

The pilot informs us that we're cleared for takeoff. Lainey hugs her mittens to her chest as we head for the runway.

"You okay?"

"I've never been on a plane this small before," she says.

"We'll be fine. I promise. I've done this at least twenty times, and I've survived every one."

Her eyes are wide as she nods, then looks out the window as we gather speed. When the wheels lift off the tarmac, she grips my forearm. "Oh! This is a lot bumpier than the big plane, isn't it?"

"Yeah. A bit. You'll get used to it."

She releases my arm and hugs her mittens again. "Today is actually the first time I've ever been on a plane."

"Really?"

"The first flight was nice. I mean, there was a very old man beside me with a lot of nose hairs who smelled like mothballs, but he was fine otherwise. You're much nicer smelling than he was." She blushes again. "Anyway, I guess on a plane this small you feel everything more."

This woman is such a breath of fresh air. And her innocence is alluring, especially since I'm going to be on my own for the next few weeks. Kodiak Island is fairly expansive, though, so there's a good chance this short flight is all I'll see of her. I'm going to make the most of this hour of normalcy. "I can't believe this is your first time flying."

"I usually take the train if I go anywhere. But there's no train to the island, and I wasn't sure I could handle the long ferry ride, so here I am." We hit a spot of turbulence, and she makes a squeaky sound, then buries her face against my shoulder. "I'm so sorry," she mumbles into my arm. "You don't even know me, and I'm using you like a teddy bear."

I laugh. "I'd climb into your lap so you can cuddle with me, but I don't think I'll fit." But she'd sure fit nicely in *my* lap.

19

"Sadly, no—you're kind of huge." She gives my biceps a squeeze and releases it on a slow exhale.

"What if I just do this?" I slip an arm around her shoulder.

"That's nice." She slides a little closer and tucks herself into my side. "That makes me feel . . . safer."

I'm not sure if she's flirting with me or just genuinely needs some kind of human contact to abate the anxiety, but I'm enjoying this, so I go with it. "Safer is good."

"It is," she agrees.

I spend the next few minutes explaining the geography as she looks out the window, but when we hit another patch of turbulence, her face pales.

"Oh no!" She covers her mouth with her palm.

"You okay?"

She shakes her head but stops abruptly, paling further. "I don't feel so well."

I reach into the seat pocket in front of us and pull out the barf bag. I blow into it to open it up and then hand it to her. "Maybe just breathe into this."

She takes it from me with shaking hands and leans forward, her hair slipping over her shoulders. I gather it up, twisting the soft, silky strands around my hand to keep it out of the way.

And then she barfs. She tries to be quiet as she retches a couple more times. I stroke my thumb along the back of her neck, and her skin pebbles with goose bumps.

With my free hand I search my pockets for a tissue, grateful when I find a handful in my hoodie. They're crumpled but unused, so I pass them over. Lainey turns her head away and wipes her mouth, dropping the soiled tissues into the bag. She rolls the top over a few times and secures it closed.

I let her hair unfurl from around my hand and run my palm down her back. "You okay?"

"Other than hugely embarrassed, I think I'm fine," she mumbles. "I don't know what to do with this." She holds up the bag.

"Here, let me deal with it."

"Oh God, no. My throw-up is in there."

"It's better if it ends up in the garbage than anywhere else, isn't it?"

"Oh yes, much better in a garbage can." She hands it over.

I unbuckle my seat belt, shimmy down the aisle, and drop the bag in the trash at the front of the plane, then make my way back to my seat. "Feel better?"

"A little. I'm so sorry. I'm the worst person to sit beside on a plane."

"Not true at all. I actually like being someone's personal teddy bear. I'd volunteer for a permanent position if it was available." I slip my hand into my pocket, root around until I find my pack of gum, and offer it to her.

She plucks the package from my hand. "I love you so much right now."

I laugh. "Mouth tastes that bad, huh?"

"The worst. I had a burrito at the airport."

"Oooh. Bad call, that."

"You're telling me." She pops a stick of gum into her mouth and closes her eyes, chewing a few times.

"Better?"

"So much." She passes the pack back, but I fold her hand around it. "It's all yours."

"Thank you." She puts it in her purse and retrieves a small bottle of hand sanitizer, squeezing a dab into her palm before passing it to me.

Before I know it, we're on our descent. Her hands are balled into fists in her lap, her eyes screwed shut.

"Hey." I slip my arm along the back of the seat again. "You're safe. Human teddy bear right here for safety cuddles."

She smiles nervously and edges closer, pressing herself right against my side. "Thank you for being so nice, RJ."

I don't know that she'd say that if she knew I was withholding who I really am. But here on this plane I'm not the NHL forward and team captain with a history of being a player on and off the ice. I'm just a guy, and she's just a girl.

CHAPTER 4

CABIN IN THE WOODS

Lainey

If this plane crashes, at least I'm going out on a high note.

RJ is the kind of attractive that makes a woman stop paying attention to what she's doing and nearly end up strangling herself with her scarf. He's tall and built, with dark hair that curls up at the nape of his neck, hazel eyes ringed with dark green, and a smile that makes my insides mushy.

I'm tucked into his side, his arm stretched out along the back of the seat, fingers curved around my shoulder, keeping me nice and safe. RJ's arm is very sturdy, and solid, and thick, like a tree trunk. He also smells great, like fresh laundry and cologne with a hint of peppermint, likely from the gum he gave me to take care of my breath.

He dealt with my bag of vomit, which is both mortifying and insanely sweet. At least the near scarf strangulation happened before I hurled. I'm currently fisting his sweatshirt in one hand and hugging my mittens to my chest with the other. I also keep trying to bury my face in his armpit. Despite the long flight from Seattle and the tiny, cramped quarters on this plane, he still manages to smell like deodorant.

He covers the hand clutching his sweatshirt.

"I'm sorry." I pry my fingers from the soft fabric, but before I can tuck my hand close to my own body, he threads his fingers through mine. It's an unexpected level of intimacy.

"A couple more minutes and we'll be on the ground again," he reassures me.

I squeeze his hand as the plane descends and squeak out my anxiety when the wheels touch down, pressing my face against RJ's chest.

Eventually, when it's clear we're bumping along the tarmac, I peek up.

RJ grins down at me; it's disarmingly charming. "We survived."

I look out the window at the mountains rising to my right, the water on the left. "We did." Now that we're on the ground I'm embarrassed all over again. "Thank you for being my personal support person and human teddy bear."

RJ smiles even wider. "It was honestly my pleasure."

"I don't know if witnessing me toss my cookies was a pleasure for anyone, but thank you for being so nice." I gather my purse and mitts, making sure I have everything before we disembark. Our luggage is waiting for us on the tarmac. The cold air coming off the water makes me shiver, probably because I've been roasting in my parka for the past hour. I shove my hands in my mitts and try to bat my hair away from my face—it's not particularly effective, given how windy it is.

"Let me give you a hand," RJ offers when he notices my struggle. He slings his huge duffel over his shoulder and grabs the handle of my suitcase, and we head for the warmth and safety of the arrival terminal. I rush to keep up with his long strides.

Once we're inside and the wind is no longer an issue, I tuck my mitts into my purse and quickly braid my hair so it's not a problem when I have to go outside again. RJ stops when we reach the car rental desk. "Where are you heading from here?"

23

"I have a cabin about ten miles past the town of Kodiak. It's supposed to be on the water. I wanted an authentic Alaskan experience." My printout with the directions from the airport to the cabin is in my purse.

"So you need a rental, then?" RJ motions to the kiosk. "I'm picking up a vehicle. If you want, I can drive you to Kodiak and you can get one there—it'll be a lot less expensive without the airport taxes."

I fidget with the end of my braid, embarrassed. "Oh, that's really nice of you, but I don't have my license."

RJ tips his head to the side, his expression curious. "How are you planning to get to your cabin?"

"I was going to shuttle to town and then cab the rest of the way."

"Or I could just drive you."

"I couldn't ask you to do that. We might be in opposite directions."

"You said you're ten miles outside of Kodiak, right? I'm already heading in that direction. I don't mind dropping you off—unless you're waiting on someone?"

"Oh no, it's just me." I try to keep my hands still instead of talking with them, which is something I do when I'm nervous. Incidentally, I'm nervous often.

RJ's brow furrows. "So you're alone here without a car?" This seems to concern him, which of course means it also starts to concern me.

"I can always call a cab when I need to go to town." I used to bike everywhere back home. And during my brief stint in Seattle I took public transit. That was definitely nerve-racking. All those people so close together.

It would be a good idea to get a bike so I can go back and forth to town for groceries and stuff. That way I won't have to worry so much about making polite chitchat with the cab drivers. Also, there are a lot of movies about psycho killers who pick up unsuspecting victims and such. I don't want to meet any of those while I'm here. I put purchasing a bike on my mental to-do list. Mostly I'm tired and in need of a shower and maybe a little rest after this long day.

"Okay." He scratches the back of his neck. "But at least let me drive you today."

"Only if it's not too much trouble." He seems safe and not like a psycho killer.

He graces me with the same brain-fritzing smile as before. "It's no trouble at all, Lainey."

I wait with our bags while he gets the keys to his vehicle. Then we head to the valet, where a huge gray truck with roll bars and waist-high tires is parked curbside.

RJ puts our bags in the back and helps me into the passenger seat before he rounds the hood and climbs in. He adjusts the radio so it's playing a local station and turns the volume down low as we follow the signs for Kodiak.

"It's just so beautiful here." I can't take my eyes off the mountains in the distance or the water to my right.

"It really is—and peaceful, especially once we're out of town and on the water," RJ says.

It doesn't take long before we're driving through the town of Kodiak, where we make a stop for groceries. It's a little awkward shopping for food with someone I don't know, but I'm happy to have a chance to stock up on essentials, since all I have in my purse are a few granola bars.

He helps me load my groceries into the truck, then programs the address to my cabin into his GPS and gives me a lopsided smile. "You're actually only about three-quarters of a mile away from where I'm staying. What're the chances?"

"It's a pretty wild coincidence, isn't it?" It also seems too good to be true.

My stomach twists as storefronts and houses give way to tall trees lining the road. I'm alone in a vehicle with a man I hardly know, and we're heading into the wilderness, where there aren't a lot of people.

Usually that is my preference, unless it's my family, who I know and trust. But right now I'm nervous and uncertain. "My cabin is supposed to have satellite TV. I really like the Discovery Channel, and of course Animal Planet is always fascinating." I realize I'm babbling, so I ask him a question. "Do you watch TV?"

"Yeah, I watch TV." He's smiling, but his focus stays on the road.

"Do you have a favorite show?" This is good. I can learn more about him. Maybe we have things in common other than liking Alaska.

"Sure, depends on my mood and how much time I have. I binge-watch shows sometimes."

"Oh, me too! Once I binge-watched an entire season of *Criminal Minds*, which was a really bad idea. I got all paranoid and thought I was going to end up kidnapped by a serial killer." I glance over at RJ, nerves going haywire.

He's huge, much bigger than me. And even though I've taken self-defense classes, I'm not sure they'd be useful against someone as large as him. What if he's planning to take me to his cabin and keep me there, like a pet? Or a hostage. I should be panicking more at that thought. As it is, my heart is racing.

He takes his eyes off the road for a second. "I promise I'm not a serial killer."

"Are you a mind reader?" What the heck was I thinking, getting into a truck with a guy I met on a plane? I can actually hear my mother losing her mind over this poor decision-making. If he does kidnap me, I'll never hear another one of her lectures again. I'm uncertain how I feel about that. I love her, but one of the reasons I'm all the way out here is because the smothering is overwhelming.

RJ laughs, reminding me that I asked a question before I got lost in the anxious spiral of my thoughts. "No, but your expression sort of says it all. I'm just a guy hanging out in the wilderness for a few weeks, planning to catch some fish. You're safe with me."

"I hope so." I wring my hands, anxiety making my mouth dry and my palms damp. Dammit. Why do I have to worry about everything?

He takes his foot off the gas, pointing to the passenger side window. We pass a red mailbox that reads Sweet View Home. "That's my driveway. You're not too far down the road."

A minute later he makes a right on a narrow dirt road, the center of which is overgrown with a strip of foot-long weeds. Tree branches brush the mirrors as we pass them. It's a bumpy ride that makes me wish I'd used a bathroom while we were in town.

The lane finally opens up to a clearing and a tiny cabin.

"Oh! It's so cute!" I clap my hands, excited that I'm finally here and I'm still alive.

For the first time in my entire life, I'm going to have a real adventure. On my own. This won't be anything like my short time at the University of Seattle. It will be peaceful, and I'll be totally safe. Nothing bad will happen to me here. It's going to be awesome. At least this is what I tell myself as enough knots to keep a professional escape artist busy form in my stomach.

As we get closer to the cabin, the cuteness becomes questionable. The cabin is actually pretty run down.

RJ frowns. "Are you sure this is the place?"

I dig around in my purse for the paper copy of the confirmation email. I smooth out the crumpled sheet. The number on the side of the cabin matches the address on the email, but the cabin looks a lot better in the picture. "Yup, this is it. Maybe the ad was old?"

"Yeah. Maybe. Can I help you get settled?"

"You've already done so much. I'm sure you have some settling of your own to do." I grip my purse strap to keep from wringing my hands again. Of course now I'm worried that I should invite him in and that he'll want to stay and hang out, but I'm tired, and I don't think I smell very nice under this parka.

"I don't mind. At least let me help you get your stuff in the cabin."

I shove down the paranoia that he's only offering so he can chain me to my bed. If he was really a serial killer, he would have just taken me to his bunker, not dropped me off at my cabin. Besides, it would be awkward for me to carry my stuff in while he sits in the cab. "Okay. Sure. Thank you."

I grab the groceries, and RJ brings my suitcase to the front door. I find the key under the mat like the instructions said and slip it in the lock, hoping the outside just needs some fresh paint and that it won't be a reflection of the inside. The door creaks its protest as I shoulder it open. I flick on the light and stare at my new home for the next six weeks, coughing as I breathe in dust.

"It's rustic." It smells musty—and possibly like something rotten.

RJ sets down my bags and also coughs several times into the crook of his arm. "That's one way to describe it."

He turns a slow circle, taking in my little home away from home. It's basically a one-room cabin with a bathroom and a closet. In one corner is a double bed made up with a comforter that may have been fashionable when my great-grandmother was my age.

A nightstand also doubles as a side table for the seventies-era recliner in a color that resembles infant poop—sort of a yellowish, browny green. A very old tube TV is set against the opposing wall, complete with rabbit ears, which I didn't even know still existed.

I'm not sure the information about satellite service was accurate, based on what I'm seeing. On the other side of the cabin is the kitchen, if one could even call it that. There's a hot plate, a microwave, a sink, and a tiny bar fridge. The kind I had when I lived—very briefly—in off-campus student housing.

The biggest piece of furniture, other than the bed, is the two-seater table pushed up against the far wall. It's conveniently located close to the tube TV, which is situated in the center of the room. Lucky me: I can watch TV from my bed, the recliner, or the table while I'm eating my noodles, which, based on the hot plate, are going to be my primary source of nourishment. And maybe fried eggs and bacon.

"This is great!" My voice is high and reedy. This place is the opposite of great, and I think I'm on the verge of a panic attack, which I'd like to avoid while RJ is here. So I fake enthusiasm, hoping I can trick my brain into believing it's true until he's gone. I clear my throat. "I love it! It's perfect."

RJ adjusts his ball cap and squeezes the back of his neck. "Are you sure you're going to be okay here?"

"It'll be great!" I pull the curtains open to let in some sunshine and release a cloud of musty dust. This time I cough for a full thirty seconds before I can speak. "It just needs a little fresh air and a good dusting!" I'm much more careful when I open the curtains over the sliding door. The glass is covered in a layer of grime, but the view beyond that is incredible. Trees dot the front yard, framing the lake and the islands beyond, the bright-blue sky reflected in the water.

I turn the lock, lift the security bar, and slide the door open. Or I try to. It takes some serious effort, at least until RJ gives me a hand. A gust of cool air comes off the water, and I pull the lapels of my jacket together. I take a couple of steps onto the deck—which creaks—and almost fall through a hole. Thankfully, RJ is there to save me with his lightning-fast reflexes.

He grabs me by the waist, pulling me up against him. "I really don't know about this place, Lainey." He sets me back down inside the cabin, away from the danger.

"It's fine. I'll just call the rental people tomorrow and let them know the deck needs a couple of new boards." Half a board is now missing, thanks to me. An animal scurries around under there. I've probably disrupted his home. On the plus side, this is going to be a great place to observe the wildlife. I pat RJ on the chest, noticing how solid it is, much like his arm. "I promise I'll be fine."

He chews on the inside of his lip and rubs the back of his neck, something he's done a couple of times now. His expression tells me he doesn't believe me, which riles me a little. He doesn't even know me, and he's making assumptions. Ones my parents would probably agree with and which are possibly accurate, but I'm determined to prove myself while I'm here.

I'm twenty-five years old. I can be independent without the world falling to pieces. I can handle living in a rustic cabin for six weeks on my own. "Honestly, RJ. I'm a big girl. I can take care of myself." I start unloading my groceries so I have something to do with my hands other than wring them.

"Okay. Well, if you've got a handle on things, I guess I'll head to my place?" It's more of a question than a statement.

I glance over my shoulder. "Thanks so much for all your help, and sorry about falling in your lap, and . . . the Cessna." I cringe, wishing I'd left it at thanks.

"No problem, and it happens to the best of us. You mind if I take your number down?" He taps the old-school rotary phone. The number is stuck to the front with one of those adhesive labels.

"Sure. Go ahead." I stuff my hands in my parka pockets. It's not particularly warm in here, but I'm still hot for some reason.

He takes the number down and shoves the piece of paper in his hoodie pocket. As an afterthought he picks up the receiver.

"What're you doing?"

"Making sure there's a dial tone." He sets it back in the cradle and rocks on his heels. "Okay. Well, I hope I'll see you around."

"Me too. I mean, yes." I try not to be too enthusiastic about my nodding. "Thanks again for everything."

"It's been a pleasure, Lainey."

I walk him to the door. He hesitates and takes a half step toward me. I decide I want to hug him, because he's been nice. And also because he's attractive, he smells good, and he's warm like a big teddy bear.

"Thanks again." I wrap my arms around his waist and let my whole body make contact with his.

"You're welcome." His arms circle me. For a second I worry that he really is a serial killer and I've just embraced my doom. But all he does is give me a squeeze before he releases me. His tongue peeks out and drags across his bottom lip, gaze fixed on my mouth.

I hope I don't have something stuck in my teeth. And that he's not thinking about me being sick on the plane. I rub my lips self-consciously, and his gaze lifts to mine again.

"I'm just down the road if you need anything. It's probably a fifteen-minute walk along the beach, but I'd wait until morning before you go exploring."

"I'm probably just going to unpack and maybe tidy up a few things. It's been a long day."

"Tell me about it. I've been going since five."

"You must be beat."

"Kinda, yeah." He glances around my cabin and seems disinclined to leave, but since there isn't much else to say, he finally heads for his truck. I wait until he's disappeared down the long driveway before I close the door.

"It's fine, Lainey. You're fine. Just put on some music and enjoy the beginning of your first-ever adventure," I mutter to myself.

I find my portable speaker in my bag, plug it in, and put on some happy, upbeat music.

I resume unpacking groceries, putting away the fridge items first. It's not very big, so it's a bit like a three-dimensional food puzzle, but if I close the door fast, everything stays put.

Next I move on to the dry goods. Everything is fine. I can totally do this. I don't need a big place or an actual oven to cook. I can get by with a hot plate and a microwave.

I open one of the cupboards and am greeted by a mousetrap—with a very dead mouse in it that smells absolutely putrid. I scream, because the black holes where its eyes used to be are staring at me, and it's disgusting. I stumble back and fall on my butt in the middle of the kitchen. The floors are rough-hewn wood, and I manage to get a palm full of splinters.

"It's fine. You're fine," I say, for what feels like the hundredth time already as I sit with a lamp aimed at my palm and pick each sliver of wood from my skin.

But I'm not fine at all. My vision blurs, and I suck in a panicky breath.

What have I gotten myself into, and how am I going to make it through the next six weeks on my own in this turd heap of a cabin?

CHAPTER 5

PRACTICE MAKES ANXIOUS

Lainey

"Hello, RJ!"

"Hi, RJ." I shake my head at my reflection. "Hey, RJ!"

I blow out a breath.

I've been standing in front of my mirror for the past twenty minutes, practicing saying hello. The thing about being really into learning is that I haven't spent a lot of time figuring out how to interact with people. I'm really good at presenting information and findings, but conversation isn't my strong suit.

RJ said his cabin is a fifteen-minute trek down the beach. I use the term *beach* loosely. It's more like a path cut into the grassy, sometimes rocky terrain with water on one side.

I've been here for two days. I have no internet reception. I've seen lots of birds and rodents and, in the distance, some whales. My only human interaction has come in the form of cashiers and a waitress at the diner I had lunch at today.

In the short time I've been here, I've made some interesting discoveries—such as, perpetual daylight sucks. Also, since I'm unable to connect to the internet, I can't check my email or do any research. I have no satellite, and I'm bad at keeping a fire going.

More than anything else, this cabin sucks. It's cold, drafty, dusty, musty, and creaky. There are a lot of spiders, and I'm pretty sure I have several rodent roommates, possibly related to the one I buried the day I arrived. Also, the hot-water tank seems to have an issue. So far my showers have been ice cold, which isn't great, because my fire keeps going out—even though I took outdoor adventuring as a Girl Scout. Although I was never allowed to actually go on the outdoor adventuring trips because, according to my mother, those were too dangerous.

I called the rental office hoping they'd be able to help, or maybe they would have alternative accommodations better suited for human habitation, but they're away on vacation and won't be back for another week. So I'm stuck in this dump with only my textbooks and two novels, both of which I've already read. I also haven't slept much, so I'm a little emotional.

This morning when I called my parents, I lied to them, which isn't something I typically do. But I'm determined to make this work, so it was necessary. I told them I'm having a great time. I had to practice faking enthusiasm for ten minutes before I made the call. I'm also grateful for the terrible cell reception. It means my parents can't video chat with me and see my puffy eyes or call me out on my lies.

After I got off the phone, I decided the best plan was to go to town and pick up a couple of tote bins to store my clothes and dry goods in. Hopefully it will make the cabin less enticing for rodents.

Two cab rides, three hours, some limited human interaction, one diner meal, and a shopping trip later, I'm back at the cabin. All of my clothes and dry goods are safely packed in totes, and now I have an entire afternoon free. With nothing to do.

So I've decided to bring RJ a thank-you gift. Well, it's also an apology gift. It's like killing two birds with one stone. Although I'd never kill a bird. But it's a thank-you for being so kind and understanding on the plane—planes—and an apology for falling into his lap, accidentally kissing him on the cheek, and getting sick on the Cessna. And a thank-you for giving me a lift here from the airport.

I picked him up a six-pack of beer while I was in town, the same kind I saw him buy when we went grocery shopping together. I run my fingers through my hair and adjust my hat. Maybe a little makeup would be advisable.

I put on some lip gloss, but it's very pink, and I don't like how much attention it draws to my mouth. The mouth I used to kiss RJ's cheek. His stubbly cheek that smelled like aftershave. The same mouth I used to toss my cookies. No. I don't want to draw attention to my mouth.

After another ten minutes of practicing, I decide I'm as ready as I'm going to be. I leave my tiny one-room cabin and walk in the direction of RJ's place.

The fresh air is nice, but the fifteen-minute walk is actually more along the lines of twenty-five, and I'm sweating under my parka by the time his cabin comes into view. If one could even call it a cabin.

The two-story A-frame has a huge deck and stairs leading all the way up from the water. It makes my place look like a derelict shack, which it kind of is. No wonder he was worried about leaving me there.

I smooth out my hair, which is blowing around my face thanks to the breeze, and take a deep breath. *You can do this, Lainey. He's just a man.* I knock before I lose my nerve.

The door swings open, and I'm greeted by a chest. A bare chest. A big, bare chest. *Oh my.* I allow my gaze to drop a little lower. Sweet heavens, he has an entire six-pack. And that V of muscle at his hips disappears into his jeans, leading my eyes down. I've only ever seen that V in magazines, never in real life. I thought maybe it was airbrushed or something, but clearly I was wrong about that. I wonder if the rest of him is just as defined . . . I snap my eyes up to his face. "Hi."

"Hey. I was just thinking about you." He rubs his lips, the hint of a smile playing on them.

"You were thinking about me while you're shirtless?" Oh God. I didn't just ask that.

He full-on grins. His smile is just so pretty. He has nice teeth. Perfect teeth, actually. "To be fair, I've thought about a lot of things while shirtless, but one of those things happened to be you."

"Right. Of course." I nod. "I would've called, but I didn't take down your number."

"I tried to call you earlier today, but you didn't answer."

"You called me?"

"I wanted to check in. See how you were getting along."

"That's sweet. I'm doing fine. Good, even." I hold up the beer. "I brought you a gift. Well, it's a thank-you—and an apology. It's both."

He inclines his head. "You wanna come in? We can have one of those."

"Oh, uh." I didn't actually plan beyond bringing the beer over. "I don't really drink beer."

"You can still come in, though. I have other liquids you can consume, unless you have somewhere else to be." A dimple pops in his cheek.

"I don't have anywhere else to be."

He steps aside and motions for me to come in. He really is a giant of a man. I'm not tall, but at five foot four I'm around average, and he makes me feel tiny.

He closes the door behind me and runs a hand over his cut abs. "I should put a shirt on."

"You don't have to do that." I gesture to his incredible chest. "I mean, unless it makes you uncomfortable to be shirtless in front of me. Then of course you can put one on, but if you're comfortable shirtless then you should just stay that way. Whatever makes you the most comfortable." I should just stop talking. I set the beer on the counter and open a cupboard. I don't actually know what I'm doing—other than trying not to gawk openly at his awesome chest. Which I sincerely hope he doesn't cover up with a shirt.

I find a couple of glasses in a cupboard and flip them over. "I can pour you one?" I ask.

He steps up beside me, looking 100 percent perfectly shirtless. "I can handle that."

"I've got it." I crack the top and pour the contents into the glass, but it foams like crazy, half the glass filling with bubbles instead of beer. "Hmm, is it supposed to be like this?"

"You really aren't big on the beer, are you?" he asks on a laugh.

"I don't like the taste. Did I ruin it?" We have two restaurants that serve beer in the tiny town I grew up in, but my family didn't eat out often, and my parents only drink alcohol on holidays. I tried beer in college, but I found it too bitter.

"You didn't ruin it. It just needs to settle." He reaches around me—he's so close I stop breathing. RJ grabs a bottle from the six-pack and twists the top off, then picks up the extra glass. Angling it to the side, he empties the bottle into it, filling it about two-thirds of the way. His only foams a little. "Do you like lemonade or grapefruit juice?" he asks.

"I love grapefruit juice!"

His smile is what sunrises are made of. He saunters to the fridge, which means I have a moment to appreciate his very defined back muscles while he retrieves a jug of juice. He tops off the glass and hands it to me. "Give it a taste."

I take a tentative sip. "Oh! This is yummy. I guess maybe I don't mind beer as much as I thought."

His smile widens. "You're the best thing in the world, you know that?"

A warm feeling spreads through my entire body. No one has ever paid me such a nice compliment before. There are a lot of amazing things in the world, and that he thinks I'm the best is, well . . . surprising. So of course I blurt out my own self-assessment. "I'm awkward and nervous."

"Well, I like it. A lot." After a few seconds of intense silence, he motions to the couch. "Sit with me for a bit? We can be awkward and nervous together."

"You're not awkward."

He shrugs. "Sometimes I am. We all can be, context and situation depending."

"Sure. Okay." I follow him to the living room.

His cabin is open concept; giant bark-stripped and sanded tree trunks function as posts with no walls to separate the rooms. The ceilings are high, and the entire front of the cabin is lined with windows, providing an unobstructed view of the water.

A fire crackles across the room, throwing off heat, which probably accounts for RJ's shirtlessness. It's definitely hot in here.

A huge framed photo of RJ and two other men—one likely his father—holding a giant fish hangs on the wall, and beside it is another photo containing two women: his mother and sister, judging from the matching dimple in the younger woman's cheek. There are also a lot of sports accents scattered around, mainly hockey related. The throw cushions read PUCK YEAH! There's a lamp in the corner, and the base is made out of a hockey stick. Even the coasters are old hockey pucks.

"Wow, so you must be huge sports fans." I pick up one of the puck coasters.

RJ rubs the back of his neck. "Pretty obvious, huh?"

"It sort of looks like my dad's room in the basement, except it was all baseball instead of hockey."

"Were you ever into sports?"

I shake my head. "Oh, no. I'm not sporty at all. My dad and my brothers always watched baseball, though. They tried to teach me how to play a couple of times, but I don't understand the rules in sports. I always had my nose in a book."

I hold on to my glass with both hands so I'm not tempted to wring them or bite my nails or any of the other fidgety things I tend to do when I'm nervous. "This is a really nice cabin."

"My dad found it a number of years back and thought it would make a nice place to vacation. I've always been really close with my younger sister, Stevie, but she and my mom aren't big on fishing, so they would stay in New York and we'd go on a boys' trip, which was good bonding for me and my brother and my dad. We've been coming here every summer since I was a teenager."

"But your brother couldn't make it this year?" I ask.

"His wife, Joy, is pregnant, and there are some complications, so he has to stay put." His smile is a little tense, as if there's more to that.

"Oh no, is everything okay?"

"Joy has gestational diabetes, which I guess isn't all that uncommon, but they're keeping a close eye on her. He says everything is okay, and I tend to take him at his word."

"What about your dad—is he still coming?" My family has never really been one for traveling. My mom is scared of airplanes and doesn't like the danger of long drives, or cars in general, so we didn't go too far from the town I was raised in.

RJ looks into his glass. "My dad passed a couple years ago."

I set my drink on the coffee table and put a hand on his knee. "I'm so sorry. That must've been hard." I've never lost anyone close to me, not even a grandparent, so I can only imagine how painful that would be.

"Thanks—and yeah, it wasn't easy. Holidays and birthdays can be tough. I've always been pretty close with my family, so we still feel the loss."

"He must've been so young." I start to shift away, worried I'm making things awkward with the prolonged physical contact, but RJ puts his hand over mine.

"He was only in his mid-fifties. He was type 1 diabetic—took really good care of himself—but some bodies are just defective, you know? Anyway, there were a lot of complications. He lost his vision, and then his body just stopped working properly. It was hardest on my mom, watching him deteriorate like that. The last summer he was around we had to cancel the trip because he just couldn't do it, but the next year Kyle and I came back here. Unfortunately, this year I'm on my own." His smile is sad. He moves his hand from mine and tips his glass back, taking a healthy swig. "What about you—are you close to your family?"

I pick my drink up to keep my hands occupied. "Oh yes, we're all very close."

"Do you have any brothers or sisters?" He seems happy to change the subject, which is understandable, all things considered.

"I have seven siblings."

He nearly chokes on his beer. "Seven?"

I nod. "Yup. I'm the youngest, and I have four older brothers. Dinner was pretty much a full-contact sport at my house."

RJ laughs. "I can imagine. What's the age span between you and the oldest?"

"Thirteen years. There are two sets of twins in there too."

"Wow, how was that, growing up?" He rests his cheek on his fist as if he finds me riveting.

It's almost unnerving to have someone as attractive as he is with his attention fully fixed on me. Also, the shirtlessness, while appreciated, makes it kind of hard to think. Not that I'll complain—I like a good challenge. "It was like having a lot of extra parents who played pranks on each other. Mostly it was nice to always have people around, but sometimes I just wanted some space, you know? They all were always in my business."

He arches a brow. "Dating must've been fun."

"Not really."

He laughs again, rich and throaty. "Did they make it impossible for you in high school?"

"Sort of. We were all homeschooled, so it was a little different for me."

RJ's eyebrows shoot up. "Homeschooled? What was that like?"

"It's probably less isolating than it sounds. There are whole communities built around homeschooling. Like, we even had dances and events and stuff." Not that I did much dancing. I was more the wallflower, standing off to the side, watching everyone else while I tried not to have a panic attack with all those people in one place at the same time.

"With your brothers and sisters?"

It's my turn to laugh at his slightly disturbed expression. "Not just my brothers and sisters, silly. Plus, most of them were a lot older, already done with college by the time I was high school age. We'd get together with all the homeschooled families in the area. They had sports teams and everything. I usually only had about three hours of instruction a day, and I learn fast. Anyway, by the time I was fifteen I'd finished all of the curriculum for my senior year of high school, so I took the college admission tests. I did well, but my parents thought I was too young to go to college, so I took courses online for a couple of years."

"So you're a genius?" RJ asks.

I shrug, embarrassed, and focus on my drink. "I'm just a fast learner. I pick things up quickly, and I have a good memory."

"Smart is sexy, Lainey."

I glance up to find RJ smiling warmly, but it's the way he's looking at me that makes my palms damp and my stomach flutter. Like I'm a fascination.

"What about you? You must have a pretty active job to look like this." I motion to all the cut lines of his torso.

Two dimples pop in his cheeks. "Is that a compliment?"

"It could be, if it doesn't offend you." I hope he doesn't think I'm objectifying him.

"It definitely doesn't offend me, so thanks."

"You're welcome." I take another sip of my drink and realize I've reached the bottom of my glass.

RJ plucks it from my hand and stands. "Here, let me get you another one. Unless you want something else? I have a few bottles of wine kicking around—and whiskey."

"Are you sure? I don't want to monopolize your afternoon."

"Are you kidding? You're the first person I've spoken to in the past two days. I gotta be honest, fishing alone isn't nearly as fun as it is when my brother is here. Why don't you stay for dinner? I was going to make steak and baked potatoes, and it's way easier to cook for two than it is for one."

Anything that isn't noodles or toast sounds amazing. And I don't really want to go back to my cold, lonely cabin any sooner than I have to. "As long as I can help cook."

"That would be great, because I can barbecue a mean steak, and I can bake a potato, but my cooking skill set is pretty limited otherwise. I'm excellent at ordering pizza, though."

"I ruin steak every time I try to cook it, but I can manage pretty much anything else, so we'll make a great team."

I can't believe I'm having dinner with an insanely attractive man. Sure, I dropped in on him unannounced, and we're both likely starving for conversation, but I can still be excited. And nervous, definitely very nervous.

I have a new friend, and he looks great without a shirt on, and that makes my damp palms and my speedy heart rate totally worth it.

CHAPTER 6

SMOOTH MOVES

Rook

When Lainey excuses herself to the bathroom, I rush upstairs and throw on a T-shirt. I know she said whatever makes me comfortable, but sitting around shirtless is such a douche move.

I make it back to the kitchen and pour her a fresh drink before she returns from the bathroom.

"How can I help with dinner?" Lainey drapes her sweater over the back of a chair.

And my mouth goes dry. Like I ate an entire sleeve of saltines and chased it with a tablespoon of salt. So far I've only seen Lainey in a giant parka or an oversize sweater. Under all that bulky fabric is one hell of a body. She's wearing a simple white waffle shirt that conforms to her curves. A pair of dark-wash skinny jeans encase her toned legs.

I'm used to bunnies throwing themselves at me, often in questionable states of undress. I stopped getting excited about miniskirts and revealing tops a long time ago. There's something infinitely sexier about a woman who can show off her body without actually showing it off at all.

Lainey tips her head to the side. Her teeth press into her full bottom lip. I want to do that. Suck that pouty, full lip between my teeth and bite it. I want to do a lot of other, far more explicit things than that, but a kiss seems like a good place to start.

"RJ? Is everything okay?" Her eyes dip down to my chest. I'm wearing a shirt from one of my endorsement campaigns. It afforded me the extensive renovations on this cabin a few years ago.

"Huh?" I give my head a shake. "Oh. Yeah. Everything's good. Sorry, zoned out there for a second."

She smiles and pushes up on her toes, her eyes twinkling—like, they legit light up, and her excitement makes her entire body vibrate. It also makes her boobs jiggle. I try to keep my eyes glued to her face. It's not easy, though.

"I do that all the time! Sometimes my brain is busy with so many thoughts I miss entire conversations. Does that happen to you too?"

I grin. I love that she seems to say whatever is on her mind. "All the time."

"It's actually a helpful skill when you're being lectured, because I can sort through stuff in my head, but it's not so great when your supervising professor is telling you what's wrong with your thesis." She pulls her hair over her shoulder and finger combs it.

"I take it that's happened to you."

"It did. Thankfully he also emailed all his criticisms, so missing out on it the first time wasn't that big of a deal." She divides her hair into three sections and deftly braids it without looking at what she's doing even once. It's pretty damn impressive. I almost want to pull it apart so I can watch her do it all over again. "Anyway, enough about that. Let's get started on dinner!" She nudges me out of the way so she can wash her hands. She dries them on her jeans and moves over to the fridge, opening it to check out the contents.

I kind of like that she makes herself at home. I'm used to women who expect to be catered to. It's refreshing to meet someone who doesn't want me to pander to her.

I start pulling things out of the fridge as she starts naming items she'll need and set them on the counter. I manage to locate most of what she asks for.

"What about garlic? Do you have any of that?" She leans over, peering into the fridge beside me. Her braid slips over her shoulder, skimming my arm.

"Uh, maybe we could forgo the garlic?"

"Are you allergic? My oldest brother gets bloated when he eats it. It took us forever to figure out what was causing it. Sometimes I'll still put some in when he's coming for dinner, because it's funny to see him look like he's expecting." She tips her head to the side. "Or you just don't like garlic?"

"I like it sometimes, but it depends."

Her brows pinch together. "On what?"

"Who I'm eating with. I mean, if I'm going out with buddies, you bet I'm gonna order the honey garlic wings, or the cheesy garlic bread, or the pasta Alfredo. But if I'm eating dinner with a pretty girl, I'm gonna pass on the garlic."

"Oh." She twists the end of her braid around her finger.

Shit. I hope I'm not reading things wrong and making her uncomfortable.

"Does that mean you think I'm pretty?"

That she sounds genuinely curious as to my answer is unexpected. "You see yourself in the mirror every day—what do you think?"

She averts her gaze, still playing with the end of her braid. "My eyes are too big, so I always look like I'm surprised. My nose is small, and my lips are too full, so my mouth doesn't really fit the rest of my face."

"Wow. I think you need a new mirror, because all I see is a whole lot of gorgeous."

She snorts a laugh and waves me off. "Once, I took a portrait class, and we learned all about proportion and symmetry of the face. Those are just my flaws based on what I was taught."

"Well, I'm a big fan of all your flaws, and I think they make you more beautiful, not less."

"Thanks. I think you're beautiful too." She cringes. "I mean handsome. You're very nice to look at, with or without a shirt on. When I fell in your lap on the airplane, I remember thinking, *At least I fell on someone nice looking.*"

"Is that so?"

"Mm-hmm." She opens a drawer, maybe to avoid looking at me. "And as much as I was mortified when you sat beside me on the Cessna, I couldn't complain about the view, inside or outside of the plane. That you turned out to be really nice, and just so helpful, was a great bonus." She hands me a roll of foil. "Why don't you wrap the potatoes? They take the longest, so we should get started on those first."

I put the potatoes on the barbecue and let Lainey order me around. She definitely knows her way around a kitchen. When I was growing up, my mom did most of the cooking, but my dad could make a mean Saturday-morning brunch. He also made great bread, which I miss a lot.

An hour later we're seated at the table, plates full of steak, twice-baked potatoes, and crispy brussels sprouts cooked in bacon fat. I open a bottle of red wine and offer Lainey a glass.

"Just a little bit? I'm not sure I like red wine."

"Maybe you just haven't had the right red wine." I pour a little into her glass.

She picks it up and gives it a swirl, then sniffs it. "I've seen people do this in the movies, but I don't really know what the point is," she admits, then tips the glass back and takes a tentative sip. Her expression turns thoughtful; then she takes another, slightly more robust sip. "This is actually really nice. I like it. Maybe the red wine I had before was bad."

"Maybe. Some of the cheap stuff tastes pretty awful." I pour more into her glass before filling mine. I hold up my glass and wait for her to raise hers. "To chance meetings."

"To new adventures and great company to share them with." We toast and take a sip, each smiling behind the rim.

Dinner is fantastic. I can get by on my own, but back home I have someone come in to prep my meals for me, because I don't have a lot of time during the season and my diet is pretty strict. Nothing beats a good meal cooked by someone who knows what they're doing.

"Tell me more about your family."

"Like what?" She pops a brussels sprout into her mouth and chews thoughtfully.

"What do your parents do for a living?"

"They're dairy farmers. I have to admit, I haven't missed getting up at the crack of dawn to milk cows the past couple of days, although there really hasn't been a dawn to speak of either." Lainey takes another sip of her wine. Her glass is almost empty.

"I grew up on a farm too. Gotta say I don't miss those early mornings either." I uncork the wine and refill her glass and mine.

Lainey sits up straighter, and her eyes go wide with that excitement I've seen a few times already tonight. "Oh! What kind of farmers?"

"Alpaca."

"Really? That must have been so fun! They're just so adorable."

"They can be—when you're not trying to shear them, anyway."

She leans in closer, eager for more information. "Tell me all about that. I want to know everything. How often do they mate? What's it like to raise them? Did you get attached? Did they all have names?" She's just so sweet.

I laugh and tell her all about my childhood growing up on an alpaca farm, happy to have something else in common that I can share with her.

"And is that what you do now? Farm alpacas?"

I hesitate, weighing my options. For the first time in years I feel . . . normal. Being here, in this place with so many good memories—of the time before hockey took over my life, when I was just RJ enjoying my summer and fishing and being a regular guy. I want to hold on to that for as long as can.

There's no pressure, no self-doubt that she's only interested because of my career and my bank account. Besides, what's the harm in telling her a little white lie? In a different life, if I hadn't been such a good hockey player, I *would* be an alpaca farmer. "It's what I grew up doing." It's not a straight answer—so not a complete lie, but not the truth either.

"That's so great. Do you have other siblings who work with you?"

"Both my brother and sister decided on other professions. My brother works in animation, and my sister wants to work in sports therapy. She's still in school."

"That's so nice. All of my brothers went into dairy farming. One of my sisters does all the bookkeeping, and my other two sisters help with distribution."

I shift the conversation away from myself, feeling uncomfortable that I just blatantly lied to her. "So you're the only one who didn't go into dairy farming? Was that hard?"

Lainey looks down at her glass and shrugs. "I still help out, but I didn't go to school for anything agriculture related. At first it was tough. My family likes to stick together, and they're pretty protective of me—being the youngest and all—but I really enjoy learning, so I keep finding new things I love to study." She leans back in her chair and cups her glass of wine in her palms, like she's holding a bowl. "What about you? Did you go to college?"

"For a couple of years, but school wasn't my favorite. I like to be moving instead of sitting."

"Mmm. Yes. I can see that." Her eyes drift over my T-shirt-covered chest, and she bites her lip. I don't think she's being coy, just honest. She clears her throat and touches the back of her hand to her flushed cheek. "I think this wine is going to my head. Is it really warm in here?"

"You've got the wine blush. It looks good on you."

"I should probably hold off on finishing this glass." She sets it down and pushes back her chair. "I'll help clear the table." She arranges her fork and knife on her plate, which she cleared impressively, and takes it to the sink to rinse it off.

I put away the condiments while Lainey rearranges the dishwasher for me. She also refuses to put the pots and pans in there, assuring me they won't come clean and it will just bake on and be ten times harder to get off.

"I can wash." Lainey bumps her hip against mine, nudging me out of the way.

"You're my guest—you don't have to do that."

"I don't mind." She puts the plug in the drain, squirts some dish soap into the sink, and turns on the tap. "The hot water is actually really nice."

I lean against the counter. "What do you mean?"

"Just a bit of trouble with the water heater at the cabin." The fact that she doesn't look at me tells me there's probably more than *a bit* of a problem.

"Do you have hot water?"

"It'll be worked out soon." She waves a soapy hand, flinging suds in the air. They land on her chest and in her hair—and also on me. "Oh! I'm so sorry!"

She wipes her sudsy hands on her jeans and starts brushing them off my chest and neck. I don't stop her, because I'm more than happy to have her hands on me.

She makes the most adorable face. "There's some in your hair. I'm really sorry—I get flaily when I'm nervous, which is a lot of the time. And then I start talking and I can't stop."

"Am I making you nervous?" I bite back a smile.

"Well, not you, exactly, but the whole situation at my cabin—and I don't want you to think I came here because I want your help or anything. Or that I'm trying to mooch a meal off of you or take over your kitchen. Really, I just wanted to see you again, and say I'm sorry, and thank you."

"First of all, you don't need to apologize for anything—and I offered to drive you to your place, mostly for selfish reasons."

"What's selfish about going out of your way for someone else?"

"I wanted to spend more time with you, Lainey, without coming across as too forward or pushy." *Or scaring you off.* Which seems likely with how nervous she is most of the time. I'm getting used to it, though, and it's pretty damn endearing.

"Oh." Her tongue sweeps across her bottom lip as she contemplates that bit of honesty. "Well, in that case, I didn't bring the beer over just as an apology and a thank-you—I wanted to see you again too."

"And here you are."

"And here I am." She blinks her big doe eyes at me, a small, shy smile on her full lips.

"If you haven't figured it out already, I'm really happy about that, and not just because you make kick-ass twice-baked potatoes."

That blush of hers amps up a couple of shades of pink.

I skim her warm cheek with a knuckle.

"Do I have something on my face?" Her voice is soft and whispery.

"No. You're blushing, and it's sweet." I tip my head down in silent request.

"I like the way that feels." Lainey takes a small step forward and reaches up. Her breasts brush against my diaphragm, and her very warm, soft fingers caress my cheek, mirroring the touch.

"Am I blushing too?"

"Maybe." She bites her lip to suppress a smile.

I dip down a little more. "Lainey?"

"Yes, RJ?"

"Can I kiss you?"

"I was hoping you would, so please, yes." She tips her chin up, and her eyes fall closed.

I curl my fingers around the delicate curve of her neck, feeling the heavy rush of blood pumping against my palm. I bend to touch my lips to hers. Her grip on my shoulders tightens, nails biting through my shirt as she makes the sweetest, softest sound. So of course I do it again—and again.

Lainey's hand slides higher, fingertips dancing along my collar until they slip into the hair at the nape of my neck and tug. She parts her lips and flicks her tongue out. It's all the confirmation I need that we're on the same page. I wrap my arm around her waist and pull her against me.

I suck her pouty bottom lip like I've wanted to since I met her and follow with a nibble. She gasps and pulls away, gaze darting from my mouth to my eyes and back. "I feel that through my whole body."

"Should I do it again?"

She nods once and whispers, "Please, yes, and thank you."

So I do it again, and I'm rewarded by yet another sweet gasp, followed by a low moan.

The kiss goes from tentative exploration to frantic in seconds. Dishes forgotten, we stand in front of the sink and make out. It feels a lot like it did when I was back in high school with my first-ever girlfriend, when everything was new. God, I've missed this: being with someone who's genuinely into me. Not because I'm an NHL player—not because I have money, or a sweet ride, or any of the other reasons that typically draw women to me—but because we're acting on a mutual attraction.

One of her hands roams over my chest and down my abs. I will it to go lower, but as soon as she reaches my belt she heads back up. I shift her a little so she's pressed up against the counter. If there weren't a pile of dirty dishes strewn all over it, I'd lift her up so I don't have to bend down quite as far.

I want to run my hands all over her body, but I take into consideration all the things I've learned about her tonight. It sounds like she's been pretty sheltered, so I let her take the lead and wait for her to make the next move.

She feels behind her, elbow bumping a pot on the counter and almost knocking over an empty glass. She makes a muffled sound of annoyance as she presses her hips into mine.

Lainey breaks the kiss long enough to suck in a deep breath and peek around me. I'm about to suggest we take it to the living room and that I'm more than happy to carry her there. Before I can say a word, she pulls my mouth back down to hers and sidesteps over to the table. The kiss grows sloppy and wet as she reaches around me. I try to figure out what she's up to, but I can't without separating our mouths again, which I'm really not inclined to do.

"Here, sit," she mumbles into my mouth as the chair scrapes across the floor. She pushes on my shoulders, and I drop into the chair. Lainey follows, her ass resting on my thighs. Maybe I'm a little off base about how sheltered she is. I definitely should've moved this to the living room when I had the chance. The couch is way more comfortable. Lots of room for stretching out and lying down.

We kiss like we've been starving for each other, hands roaming but staying in mostly safe zones.

She rolls her hips, and I groan at the friction. Lainey goes stiff and still, gasping when she feels me. Her hands rest on my shoulders, and she pushes away, eyes wide.

"Oh my God." She clambers out of my lap and backs up into the counter. "I am *so* sorry."

Me too. Because I'm missing all of that soft and hot rubbing up on my aching, disappointed hard-on. "For what?" It's mostly a croak.

"For throwing myself at you. I'm not usually so forward. I really don't know what got into me." The color rises in her cheeks. "I should probably head back to my cabin." She smooths out her shirt and adjusts her jeans.

"Whoa, wait." I stand and snag her wrist before she can make a move to actually leave. "I need to sober up a little before I can drive you back." I don't want to take her back to that shitty cabin at all, but I also don't want to make her more uncomfortable than she already is.

Her eyes are fixed on my chin, cheeks flaming. "It's okay—you don't need to do that. I can just walk."

"It's midnight, Lainey—there's no way you're walking anywhere."

Her eyes flip up to mine, and her lips flatten into a line. She looks like she's about to fight me on that, so I release her wrist and barrel on.

"It's dangerous this time of night. I know it's not dark, but bears will be out, and you've had a few drinks."

"I'm not—"

"Sober or not, the walk down the beach is rocky, plus the temperature drops and it's cold out. Just stay the night."

"Stay here? With you?" She twists her hands together.

"There are four bedrooms—you can pick whichever one you want." *But you're more than welcome to sleep in my bed—with me.* "Oh, and for the record, you can totally throw yourself at me whenever you want. I won't mind in the least."

She ducks her head and huffs a laugh.

"If you really want to go back to your place, I can call you a cab, but I'd like you to stay."

She tips her chin up, wide eyes meeting mine. "You would?"

"Yeah, Lainey—in case you couldn't tell, I'm way into you. I don't want you to be uncomfortable, though, so it's totally up to you, but there's plenty of space here."

Her cheeks flush yet again. "You really won't mind if I spend the night?"

"I'd love more time with you, talking or kissing. I'm good with either—or both."

She looks away, a shy smile flirting on her lips. "Okay. I'll stay."

I try not to get too excited as I lead her upstairs to the second floor where all the bedrooms are. I'm pretty positive I'm not getting laid tonight. And I'm okay with that, but my dick seems to have missed the memo, considering how hard I still am.

I pause at the first door. "This is my room."

Lainey peeks inside. "It's so big."

I bite back a dirty reply. "Yeah, lots of space, which is nice. Come on, I'll show you the other rooms." She follows me down the hall to the next bedroom. I push the door open and flick on the light. "It has a private bath and everything."

"Oh wow!" She slips past me and beelines it to the bed. Throwing herself on the plaid comforter, she rolls onto her back and spreads her arms out, making her shirt pull up, exposing an inch of smooth skin. "This is amazing."

I lean against the jamb and cross my arms over my chest, smiling, and bite the inside of my cheek to keep from saying things that will embarrass her or me. Such as, *Imagine how amazing it would be if you were naked under me.* "You want to see the other rooms before you make a decision?"

"I don't think I need to. This is perfect." She props herself up on her elbows, stifling a yawn.

"Why don't I grab you something to sleep in? There should be a brand-new toothbrush in the bathroom—and anything else you might need."

"Okay. That would be great. Thank you, RJ."

"It's no problem."

She slides off the bed and pads over to the bathroom. I head back to my room, unsurprised that she'll be sleeping in the room next to mine instead of with me. And if I'm totally honest with myself, I'm actually kind of glad, even if other parts of my body aren't in agreement. Now that I think about it, it's nice to get to know someone before jumping into bed with them. Make a connection in more than just the physical sense.

I think that's probably what I've missed the most since I started playing professional hockey. Don't get me wrong—I had my fair share of fun. And I tried to date a few women, but most of them thought they already knew me, so dates started on uneven footing. When I didn't match the idea they had of me, it left a bitter taste in my mouth.

Much like the lie I told her about my job. I should've just been straight with her, but then maybe she would look at me differently. I decide I'll tell her the truth . . . when she's a little more comfortable around me and the time feels right.

Once I'm in my room, I rearrange my hard-on into a more comfortable position and give it a pat. "Patience, little man. This one will be worth the wait." I roll my eyes at myself, feeling like an idiot for talking to my dick.

I open my dresser, riffling through my T-shirts until I find a plain white one. I also grab a pair of boxer shorts for her, although I have a feeling they'll be way too big. She's still in the bathroom, so I leave the shirt and boxers on the bed and go back downstairs so I can get us each a glass of water, set up the coffee maker for the morning, and turn off all the lights.

By the time I come back upstairs, she's already changed into my T-shirt. Her back is to me, so I have a moment to observe her. The hem hits her mid-thigh, showing off her lean legs. She bends over and pulls the comforter back, exposing the flannel sheets.

I clear my throat, and she jumps.

"Sorry, I didn't mean to startle you. I brought you a glass of water." I cross the room and set it on the nightstand.

"Oh, thank you, that was thoughtful."

"You have everything you need?" I ask, wishing she weren't so nervous around me and that our make-out session hadn't brought with it an awkwardness to our interactions.

"Yup. All set. And thank you for this." She tugs at the sleeve, which almost reaches her elbow.

My gaze drops and catches on her chest, where her nipples pop against the white fabric. I drag my eyes back up to her face. "No problem." I have to clear the frog out of my throat. "I'm not sure if you're an early riser, but the coffee is ready to go, so if you're up before me, just make yourself at home."

"Okay." She takes a tentative step forward and wraps her arms around me. I return the hug but try to keep everything below the waist from making contact with any part of her.

I wait for her to let me go before I slip a single finger under her chin and press a chaste kiss to her minty, soft lips. "Night, Lainey."

"Night, RJ."

CHAPTER 7

MORNING AFTER

Lainey

I sleep for almost ten blissful hours. I could probably lie in this bed forever, but it's after ten, and I can hear RJ downstairs in the kitchen.

I roll out of bed and pad across the floor to the bathroom. Once I get an eyeful of my hair, I decide it would be best to indulge in a shower before I go downstairs, especially since my cabin lacks hot water. While I enjoy the perks of a functioning hot-water tank, I replay that kiss—make-out session—from last night over and over in my head. I wonder if he'll kiss me like that again before I leave. I hope so.

I don't have a choice but to put back on my clothes from yesterday once I'm done, but at least I'm clean and warm. I'm nervous all over again, unsure how not to be awkward as I head downstairs. I plan to thank him for being so hospitable, and then I'll head back to my cabin. RJ is in the kitchen, pushing something around in a frying pan. He's wearing a pair of low-slung sweatpants and a white T-shirt that pulls tight across his back. All my words disappear as I watch his muscles flex under the cotton. I would like to be that cotton.

"Morning. How'd you sleep?" RJ gives me that smile that seems to make my brain short out for a moment.

"I slept great, thank you. I'm sorry it's so late. Those blinds keep out all the light, don't they?" My sweater is hanging over the back of the chair, so I pick it up. "I should probably be going."

"Or you could stay for breakfast," RJ suggests.

"Oh, I couldn't do that—I've already overstayed my welcome. I'm sure you have a busy day." I pull the sweater over my head, even though I'm already hot. If I go now, maybe I'll get that goodbye kiss I'm hoping for.

RJ props a hip against the counter. "Actually, my day is wide open. I mean, there's a chance I'll go fishing at some point, but otherwise I'm totally free. Do you have plans?"

"Uh, no, no plans."

"So you can stay? Have breakfast with me, and then maybe—if you're feeling up to it—we could go to town, or whatever you want, really."

"Are you sure? I don't want to impose." Staying means no goodbye kiss, but maybe we can spend some of the day with our lips against each other's.

"You're not imposing at all, Lainey. I'm happy you're here, and to be honest, I'm still looking for any excuse I can find to spend more time with you."

"Well, in that case, breakfast sounds great. What can I do to help?" And just like that, the awkwardness is gone.

RJ pours me a coffee. "You drink this, and I'll take care of the rest."

I add a little sugar and cream, stir, test, and repeat until it's perfect. "This coffee is amazing."

"You sure you got the cream-to-sugar ratio right?" RJ asks.

"Are you making fun of me?"

He holds his thumb and finger close together. "Maybe a little."

"Too much cream and sugar ruins coffee. I err on the side of caution." I poke his chest.

RJ wraps his arms around me, pulling me up against him. It looks like that kiss I was hoping for is going to happen a lot sooner than I anticipated. He drops his head, and our lips meet and part, tongues stroking in a wet, velvet caress.

I try not to get carried away like I did last night, but kissing RJ is like eating birthday cake. Once I start, I can't seem to stop. I run my hands over his chest and grip the back of his neck to keep them from wandering too much. RJ's hands move in the opposite direction, and he palms my bottom, pulling me closer.

With his free hand, RJ shoves aside whatever's on the counter and knocks the cutting board into the sink with a loud crash. We break apart for a second to check the damage, but everything seems fine.

RJ turns his attention back to me, lifting me onto the counter. "God, I love your mouth."

"Every time you kiss me, I feel like I've just consumed a gallon of coffee spiked with alcohol," I tell him.

"Is that a good or a bad thing?" He drags his lips along the column of my throat.

"It's good. I think." I tip my head to the side. "Although both are highly addictive. Do you think people can get addicted to kissing? I suppose it's possible, since people can be addicted to sex. I guess you can be addicted to anything, really." Crap, I'm babbling.

RJ chuckles and nibbles along the edge of my jaw. "I'm definitely developing an addiction to you."

I part my legs, and RJ steps into the space, groaning when his erection presses against me. I wrap my legs around his waist and hook my feet behind his back, sinking deeper into lust.

Just as RJ slips his fingers under the hem of my shirt, the pungent aroma of something burning—not related to the fireplace—causes him to break the kiss. "Oh shit!" He reaches over to shut off the burner and move the frying pan, now filled with semicharred hash browns, to an unused burner. In his haste, he knocks over my coffee, which spills across the counter.

I jump down before it can reach me, but it drips over the edge onto the floor, splattering our feet.

RJ nabs a dishtowel to sop it up, cheeks flaming just like mine. "That went wrong fast."

"Maybe we should save the make-out sessions for after meals," I suggest, breathless and a little embarrassed that once again I've gotten totally carried away. At least it's not one-sided.

"Probably a good idea." He pushes the charred hash browns around in the pan. "So . . . bacon, eggs, and toast?"

I pat his chest. "I'll make the toast, and you take care of the eggs?"

After breakfast RJ takes me for a ride in his boat. The only kind I've ever been in is a canoe, which tipped over, and yesterday I tried to put the one at my cabin into the water, but a family of squirrels was living in it, so that put an end to that.

Being on open water makes me nervous, so RJ distracts me with more making out. My lips are probably going to be seriously chapped after today, so I'll have to use some lip balm tonight to keep them from peeling.

By the time we get back from our boating trip—I didn't see one dolphin or whale, although I wasn't paying much attention to anything besides RJ—it's well past lunchtime. We make steak sandwiches with last night's leftovers, and RJ suggests a trip into town. I have a list of things I need to pick up, like a new space heater, so I'm all for it.

After a brief stop at my cabin so I can change into fresh clothes, we spend the afternoon shopping. We tour the quaint downtown and grab dinner at a pub. It's after eight by the time we head back to his truck.

"Do you want to come back to my place?" RJ asks once we're on the way to our cabins. Well, my cabin, his rustic house on the water.

The answer to that question is yes. I definitely do. However, I'm concerned about my ability to manage myself around RJ. I worry that things are moving too quickly, and as much as I dislike my cabin, it might be a good idea to spend the night on my own. "That's really sweet of you, but I don't want to impose, and I should probably do some work on my thesis paper, since that's why I'm supposed to be here."

"It's really no imposition, Lainey." He pauses, and I almost want him to try to convince me otherwise. I don't think it would take much. "But I totally understand if you need to work."

We pass RJ's cabin and continue to mine. He helps me carry all my purchases inside. While I set up the new space heater, RJ helps get the fire going.

Once that's taken care of, he hooks his thumbs in his pockets and rocks back on his heels. "Can I call you tomorrow? See what you're up to?"

I'm still bundled up in my parka, but I'm nervous again, which means I start to sweat—so I tug off my hat, then realize I probably have hat head since I've been wearing it all day. I can feel my bangs sticking to my forehead and static working its magic elsewhere. I want to put it back on, but I drop it on the lounge chair and fiddle with the end of my braid instead. "I'd like that."

"Okay. Well, if you have any problems tonight, I'm just a phone call away." He scribbles down the number for his cabin on a piece of paper, then pulls me in for a hug. I let my gloves drop to the floor and curve my palm around the back of his neck. I know he's leaving, so I might as well get in one last good-night kiss. It goes from soft to needy between one heartbeat and the next.

Several minutes later we come up for air.

"I'll call you tomorrow." This time it's not a question.

He comes in for another kiss that, once again, turns into a dance of tongues and a grinding session.

"If you don't go, I'm not getting anything done tonight, and no one gets any kind of reward tomorrow." I shimmy us toward the door.

"It'd be a lot easier if you weren't such an active, enticing participant," RJ mutters as our tongues tangle again.

"It would be a lot easier for me if kissing you didn't make my whole body feel like it's been dipped in some kind of sensory-heightening serum." I fumble with the doorknob, sucking on his bottom lip at the same time.

Eventually I manage to get the door open. The shock of frigid air is enough to finally get us to separate. I pry my fingers from RJ's neck, and he releases me, taking a step back.

He slips a hand into his pocket and does some blatant rearranging, which both thrills me and makes me blush.

He smirks. "What can I say? We both like you."

I laugh and roll my eyes. "You're incorrigible. Now go, so I can make an attempt at being productive."

RJ holds up a finger. "Just one more kiss to tide me over?"

"Just one."

He leans in, and I put my hand on his chest, allowing only a couple of sweeps of tongue before I step back. "I'll talk to you tomorrow."

He walks backward to his truck, and I stand in the doorway, staying there until the taillights disappear down the driveway.

I'm probably going to regret not staying at his place tonight, but I think I should at least try to resist him. Besides, this will inevitably heighten the very present chemistry between us. Theoretically, it should. I guess I'll find out tomorrow if I'm right.

CHAPTER 8

SCAREDY-CAT

Lainey

I can list the things I like about my cabin on one finger: not being in it.

I spend a good part of the evening trying to work on my thesis. *Trying* being the operative word. Mostly, all I can think about is kissing RJ and the feel of his erection pressing against my stomach through all the barriers of fabric.

While I have spent some time on the water, it hasn't been studying the animals in it. So I review some of my preliminary research and manage to make notes on the correlations I intend to focus on when I actually put some time and energy into the real reason I'm here. Which is not making out with RJ.

But he's so good at it.

It makes me wonder how many other women have had the opportunity to experience his kissing skills. It also makes me wonder what else he's good at. Probably everything, I decide. He seems to know exactly what he's doing. While I have a master's in sex therapy, most of my knowledge is theory and text based.

And now I'm thinking about sex for what seems like the millionth time since I fell into RJ's lap on the plane a few days ago. And I'm thinking about how uncomfortable this bed is in comparison to the one in his spare room. Right next to his bedroom. Where he's probably sleeping right now. Unlike me.

Instead, I'm lying on a lumpy mattress, staring at the ceiling, freezing under a pile of musty-smelling blankets, wishing I'd taken him up on his offer.

I know without an ounce of doubt that I would not be sleeping in the room beside his if I went back to his place. I don't think there's anything wrong with people being attracted to each other. In theory, it's a natural human reaction. But I have never been this wildly attracted to anyone before in my life, and I worry that my lack of restraint may be a problem.

I roll over onto my stomach and pull one of the dank pillows over my head, close my eyes, and try to shut my brain off. It's pointless, though. I'm wide awake. It's only four o'clock in the morning, but I give up on trying to sleep.

I make myself a coffee, toast a bagel and slather it in cream cheese, and head outside with a pair of binoculars. While we were in town yesterday I was able to borrow a couple of books on my e-reader, and I picked up a million brochures so I'll have some reading for comparative data analysis.

I get lost in my reading and watching for dolphins and whales on the water for the next few hours. I would probably spend the entire day sitting outside, despite it being cold and my fingers being mostly numb, just to avoid the cabin.

Eventually I need to use the bathroom, and I could definitely use a fresh pot of coffee, since my eyeballs feel a lot like eggs covered in sand when I blink. The phone rings just as I'm finishing up in the bathroom. I don't even bother to wash my hands. Instead, I rush out with my pants still half-down and answer the call before the phone stops ringing.

"Hello!" I shout and then cringe because I'm too loud.

"Lainey?"

My excitement deflates like a sad balloon, but I try to keep the disappointment out of my voice. "Oh, hi, Mom."

"Thank God you answered. I was getting worried. I emailed four times already this morning, and I've been calling for the past two hours."

"Oh, sorry, I was outside and I couldn't hear the phone, and cell service really isn't reliable here. Is everything okay?"

"Oh, oh yes. Everything is fine. I was just worried about you since you didn't call yesterday. I read an article about bear attacks up there in Alaska. Did you know you can't keep your garbage outside because of the bears? And did you know that brown bears are related to grizzlies? They'll come sniffing around if you leave any food out. You have bear spray, don't you? I should have insisted you take shooting lessons over archery when you were a teenager."

"I know all about the garbage, Mom, and you know how I feel about guns." I shudder at the thought of ever having to hold one.

"I know, I know. But what about the bear spray? Do you at least have that?"

"I do."

"Okay. Well, that's good. How are things going? You know it's all right if you get homesick and decide to come back early. Your ticket is open ended, so you can fly home anytime."

"I'm actually having a great time."

"Oh. Well . . . that's good. You're managing the anxiety okay, then? You have all your visualization techniques for when things get stressful?"

"I'm managing everything just fine, and yes, I know what to do when things get stressful. It's pretty quiet around here, though."

"I'm glad to hear that." She doesn't sound glad at all. "Have you made any friends? You can be so focused on your studies and sometimes making friends is hard for you. Are there any other students there?"

"No other students, but I did make a friend."

"Really? That's so wonderful!"

I try not to be affronted by her shock.

"Where did you meet her? Have you done fun things together? If she's not a student, what does she do? Is she local?"

"I met them on the plane. They're not local—they actually have an alpaca farm in New York, which is really cool. We went boating yesterday."

"Well, that sounds fun! Did you wear a life jacket? What's her name?"

"RJ."

"RJ? That doesn't sound like a girl's name."

I hate that I'm twenty-five and telling my mother that I met someone who isn't female is still a thing. "That's because RJ isn't a girl."

I'm met with silence—a long, heavy silence. I'm aware it won't last. "You're spending time with a boy? What do you even know about him? And who goes by initials? I don't like this at all, and I don't think your father is going to like it either."

I bite back the scathing remarks I'd like to let fly, aware I'll regret it if I get into an argument with my mother with no way to patch things up from this far away. "He's very nice, Mom. He's been very helpful and kind. He's taken me grocery shopping, and we had a nice afternoon exploring the town together."

"Do you really think this is a good idea, Lainey? You know how attached you get to people. You're only there for six weeks, and you already sound smitten!"

"I'm not smitten." I don't like how sour those words are. "I'm only here for a short time, and he's only here for a few weeks. There's no harm in spending time with someone I like."

"Boys only want one thing, Lainey."

"He's not a boy, Mom, he's a man—and I'm not a girl. I'm a twenty-five-year-old woman. We have fun together, and I'm going to enjoy my time with him," I snap.

More silence follows.

"Please, Mom, don't make this hard for me."

She sighs. "You know how much I worry about you."

"I know, but I'm having fun, and he really is nice." *And very good at kissing.* "How's everyone doing? How is Mooreen? She must be ready to have her calf soon. Is Dr. Flood coming to take care of that?" It's not a subtle shift, but it does the trick.

My mom goes off on a rant about the animals, then goes on to gossip about the neighbors.

Eventually she lets me go so she can get back to laundry. I decide to call my friend Eden, who recently moved out to Chicago for a great job. I miss her, but we still keep in touch through phone calls and email. She's much more enthusiastic about my new friend.

By the time I end the call with her, it's already two o'clock in the afternoon, and I'm tired and hungry. I eat a handful of crackers, too exhausted from being up since four o'clock in the morning to be bothered with boiling water and making noodles. The sun is no longer shining, clouds having rolled in while I was on the phone, darkening the afternoon sky.

I decide a twenty-minute nap will do the trick and that I might be able to make it through the rest of the day, and I have half a hope of getting a decent night's sleep. After my nap I can call RJ and see if he's still up for doing something.

I put on some relaxing music and lie down on my lumpy bed. The moment I close my eyes, RJ's toned chest appears behind my lids. I allow the memory of his lips on mine and the way it felt to be pressed up against all those hard muscles to take over as I sink into blissful sleep.

A huge bang startles me awake. I bolt upright and reach for the closest object, which happens to be a textbook on my nightstand. No lights are on, which doesn't make a lot of sense, since I could've sworn they were when I fell asleep. A flash of lightning startles me, and seconds later a crash of thunder makes the entire cabin shake. Shadows crawl across the walls for the short span of time that there's light, so, of course, I scream.

I hate thunderstorms. The thunder sounds a lot like gunshots, and it reminds me of my time at college in Seattle. That, along with the fact that I'm in a rickety cabin, the fire has gone out, and there are no lights on, sends me right into Anxiousville.

Rain pounds on the roof, and more thunder and lightning have me hiding under my covers. I try to slow my panicked breathing, but it's coming too fast and I'm already spiraling out of control—all my thoughts are fleeting. I need light.

"Take a breath, Lainey. Take a breath and figure it out," I tell myself. I inhale deeply and exhale slowly. *Breathe in. Breathe out.*

There has to be a flashlight somewhere in here. Or some candles. I gave up on charging my cell phone yesterday, since I have one of those cheap carrier services and I haven't been getting reception at all. Still, it doesn't hurt to see if it's holding a charge so I can at least use the screen to find something more reliable. Unfortunately, it's dead, just like all the lights in this place.

A cold drop of water hits me on the back of the neck—and then another on my arm.

The momentary reprieve in my panic dissolves as I stumble around in the strange inky darkness, searching the cupboards for anything other than the pack of matches I keep using to light the fire. I finally find a lighter, but all it does is spark without giving me a flame. Eventually I manage to find a flashlight, but it flickers once and dies. "Is nothing about this stupid place reliable?" I yell to no one.

The only answer is a strike of lightning and a boom of thunder.

The wind picks up, howling through the walls, making it sound like there are wolves outside my cabin. Which is when I totally lose it. Because here I am, alone in this cabin with no lights, no flashlight, no candles—and the roof is leaking in a bunch of places, based on the number of times I'm getting dripped on.

"You need to get a grip, Lainey," I tell myself through a sob. I suck in a deep breath and release it through my nose, trying to focus on the visualization strategy my therapist always tells me to use when the panic gets too big.

I go through my senses: five things I can taste, four things I can touch, three things I can smell, two things I can hear—that doesn't help the anxiety at all, since thunder happens right at that moment.

I work to block out the memories from college. The storm. The lightning and thunder, how they overlapped with the repetitive rat-a-tat. The crashing open of the lecture hall doors. The screaming . . .

I'm startled once again when the phone rings. If it's my parents, there's no way they're going to believe I'm okay. Because I'm not. I'm terrified. But I really don't want to be alone in this storm right now, so I answer it, even if it's going to bring me nothing but grief.

"Hello?" I croak.

The line crackles with static. "Lainey?"

It's not my parents, thank God. "RJ?"

"Hey, I'm glad you answered. I tried to call earlier, but the line was busy—" He cuts out when a huge crack of thunder makes the cabin shake. I also shriek, which makes it hard to hear. "Are you all right?"

"Uh . . ." I consider lying but realize there isn't much of a point. "I don't have any power."

"Yeah, all the lines are down. The summer storms can be harsh here, and we can lose power for a couple of days."

"A couple of days?" There's that high pitch again.

"Yeah, I have a generator in case of power failures. I'll come get you, okay? I'll be there in five minutes, maybe ten at the most."

"Okay. That would be nice." I whimper at the next flash of lightning. "I don't really like thunderstorms."

"I'll be there as quick as I can."

"Can you bring a flashlight? The ones here don't have any batteries."

"Shit. Yeah, of course. I'm already on my way out the door. See you in a few."

"Okay. Thank you." I reluctantly hang up the phone. I want to pack a bag, but I can't do that without some kind of light source.

Minutes drag on for what feels like hours, until a knock scares me—although pretty much everything is scaring me right now. I flip the lock and throw open the door. Standing on the rickety, unsafe back steps, getting pounded by the rain, is RJ, dressed in a yellow rain slicker, holding a flashlight bright enough to land a plane.

I step back, letting him in. His hood falls back, exposing his gorgeous face, flushed and dotted with raindrops. I close the door behind him and throw myself into his arms, not caring that he's soaking wet. Or that I look desperate. A crash of thunder has me trying to bury my face in his chest.

He stands there for a moment, unmoving, possibly shocked, before he finally wraps his wet arms around me. "Hey, you're okay."

"I really hate thunderstorms," I mumble into his rain slicker.

He runs a soothing hand down my back. "Totally understandable when it's raining almost as hard inside as it is outside."

I take several deep, steadying breaths, trying to regain a little composure so I don't come across as a complete head case, but I've been crying, and my face always gets blotchy and my eyes get puffy. At least the lighting is bad.

Eventually I loosen my hold, aware I can't koala bear him forever. "I'm okay. I'm fine. Thanks so much for coming."

"I would've been here sooner if I'd known it was this bad." He cringes as drops of water land on his head from the ceiling above. "Let's pack you a bag and get you out of here."

I nod. "I'd like that."

With the help of his flashlight I stuff clothes into my suitcase. I throw in my laptop and any other electronics, worried that they'll get wet and ruined with how much rain is coming through the roof.

I toss my toiletries in as well and throw on my coat. "I think I'm ready." I shove my hands in my pockets so he can't see how much I'm shaking.

RJ stuffs my suitcase into a big black garbage bag before we head out. The rain is so heavy I can barely see the truck, still running, sitting less than twenty feet from the back door. "Let's go," he shouts, voice drowned out by the driving downpour.

I make a break for it as another boom of thunder shakes the ground. My feet slide out from under me, but RJ's strong arm wraps around my waist, dragging me back up.

"Got you." RJ half carries me the rest of the way to the truck, only letting me go when he's sure I have my footing. I wrench the door open, scrambling into the passenger seat with help from RJ. Once I'm safe inside, he tosses my suitcase into the back seat and rushes around the hood.

It's warm and dry inside, apart from where I'm dripping all over the seat and the floor. In the short distance between the cabin and the truck, my coat got soaked through to my shirt. RJ blasts the heat, and I buckle myself in.

The windshield wipers are on full speed, but the rain is coming down faster and harder than they can do their job. It takes twice as long to get back to his place, because branches have fallen on the road and he has to swerve around some of the larger ones.

Once we reach Sweet View Home, he presses an automatic garage-door opener and pulls in. Shifting into park, he cuts the engine. "Come on, let's get you inside and dried off."

Despite the blasting heat, my teeth are still chattering—I'm not sure if it's from the cold or the anxiety. "That w-would be n-nice."

RJ is out of the truck and around the passenger side before I even have my seat belt unfastened. Although I can't really feel my fingers, so hitting the release button is more difficult than usual. I manage to free myself as RJ opens the door. He wraps his wide palms around my waist and lifts me out of the truck. I brace my hands on his shoulders, embarrassed and strangely turned on by how easy it is for him to pick me up like I weigh no more than a toddler.

He sets me down, and I huddle into myself, still shivering, as I wait for him to grab my stuff from the back seat. I follow him inside, not knowing what to say. My shoes make a squishy sound as I step onto a mat in what's clearly the mudroom. This space alone is probably bigger than my entire cabin.

I drop to one knee and focus on the task of untying my shoes. The laces are soaked, and they pull tighter instead of looser when I tug the loops. I'm frustrated, embarrassed, and still trying to get a handle on how anxious I am.

"Hey." RJ drops down into a crouch in front of me. He's still wearing rain boots, which are far more practical than my running shoes.

"I keep making the knots tighter." I avoid making eye contact by continuing the futile task of untying my shoes.

His warm hand covers mine. "You're freezing. Let me help, Lainey."

I stop fighting with the knots and let him take over. He leaves the laces and pulls my shoes off. My socks are soaked, along with every other part of me, and they stick to the shoes, coming off with a wet suction sound. I'm sure the bottoms of my feet are wrinkly, and the rest of me looks like a splotchy drowned rat.

My teeth won't stop chattering as RJ helps me to my feet and unzips my coat. It lands on the floor with a heavy thud. His own yellow raincoat is gone. I shiver violently, and RJ runs his hands up and down my arms. It feels nice, but it doesn't do much good since I'm soaked to the bone.

"Come on. You need to get warm, and that's not going to happen in these wet clothes." He tucks me into his side and grabs my suitcase, leading me down the hall and upstairs to the bedroom I stayed in two nights ago. RJ drops his arm from around my shoulder and sets my suitcase on the bed.

I hug myself, trying to control the shivering. I'm embarrassed that I'm in such a state. Another roll of thunder and flash of lightning makes me jump.

He moves closer until his socked feet touch my bare toes. "God, you're like a scared little kitten, aren't you?" He skims my cheek with the back of his hand.

"I'm sorry. I know it's silly and it's j-just a th-thunderstorm."

"You don't have to be sorry. That cabin is the prime setting for a horror movie." He tips my chin up, his expression soft. "Why don't you warm up with a shower and put on some dry clothes? I'll make you something hot to drink."

"I would l-like that."

"Great. I'll put a few extra logs on the fire. Take your time." He presses a kiss to my cheek, then leaves the room, closing the door behind him with a quiet click.

I exhale a long breath as soon as I'm alone. Thank God I managed not to cry in front of him. That would be insanely embarrassing. I turn on the shower, strip out of my soaked clothes, and step under the hot spray. I can't hear the thunder or lightning in here, so I'm finally able to relax a little. I don't know how long I stay there, but by the time I'm done my hands are as pruney as my feet and my skin is bright pink.

I rummage around in my suitcase for a nice pair of underwear. I have to settle on pink cotton ones since I didn't bring anything sexy for this trip, thinking the only guys I'd be hanging around with would be of the whale or dolphin variety.

I pull on a pair of thermal leggings, a thermal undershirt, an over-size sweater, and wool socks. I check my reflection in the mirror, relieved my cheeks aren't blotchy anymore, and head downstairs.

I find RJ in the living room, stoking the fire. There are pillows laid out on the floor and big fluffy blankets. On a tray next to the pillows and blankets are two steaming mugs of hot chocolate piled high with marshmallows. A plate of cookies and pastries sits between them. The rain has slowed, the pounding now a light patter.

"This looks cozy." I clasp my hands to keep from wringing them. Now that I'm not panicking, I'm more than a little embarrassed by the way I acted when RJ picked me up.

"And you look much warmer." He pats the pile of blankets. "Wanna come sit with me?"

"Sure." I drop onto one of the cushions and cross my legs as RJ does the same. "Sorry I was so . . . freaked out when you came and got me."

He props himself up on one elbow. "Can I be completely honest?"

I glance quickly at him and then away. "Of course."

"I'm just glad I get to spend more time with you. And I actually really like that I get to protect you, even if it's just from getting rained on—which probably sounds wrong. It's just . . . nice to take care of someone else? Feel . . . needed?" He blows out a breath and cringes. "I'm going to stop while I'm ahead. Or maybe behind."

"I think I get what you mean." I run my fingertip along the seam of my leggings so I have somewhere to focus that isn't RJ's face—or specifically his mouth. Now that the worst of the storm seems to have passed and I can do something other than panic, I'm remembering what it was like to be kissed by him. "It's kind of nice to be taken care of. Normally I'm just dealing with overprotective parents, so this is much more welcome."

He relaxes a little. "Okay. Good. I'm glad you feel that way. And I can completely understand why your parents are overprotective."

"I can take care of myself—I just don't like thunderstorms," I say rather defensively.

He runs a gentle finger along the back of my hand. "I think you can take care of yourself just fine, considering you survived in that shithole cabin the past few days. But I'd be overprotective, too, if I had a daughter and she was gorgeous and sweet like you. I wouldn't want anyone to take advantage of what's mine." He shakes his head. "I think I'm digging myself a bigger hole, aren't I?"

I laugh. "There weren't many opportunities for me to get taken advantage of with four older brothers."

"Can't say I blame them for wanting to keep the wolves at bay." His gaze moves over me in a hot, familiar way.

"You're not a wolf, though, are you, RJ? You're a teddy bear."

His dimpled grin appears. "I'm glad you think that. You feeling better now?"

"Much, thank you. I don't know what I would've done tonight if you hadn't come to get me." Other than cry, anyway.

"I'm glad I could. Tomorrow we can go back and get the rest of your stuff."

"The owners of the cabin will be back at the end of the week, I think. I can let them know the roof needs to be fixed." I work on sounding flippant about it, because I've already been the damsel in distress more times than I'd like with RJ.

RJ cocks a brow. "At the risk of sounding like I'm telling you what to do, you can't stay there anymore, Lainey."

"I've already paid for it, though, and I can't afford to rent something else."

"You don't have to rent something else. You can stay here. Four bedrooms, remember? And you're already set up in one of them. Unless you don't want to stay here. If that's the case, then I can drive you to town and we can see what's available there, but that cabin is a total shithole, and I can't in good conscience take you back there unless it's to get your things."

CHAPTER 9

SENSORY EXPLORATION

Rook

Shit. That might not have been the right thing to say.

Lainey's expression remains flat for several more seconds before she finally cracks a smile. "It really is a dump, isn't it?"

I'm relieved she didn't take that the wrong way. "I gotta be honest—I felt bad leaving you there the first night."

"I felt bad about that too."

I laugh at her wry grin. "So you'll stay here? I don't have to worry about that roof caving in on you or the raccoons cuddling in bed with you?"

"I think mice and spiders are the more likely cuddlers." Lainey shudders. "Yes, I'll stay for now."

We sit by the fire, drinking spiked hot chocolate and talking about what it's like to grow up with four older brothers and three older sisters. I like that I can talk about my siblings and my family with her. As we share stories, I decide I should come out and tell her the truth about my job and hope that she isn't upset that I wasn't honest in the first place. I prop myself up on one arm so I can look directly at her. She's reclined against a pile of pillows, long hair spilling over her shoulders, eyes soft, cheeks pink with the heat from the fire and the spiked hot chocolate.

"I want to tell you something." I finger a lock of silky hair, nervous and second-guessing myself. I really don't want this to change things.

She smiles and bites her lip. "Okay. Sure. You can tell me anything, RJ."

I return her smile, but I doubt mine is as easy. "So you know how I said—"

A flash of lightning makes Lainey's eyes flare with panic and her face pale. "Oh no. I thought the storm was over."

An impressive crack of thunder follows that statement, and she sits up, pulling her knees to her chest so she's almost a little ball.

Obviously my truth has to wait. "Hey, it's okay. You're safe." I shift so I can put an arm around her.

"It's silly to be afraid of thunder." She turns to me, her entire body shaking.

I slip an arm under her legs and move her so she's in my lap. "Human teddy bear right here, offering safety cuddles, free of judgment."

"Thank you. I'm sorry." She presses her forehead against the side of my neck, warmth feathering across my throat with her panicked breaths.

"You don't need to apologize for being scared, Lainey. Did you have a bad experience during a storm?" It's the only reason I can come up with for her to be so freaked out.

She nods against my shoulder.

"Do you want to talk about it?"

She's quiet for long enough that I almost backtrack.

"Remember how I said I went to Seattle for college?"

"But you didn't stay long." She said she was only there a month. I assumed the city was too much for her.

"No. I didn't."

"What happened?" Now I'm trying to figure out how thunderstorms and leaving her college program fit together.

"I lived off campus in the student apartments. There was a thunderstorm one night, and the building lost power—so when I woke up, it was only about twenty minutes before class. We were getting tests back that day, and I decided I'd rather be late than miss it altogether, so I got ready and rushed to campus. I was only about five minutes late. It was still storming, lots of thunder and lightning." She shudders and curls up tight against me. "I was on my way up the stairs into the lecture hall. There was this sound, and at first I thought it was thunder."

I stroke up and down her back, hoping to soothe her, aware that this story is going nowhere good. "But it wasn't?"

"No." Her voice is so small, like she's trying to hide from her own memories.

"What happened then?"

She shifts a little so she can meet my gaze, her own swimming with ghosts and tears. "There was a boy in my class—or a man, I guess. He was kind of a loner, like me a bit. Quiet. Shy, but also . . . dark? He never really looked happy about anything. Just sort of cynical. But I always said hi to him even though he never looked very friendly, because no one really wants to be alone, you know? And he always nodded. It was never anything more, but I tried." She clears her throat. "Anyway, that day he brought a semiautomatic to class, and the sound I mistook for thunder was him firing into the lecture hall. A few people got hit before he turned the gun on himself."

"Oh God, Lainey, that must have been awful. I can't even imagine what would make a person do that." I tighten my hold on her as I consider how terrified she must have been.

Her eyes are sad and distant. "He failed the test, so maybe that set him off? I wondered if maybe—if I'd tried a little harder—he would have talked to me. Maybe, if he had a connection to someone in there, that would have stopped him? It's probably stupid to think that. I mean, clearly there was something wrong with him—he wasn't balanced—but still . . ."

I brush away her tears as they fall. "You can't take that on, Lainey. He was mentally ill. The only time a person does something that extreme is if they're not well. You're lucky you were late." *I'm lucky you were late, or you might not be here.*

"That's what my family kept telling me. They still do. Because I'm here—and I didn't see it happen, I just heard it and witnessed the aftermath." She looks haunted in that way only people who have experienced deep trauma can be. "This isn't . . . I haven't really talked about this with anyone but my family and my therapist. It's just . . . not good conversation. I couldn't talk about it with my mom—she couldn't handle it."

"How do you mean?"

"She worries more than I do. And the news coverage of the incident made it so much worse." Her fingers drift slowly along the collar of my T-shirt, eyes following the movement.

"I'm glad you feel safe enough with me to talk about it—and as hard as it is to do, sometimes it's better to get it out rather than keep it all locked up inside."

"I used to worry that talking about it would make the fears worse instead of better."

"Because it makes the memories fresh again?" I rub her back, not really knowing what else to do for her.

"Mm-hmm." She nods. "But it feels good not to hold on to it alone anymore."

"Good. It shouldn't be yours to hold on to."

"That boy, the shooter, he didn't survive." Lainey drags her finger along my clavicle, body jolting with the next rumble of thunder. She exhales a shaky breath before she continues. "People came rushing out of the lecture hall. Everyone was screaming." She presses her palm against the side of my neck, thumb brushing back and forth slowly along the edge of my jaw. "I was just . . . frozen on the steps. I knew I needed to move, but I couldn't make my body follow the command. By the time I turned to run, everyone was on me. I twisted my ankle on the steps, but someone grabbed my hand and pulled me out of the way before I could get trampled. I was lucky I didn't see any of it firsthand."

The last part sounds more like something she says as self-reassurance. "I'm so sorry you went through that." No wonder she was so terrified when I came to pick her up. And I realize that Lainey is far stronger than I ever could have imagined. To survive something like that and still be able to look at life with such positivity is a miracle.

"My classmates went through much worse, but now you know why I hate thunderstorms so much. I've always been anxious, but after that . . . I have a very hard time with crowds, so the airport was a challenge for me. And being on a plane with no way of escaping, that wasn't pleasant either. But I used all the strategies I have to stay calm, and I made it through just fine—and then you were on the Cessna, so that helped. I should be able to handle a thunderstorm, but the memories are hard to deal with sometimes."

"Is there anything I can do? Some way I can help now?"

"Being here with you makes me feel safer." She smooths her hand over my shoulder and down my biceps, slipping under the hem of the sleeve. "I don't like to rely too much on people to help calm me, because it's not always effective—especially if those people aren't there when the anxiety becomes intolerable—so I usually do a sensory calming exercise."

"What is that?"

"I focus on the five senses, counting down from five to one. So unless it's dark, I usually start with five things I can see." A flash of lightning startles her, and she digs her nails into my biceps.

I tuck a finger under her chin and turn her head away from the windows behind us, since she's waiting for the next rumble of thunder. "Tell me what you see right now, Lainey."

Her eyes search mine, bottom lip trembling. "I-I see flecks of blue and gold near your iris when I'm this close to you."

"That's one. What else?"

"You have a dimple high on your left cheek. It's always there, but it's more obvious when you smile or laugh." She skims my eyebrow with her fingertip. "You have a scar above your eyebrow that makes it look arched all the time."

I laugh, and she smiles. "You have a tiny freckle right here." She taps my bottom lip, then drags her finger down the side of my throat. "And this vein right here shows me exactly how calm you are right now."

"What's next? Touch? Or do I get to play this game too?"

"That depends."

"On?"

"Are you anxious?"

"Maybe a little."

She frowns as if she's concerned, which is ironic considering what she's been through and how it's affecting her right now. "About what?"

"I have a gorgeous woman that I really like who's anxious because she's been through something bad that I can't fix, even though I want to be able to. I don't want to mess this up by saying or doing the wrong thing."

She shifts, and for a moment I think she's going to move off my lap, but instead she straddles my thighs. "Everything you say is perfect, so you have nothing to worry about."

A flash of lightning has her sucking in a breath.

"Hey, hey, stay with me, right here. Focus on me. Tell me what you feel." I cup her face in my palms to keep her eyes locked with mine.

"I feel . . . my heart racing, the warmth of your palms against my skin, the heat of your body under me even through our clothes, and an ache . . ." She bites her lip and her cheeks flush.

"What kind of ache?"

"For you to touch more of me," she whispers, almost shyly.

I skim her throat lightly. "Like this?"

"Yes, please."

I drag my fingers over her collarbone and down her arms until I reach her hands. I bring one to my lips so I can kiss her knuckle. "Is taste next?"

She nods, eyes staying on mine. "It is."

"What do you want to taste, Lainey?" I run my hands up the outside of her thighs, wishing I were touching bare skin. I know what I want to taste, but I'm not exactly sure what direction we're heading, and I'd like her to lead.

"Your skin." She leans in, nose brushing along my jaw as her lips find my throat, right over the pulse point. Her soft, warm tongue strokes along my skin before she kisses her way up to my ear. "I taste salt and the bitterness of aftershave." Her lips travel over my cheek until they finally brush over mine. She sucks my bottom lip. "I taste mint and chocolate and marshmallows."

She angles her head, lips parting as she comes in for another kiss, this time with tongue. I keep my hands on her thighs, even though I desperately want to touch more of her. Her tongue strokes mine, and she whimpers quietly.

She slides her fingers into my hair and latches on. Lainey shimmies forward until her chest is flush with mine, and I'm sure she realizes that her calming exercise has been having the opposite effect on me. I groan into her mouth.

"I hear desire." She drops her hands and grabs the hem of her sweater. "And the soft rustle of fabric." She lifts it over her head, along with the thermal shirt under it, skin pebbling—possibly because it's cold, maybe because she's still anxious . . . or turned on.

She's gloriously topless, and my imagination has proven absolutely abysmal in concocting anything close to the reality of what this would look like, feel like, be like.

I couldn't have predicted a set of circumstances that would bring us into each other's lives like this, let alone to this point. It feels . . . different. Like there's significance in every single touch and caress, and I feel the sharp bite of guilt over not being completely honest with her about who I am. But I won't ruin it now, not when she's shared something so obviously painful for her. Not when she's here, looking for me to take it away for a while in whatever way I can.

"You're gorgeous." I smooth my hands down the sides of her neck and kiss her.

"We never got to smell," she murmurs against my lips.

"I smell mint and cucumber shampoo." I brush my nose along the column of her throat. "And the sweetness of your vanilla lotion. What about you?"

"I smell need and lust and wanting."

"We should do something about that, shouldn't we?" I settle my hands on her waist.

"Yes, please."

I kiss her again, and this time restraint becomes unnecessary. Like every other time we've kissed, it's as if someone has flicked a lighter in an ocean of gasoline. She wraps herself around me, and I have to coax her to loosen her hold. "I want to taste every inch of you, Lainey, starting right here." I touch a finger to her lips and drag it down between her breasts. "And I'll make a stop here, before I continue"—I draw a line straight down, circling her navel, and stop at the waistband of her leggings—"under here. Do you think that would be a good sensory calming exercise?"

"I guess we'll have to try it out to see if it works." She gives me a tentative, saucy grin.

And I make good on my sensory exploration promise. We undress each other slowly, savoring the experience. I kiss every bare, sweet inch of her, spending the most time between her thighs, licking and kissing until she's writhing under me and calling out my name as an orgasm rolls through her.

I'm fully prepared for that to be where it ends, but Lainey tugs me back up and wraps her legs around my waist. She's already slick from my mouth and her orgasm. "Lainey," I groan when I settle against her, warm and wet.

"I want to know what it feels like to have you inside me."

I lift my head and meet her hazy, lust-soaked gaze. "Are you sure? We don't have to—"

She looks suddenly unsure. "You don't want to know what I feel like from the inside?"

"That's not—" I have to clear my throat. "Yes. Of course I do, I just don't want you to feel pressured—"

"I don't feel pressured. I feel like I'm under pressure. Like one of those mints dropped into a bottle of soda and shaken with the top on. That's what it's like when you kiss me, so I want to know what it's like when you're in me."

"Is this . . . have you . . ." I don't know how to ask without making it awkward.

She tips her head to the side, brows furrowing for a moment until they pop back up. "Oh! You think—" She bites her lip. "I'm not *that* inexperienced, RJ."

There's no good way to respond, so I drop my head and kiss the side of her neck. "I just wanted to be sure, and I want this to feel good for you—for both of us. Let me grab a condom." I'm grateful that there's one in my wallet, because the box I bought the day after I met Lainey—hopeful that at some point we'd get here—is upstairs in my nightstand.

I kneel between her thighs, and Lainey sits up, taking the foil square from me. She strokes me a few times, then bends to kiss the head, wetting it with her lips before she tears the wrapper open and rolls the condom on. It's sexy and sweet and so damn hot. Especially when she straddles me, positions me at her entrance, and sinks into my lap.

This is nothing like our frantic make-out sessions. It's slow and gentle, a leisurely climb to the peak. When I feel myself getting close, I still her with my hands on her hips and kiss her as a distraction. Over and over, I balance at the edge and back off until Lainey can't stop the orgasm from stealing her breath.

I flip her over so I can keep the rhythm, chasing down my own orgasm. I try to bury my face against her neck, but she cups my face in her hands. "I want to see you," she murmurs, eyes soft and searching.

I meet her gaze, and my ego pretty much expands to fill the entire universe. Lainey's eyes hold fascinated awe, like there's nothing more enthralling than me in this moment. I come hard, eyes locked on her gorgeous face, wishing there were no end to this feeling.

I drop my forehead to hers, breathing hard. She kisses the corner of my mouth. "I would do that again and again and again just so I could see that look on your face."

"What look?"

"Pure rapture."

"That belongs to you and you alone."

Orgasm drugged, we kiss until exhaustion creeps in. I remove the used condom, tie it off, and toss it near the fireplace. I pull the blankets over us, and Lainey curls into me.

I think about how I could get used to this—not just the sex, but her. And I wish I'd started this with the truth instead of a lie, because it's too late to take it back . . . but I promise myself I'll find a way to tell her before we leave Alaska. And I hope like hell it won't ruin what we have here.

CHAPTER 10

THE FALL IN

Lainey

Having grown up on a farm, in a rural area, homeschooled, and with social anxiety doesn't mean I never had a boyfriend. I did. Not a lot, but a few, and most of them were long term. Well, longish term.

Also, having four older brothers meant dating could be difficult—and often secretive. In addition to the secrecy came the challenge of finding opportunities for privacy. Even now, at twenty-five, I've never lived away from home for long. Because of the farm, none of my siblings have strayed very far from the hub of the family wheel. Everyone lives within a few miles of each other.

Sure, the house we all grew up in was big, with lots of places to sneak off to—barns are decent places to make out in, if you can get over the smell. And animals don't generally rat you out—unless you happen to kick over a bucket and it lands in a cow stall, scaring the crap out of them.

Even with the challenges I faced in the dating world, I went out with a guy who had his own place for a while. That proved helpful in expanding my sexual repertoire and putting theory into practice; however, based on my most current experience, that guy wasn't all that great in bed. Certainly not as giving, skilled, or well endowed as RJ.

Suffice it to say, I don't put up a fight the next morning when RJ suggests we get the rest of my things and bring them back to his place. But first we have more sex. And then a shower, which leads to more sex. I can see how that particular location might be a little dangerous with someone who isn't as strong or agile as RJ.

Being intimate with someone who is in such amazing physical condition is pretty fantastic. Not only can he pick me up and carry me around like I weigh as much as a bag of potatoes, he can also hold me up—with the help of the shower wall—and give me an orgasm. It's extraordinary.

He's rather extraordinary, really.

After last night there's a shift between us. It feels like we're connected in ways beyond intimacy.

We make a quick breakfast, get the rest of my personal effects from my crappy cabin, and return to his place. And yes, we have more sex. Actually, that's pretty much all we do for the rest of the day. That and eat. I wander around in one of his button-down plaid shirts, and he wanders around in his boxer briefs—my request, obviously.

I've never had a fling before, and I'm aware that's what this is. He lives in New York, and I live in Washington. He has to run an alpaca farm, and I have to finish my master's and get a job, eventually—or start my PhD, whichever makes more sense.

So I try not to worry about what will happen when I go back home. Instead, for the first time in my life, I just let myself enjoy the time I have with RJ and hope that my heart can handle it. I also enjoy sex with him. A lot. So that helps too.

Days bleed into each other as RJ and I settle into a routine. We make meals together and go boating almost every day, and I even manage to work on my thesis paper. His internet reception is far superior to what mine was, so I'm actually able to get quite a bit done . . . all things considered. As the days on the calendar count down to his impending departure, everything that doesn't involve spending time with him takes a back seat.

A few days before he's supposed to go home, RJ changes his plans. My ticket is open ended, and he doesn't have any obligations until the middle of July, so he suggests that he stay longer. My heart skips a few dangerous beats at the thought of more time with him. I'm so attached to him already, and this is only going to make it that much harder when we have to leave. But I'll take a bruised heart in exchange for more time, and he delays his departure so we both leave closer to mid-July.

Two weeks before we're supposed to fly back to Seattle, we run out of condoms. It's not really a surprise, considering how quickly we've been going through them. We're in the kitchen, making coffee and toasting bagels, me in my favorite uniform—one of RJ's flannel plaid shirts—and him in his boxer briefs.

He reaches over me, erection poking me in the hip as he grabs two mugs from the cupboard above my head. He sets them in front of me, moves my hair aside, and presses a wet kiss to my neck. He follows that with the gentle scrape of teeth.

"RJ." It's more moan than warning.

"How am I supposed to resist you, especially when I know there's nothing under that shirt." His fingers dip beneath the hem and skim along bare skin. I bat his hand away, spin to face him, and put a palm on his chest. Not that it's much of a deterrent, since I hum in appreciation instead of pushing him away—and brush my thumb over his nipple. In the short weeks RJ and I have had to explore each other's bodies, I've discovered that his nipples are a hot zone. So are his neck and the V of muscle at his hips, leading to the hottest hot zone of all.

He grabs me by the waist, picks me up, and deposits me on the counter. His palms curl over my knees.

"It's been, what, two hours?" I drag my nails down the side of his neck and relish his low groan.

"Two hours too long. I'm going through withdrawal." He puts pressure on the insides of my knees, a silent request to let him in.

I spread my legs, my appetite for him as voracious as his is for me. "We need to go to town."

"We will, but breakfast and orgasms first, and not necessarily in that order." RJ slides his warm, rough palms up my thighs, biting his lip as he pushes the flannel up, exposing me. I'm already wet. It's pretty much perpetual with RJ. "Fuck, Lainey."

"Not until after we go to town." The statement comes out a little breathless—but also with conviction. I internally pat myself on the back for being responsible.

RJ rests his forehead against mine. "I could just slip it in there for a couple of strokes, like two or three. That'd be okay, right?"

I snort a laugh. It's definitely not a becoming sound at all. And it turns into a moan when RJ pulls his boxer briefs down and rubs the head of his erection along the inside of my thigh.

"I told you we should've gone to town yesterday," I murmur, half-entranced by the way he keeps rubbing the head along the crease in my thigh, up one side and then down the other, over and over again.

"You feel so good." He circles my most sensitive skin, and I moan. "Just two strokes bare, Lainey, please."

The toaster pops behind me. "The bagels are ready."

"Fuck the bagels."

"That might hurt." I suck in a breath as he drags the head of his erection down, parting my lips, passing my entrance. "One stroke. In and out. That's it," I say before I fully consider the ramifications.

RJ's eyes flip up to mine, and his chest rises and falls. His gaze drops, and so does mine. "You're sure?" He's right there, hand shaking, erection kicking in his fist.

"Once. One time."

The head slips in, both of us look down, and I clench around him. It's such a terrible, wonderful idea. He pushes in another inch on a low groan. "God, Lainey, look at you." He frames my sex with his hands, thumbs sweeping over me, and pushes all the way in.

I moan, long and low and desperate. Because it feels so good, and I know it's so wrong and bad and dangerous. But I wrap my legs around his waist anyway, keeping him in me as I roll my hips. His mouth drops open, and his lids flutter, his fingertips digging into my thighs as his forehead comes to rest against mine. "You feel so good like this—so fucking good, Lainey."

"You too." I unhook my legs from his waist and put a hand on his chest. "But it's not safe."

His lust-heavy gaze meets mine, torn and desperate. He looks down, and I follow his eyes, watching as he eases out on a plaintive groan. As soon as the ridge appears, I push him back and slip off the counter, dropping to my knees. Engulfing the head, I taste my own need. RJ's hands slide into my hair as I take him in as far as I can.

We end up on the floor, me straddling his face while I take him in my mouth, competing to see who can make the other come first. I would've won if he hadn't added his fingers.

Afterward we toast new bagels and drink lukewarm coffee for breakfast. "That can't happen again," I say between bites of bagel.

"I know. I'm sorry. I promise I've always been safe in the past and that we'll be safe from here on out. I got carried away. Right after this we'll go to town and stock up, okay?" He leans in and kisses my cheek, lips moving to my ear. "You feel like velvet, and you taste like heaven. I would stay inside you forever if I could."

I push away from the table. "I'm getting dressed so we can go."

"Good idea."

Fifteen minutes later, RJ and I are fully dressed and ready for an outing so we can restock condoms—and maybe food, although that is definitely second on the to-do list.

It's fairly warm today, crisp like that time between spring and summer in Washington.

He spins the truck keys on his finger. "You know what we should do?"

"If it involves your penis and my vagina, it needs to wait until we get back from our shopping trip."

He grins wolfishly. "You have a one-track mind, don't you?"

"Only when I'm around you, apparently," I mutter.

"Lainey! Catch!" RJ shouts.

I raise both hands defensively, because I am not known for my excellent reaction time, and am rather surprised when my fist closes around the object he's tossed my way. "I am not good at catching things, so I don't suggest you do that again."

"You can be good at anything if you practice enough," RJ replies.

I glance down at my palm and find I'm holding his truck keys. "I don't have my license, remember?"

"I know. I'm going to teach you how to drive."

I glance at his monster rental truck with all the bells and whistles. "No. Nope. No way." I toss the keys back to him. My aim is terrible, but he still manages to snag them out of the air before they hit the ground.

"Why not?"

"What happens if I ruin that truck?" My father has the base model, and it's expensive as heck. I can't afford to ruin a truck.

"You're not going to ruin it, Lainey. I'll be right beside you, teaching you what to do. We'll take it slow."

"But I might scratch the paint. Or hit something." I've seen a lot of roadkill on our trips to town. I would prefer not to add to that body count.

RJ arches a brow. "You grew up on a farm. You have to have driven a tractor."

I cross my arms over my chest. Of course I've driven a tractor. "Not the same, and you know it." I can back up into the fence or accidentally hit the side of the barn and no one will get mad at me for scratching it, since farm machinery is meant to get beaten up.

A half grin tips up the corner of RJ's mouth. "You're right, not the same at all. A tractor is way more difficult to drive than a truck. You'll be a pro in no time."

"Tractors are meant to be ridden hard—trucks like this one, not so much." I make a flaily gesture toward his sporty, unscratched, undented rental. It's rather intimidating and fancy.

His half smile turns into a full-on grin, and his eyes move over me in a slow, hot sweep. "I'll make you a deal."

"What kind of deal?"

"I'll let you ride me however you want if you give it a try."

"How would that be different than any other day?"

He taps his lip thoughtfully. "Hmm, you have a point. You're pretty demanding when you're naked."

"I'm trying to be helpful!" I defend myself. "I don't see the point in being a passive recipient. Unless you'd prefer I keep you guessing as to what I like and what I don't."

RJ drags his tongue along his bottom lip. "I fucking love how expressive you are." Palm flattening against my lower back, he pulls me into him, his erection pressed against my stomach. "Please, Lainey. Let me teach you something new."

I glance at the truck and back at RJ. He looks so excited and turned on by the prospect. When I said I didn't have a license, I didn't mean that I can't drive. I can. But I'm not comfortable on highways, and I've only ever driven on country roads—and always in a beat-up pickup truck, not something nice like his rental. Still, RJ thinks I don't know how, and if he wants to persuade me to learn, who am I to take the opportunity away from him?

I'm sure I can handle driving on the road into town. Plus, I won't have my mother beside me, freaking out when I get even close to the speed limit. She drives like an eighty-year-old on Sunday.

"Okay. I'll give it a try."

RJ helps me into the driver's seat—which is mostly just an excuse to touch my butt—and adjusts the seat so I'm closer to the gas and brake pedals. He rolls down the window, closes the door, and pulls his phone out of his pocket. "Smile, baby."

I give him a cheesy grin, excitement and nerves battling as he snaps a picture and rounds the hood. He gives me a brief rundown of all the dials and knobs before I slip the key in and turn the ignition over. The engine rumbles to life. I wipe my hands on my thighs, since I put lotion on before we left the cabin.

"Hey." RJ places his hand over mine and gives it a gentle squeeze. "Don't doubt yourself, Lainey. You got this."

I realize he must think I'm anxious, so I follow his instructions, shifting the truck into gear and tapping lightly on the gas pedal, sort of like I would when I'm driving a tractor. He lets me get the feel for the gas and the brakes by circling the wide-open driveway a few times. Every time I hit the brake, the truck lurches to a stop, gravel spitting from the tires. At first it's not purposeful—the brakes on his truck are particularly touchy—but I'm having fun watching RJ be so attentive and concerned, so I keep doing it.

"Sorry." I bite back a smile when he not-so-subtly braces a hand on the dash.

"You're doing great—you just need to get a feel for how sensitive the gas and brake pedals are. Kinda like when I go down on you. If I want to make you come fast and hard, I need to hit your buttons like I mean it, but if I want to drag it out, then I'm gentle. Same principle."

I cock a brow. "Is this whole driving lesson going to be explained in sexual analogies?"

He grins and shrugs. "Seemed like a good comparison."

I roll my eyes but take his advice, barely tapping the gas when I want to speed up and gently moving to the brake when I want to stop. It's actually a pretty accurate analogy. Eventually I make my way down the long driveway. When I reach the main road, my nerves become real. While it's not a busy road, logging and transport trucks use it frequently, and the speed limit is higher than I'm usually comfortable with.

RJ stretches his arm across the backrest and gives my neck a reassuring squeeze. "You got this. Just take it slow, and you'll be fine."

The road is clear of traffic, no one coming in either direction. As far as "learning" to drive goes, this is probably ideal. I signal left, toward town, and ease out of the driveway. I'm currently only doing about twenty-five miles an hour, much lower than the posted speed limit. I check the rearview mirror. "What happens if someone comes up behind me?"

"You can always pull over and let them pass. Give it a bit more gas, gorgeous." The pet name warms me from the inside.

I do as he instructs until I reach about forty-five miles an hour. "How do people drive on the freeway when everyone is going this fast and they're all so close to each other?"

"You get used to it. You're doing great."

I like the praise, so I keep easing the speedometer up until I'm going the posted speed limit. "This is a rush!" I tell RJ.

He laughs. "It's fun, right?"

"It is!" I glance over at him, taking my eyes off the road for a split second. Or maybe it's a little longer than a split second, because when I shift my focus back to the road, a little red squirrel is bounding across the pavement. "Oh shoot!" I put on the brakes, tires squealing as the tiny rodent freezes. No one is coming in the other direction, so I swerve around it, managing to avoid turning him into a pancake. A few minutes later I pull into the parking lot of the pharmacy without additional animals playing chicken with the truck.

RJ reaches for the door handle. "I'll be right back, unless you want to come in with me?"

"Um, I'm okay to wait in the truck."

He leans over, drops a kiss on my cheek, and jumps out. As soon as he's inside the store, I unbuckle my seat belt and switch to the passenger seat. Five minutes later RJ leaves the store as a blonde woman dressed in skintight jeans and a fitted sweater is about to go inside. She looks like she belongs in a commercial for perfect hair. Perfect everything, actually. I immediately hate her when she smiles at RJ in a way that tells me she appreciates what she sees.

His eyes flare, and for a moment his gaze shifts to the truck. He accepts a hug from her, and a tight feeling settles in my stomach as she runs her hands down his arms. It's familiar. I don't like it. She glances down at the bag, a coy smile on her lips as she tries to peek inside.

When he moves it behind his back, she flips her blonde hair over her shoulder and grabs the lapels of his down vest. RJ's expression hardens, and he shakes his head, prying her fingers from his vest. Her expression shifts from friendly to irritated.

RJ motions to the truck. Her gaze follows his, and her eyes widen. I look down at my lap, suddenly uncomfortable. RJ said he's been coming here for years. I'm not the only woman to notice how attractive he is, and based on how good he is in bed, I'm definitely not the only woman to experience his skill set there.

The rest of their conversation is short and stilted. He holds the door open for her and returns to the truck, his expression tense, which tells me more than I'd like—not just about who they are to each other but also about my feelings for this man. I shouldn't be jealous. This is a summer fling. But somewhere along the way my heart forgot to consider what my brain knows: that this has to end.

RJ opens the driver's side door and climbs in, tossing the plastic bag on the center console. "Sorry about that."

"Sorry about what?" I keep my hands clasped in my lap so I don't give in to the urge to bite my nails or fidget.

He makes a general hand motion toward the store.

"Oh, you mean your friend? She was flirty." I hate that it comes out sounding bitter, catty, and insecure.

"Charity flirts with everyone who has a dick. Doesn't matter if they're twenty or eighty." RJ smooths his thumb down the back of my neck, and I jerk away.

"You don't need to placate me, RJ. It's obvious there's something between you. I know I'm not the first woman to share your bed." *And I'm well aware that I won't be the last either.*

"Hey, can you look at me for a second, please?"

I reluctantly shift my gaze to meet his.

"Charity works at one of the bars here. She's stuck and looking for a way out, or an escape, and I've made it clear I'm not going to be that guy. When I come here—it's always been to spend time with my dad and my brother, not hook up with random women."

"She's beautiful, though."

He shrugs. "She's not my type."

"And I am?"

"Yes. You're exactly my type. You're gorgeous, smart, funny, adventurous, and just so fucking sweet. You don't have anything to be jealous of, Lainey."

"I'm sorry. I shouldn't have gotten short with you."

"I'm going to say something, and I hope you don't take it the wrong way, okay?"

"Okay?" It's more of a question than a statement.

"I like that you're jealous."

"You do? Why?" I've never considered jealousy a positive emotion. It indicates a level of insecurity and vulnerability.

"It means we're on the same page, because if the tables were turned and it was you coming out of that store and me sitting here watching some guy flirt with you, I probably would've made a huge ass out of myself."

"How do you mean?"

"There's no way I could've played it cool. I would've been out of the truck making sure he knew you were mine and that he should back the fuck off." RJ cringes. "I probably should've stopped while I was ahead—now I sound like a possessive douche. What I mean is, I want to be the only one you get jealous over, that's all. Does that make sense?"

"Yes, it makes sense."

With that, we head back to the cabin and make good use of that residual jealousy—and the condoms.

CHAPTER 11

ALL GOOD THINGS

Lainey

"Lainey, baby, wake up."

I groan and snuggle into the pillow. "Just let me sleep for five more minutes, RJ, then you can sex me."

He presses his lips to my cheek, and when he speaks again, his tone makes the hairs on the back of my neck stand on end. "Baby, please. I need you to wake up. I have to go."

I blink a couple of times and roll over. RJ is sitting on the edge of the bed, fully dressed. His expression is pained. "What's going on?"

"It's my brother. Well, it's actually Joy. She went into labor. She's more than a month early, and there are complications. I know we're supposed to fly out together, but he needs me right now."

I'm still half-asleep, so it takes me a few seconds to absorb what he's said. "Is the baby going to be okay? Is Joy?"

"I don't know. It's pretty touch and go. I need to get out there so he has some support. So they all do, just in case."

I scrub a hand over my face, trying to process it all. "Right. He definitely needs you. When will you leave?"

"I have a flight in less than two hours. I have to go now." He keeps skimming my cheek with the back of his hand.

"Now?" I push up on my arms, the weight of his words finally settling.

"I'm sorry, Lainey. I wanted to fly back to Seattle with you." His expression is pained. "I really don't want to go, but I have to."

"No, no, I get it. Your family needs you—you have to be with them." If it were one of my brothers or sisters, I would do exactly the same thing.

"I'll call, okay? When I get there, I'll call and let you know I landed and how everything is going—so you don't worry."

"Okay. Yes. Please."

"I'm sorry I have to leave." He cups my face in his hands and kisses me, evidently not caring about my sleep breath.

My stomach hollows out when I realize this is goodbye. I thought we had another day—time to talk, to figure things out. I'm not going to see him again. Not anytime soon. Part of me wants to offer to come with him, but it's just prolonging the inevitable.

A desperate, forlorn sound bubbles up as he pulls back, eyes roaming over my face. "I need you one last time."

"Please. Yes." I can already feel the ache in my chest, and he's still here with me. I'm terrified of what it will be like when he's really gone. I shove down the anxiety and focus on the moment.

He pulls my sleep shirt over my head, so it's just a matter of unclasping his belt and unbuttoning his fly. "I'm sorry I can't take care of you the way I want to." His mouth covers mine again, and his kiss is full of the same desperation I feel.

I climb into his lap while he's still fully dressed and free him from his boxer briefs.

There's no finessing our way through this—it's sheer desperate need driving us as I sink down and cry out from the invasion. Everything is magnified, including the sensation of having him inside me, knowing it's the last time.

I keep our mouths fused, holding him tightly as he moves me over him, slow at first, gentle—but it doesn't last; we grip and cling, teeth clashing, tongues warring, bodies battling as we crash into each other, taking what we both need because we're out of time.

RJ tears his mouth from mine. "I need you to come."

"I'm close," I assure him.

He lifts and lowers me, faster, harder, pushing my body to the limit. The orgasm steals my breath, and I cry out, wishing the sensation were something I could hold on to.

"Lainey." The single word is as much a demand as it is a plea. I open my eyes and focus on his face, on the torment in his eyes, on the regrets I can feel creating a hole in my heart in the form of a love I'll never fully experience apart from these brief weeks.

He comes, eyes on mine, body shaking with his release. He kisses me, hard at first and then softer. Eventually he wraps his arms around me and squeezes tightly, lips pressed against my throat. He murmurs something against my skin that I don't catch.

Fragile moments pass, and his imminent departure looms. His palms smooth up my back, tangling briefly in my hair before he finally pulls back and exhales an unsteady breath. His eyes are glassy and sad. "I have to go."

"I know."

"I wanted more time with you."

"Me too. I'll walk you out?"

"That would be good. Let me get you a shirt."

I move off his lap, feeling the absence of him everywhere as we lose our physical connection. He tucks himself back into his pants and crosses to the closet, grabbing one of his shirts that he leaves at the cabin. He helps me into it, fastening a couple of buttons with shaking hands.

"That's good enough—I know you're out of time."

He laces our fingers together, and I follow him down the hall. I slip my feet into a pair of flats and curl into him as we step outside into the near dawn. Dark clouds blanket the sky, a complement to my gloomy mood. Goose bumps rise on my legs and arms, prickling all the way to my scalp. The truck is already running, his duffel in the passenger seat.

He brushes my hair away from my face. "Lainey, I . . ." He shakes his head and presses his lips to mine. "I'll call as soon as I'm in LA."

"Okay."

He pulls me against him, hugging me tightly. He kisses me one last time, a slow, sad goodbye. I'm the one who breaks the kiss first, aware that the longer this takes, the closer I get to losing it in front of him.

He cups my face in his hands. "I have so many things I needed to say to you. Things I wanted to tell you."

I fight back a sob. "It's okay. You can tell me later."

"I miss you already."

I turn my head and kiss his palm. "Me too."

He presses his lips to mine one last time. "I'll talk to you soon."

"Drive careful." I step back as he gets in and closes the door.

I watch as he pulls away. The window rolls down, and he waves before he turns onto the main road. I wait until his taillights disappear before I let the tears fall. And with them comes the first drop of rain.

I stand there, staring at the end of the driveway, feeling very much like I just lost my heart.

By nine a summer storm has set in, complete with lightning and thunder. I'm too sad to be scared as I pack up my things. At noon I lose power and wait for the generator to kick on, but it doesn't. I have candles and flashlights here, so I'm relieved that I don't have to sit in the dark through the storm, but it feels like a bad omen.

At one o'clock in the afternoon, a flash of lightning is followed by a huge crack of thunder. A second boom makes the entire cabin shake and the candles flicker for a moment, and everything goes stark and still. I try to manage the crushing panic, but the sensory calming exercise only makes me think of RJ, and the tears keep falling like the rain. By three o'clock in the afternoon I get antsy, having expected to hear from RJ already. I check the phone, thinking I'm being paranoid until I realize there's no dial tone.

"No, no, no." Without a phone RJ can't call me and tell me he made it safely, that his brother is fine, that Joy and the baby are okay.

And I can't tell him any of the things I planned to today. Like I want to come visit him in New York. Or that I think I'm falling in love with him.

As the next morning arrives, the phone lines finally come back on, but my time in Alaska has run out. And just like that, all my hope vanishes, and my heart breaks.

CHAPTER 12

DOLPHIN D*CK

Lainey
Present Day

Today is not my day. At all. After a night of little sleep, I arrived at work to be told two of our staff are off sick with the flu. Since it's a Saturday, and they happen to be friends and college aged, I'm guessing the flu is code for *hungover*. Must be nice to have zero in the way of responsibilities.

Since we're short staffed and one of the girls on today is new, I've been given the job of running the birthday party tour for a pair of three-year-old twins. This typically isn't in my job description.

For the most part, I get to avoid the swarms of people who visit the exhibits every day, which is usually fine with me. Peopling takes a lot of energy, and I don't have much of that to spare these days.

Unfortunately for me, today I'm the resident expert on all things aquatic, which apparently makes me the best candidate to run a tour. I was handling the responsibility well until about twenty minutes ago, when I found out the birthday party is for the sons of an NHL player.

Apparently a very attractive, popular one, based on the way the girls who work here are freaking out.

I don't know much about hockey, but I understand the basics: it takes place on an ice rink, and there are sticks, pucks, and helmets involved. Also, based on the fact that this hockey player has rented out the entire aquarium for the afternoon, NHL players have a lot of money to throw around.

The cake alone must have cost a small fortune. It's in the shape of a shark head coming out of the water. It's very realistic. I saw the price list for this event—it was on my manager's desk—and I could pay my rent for an entire year with what this hockey player shelled out for an afternoon looking at aquatic animals.

In addition to this extravagant party, Miller Butterson—what an odd last name—and his gorgeous wife have donated a huge amount of money to fund the dolphin project I'm working on with one of the senior staff members here. It's all very exciting. And the reason I'm currently trying not to hyperventilate.

I perform my sensory calming exercise for the third time in a row, hoping that I'll be able to make it through this experience without embarrassing myself. On the positive side, at least I only have to contend with one group of kids and their parents, rather than hundreds of families.

I fidget with the end of my braid as I stand at the front of the group of adorable, well-dressed children. Their mothers are all very put together and attractive, making me feel dowdy in my beige-on-beige uniform. I stand with my back to the huge glass wall as I tell the children all about Daphne and Dillon, our dolphins. I can totally do this. I can pretend I'm presenting my findings to a panel of very small, cute professors.

Everything seems to be going smoothly until a dark-haired little boy tugs on my arm. "Is that the daddy dolphin?"

I look over my shoulder just in time to see what has his attention. "Oh my goodness." I spread my arms and try to block the children's view, but it's futile. The dolphins have decided that right now, during this very expensive birthday party, is an excellent time to mate. They couldn't wait for the aquarium to be empty. Oh no, they have to get their stupid hump on right here.

"It's like a big pink lightsaber!" the dark-haired boy says gleefully to the redheaded little boy beside him. The redheaded boy holds his hands in front of his crotch and makes lightsaber sounds, and the dark-haired boy joins in for a few seconds, pretending to have a sword fight with their invisible lightsaber penises.

"Mommy! Look! That's like Daddy's peepee!" the dark-haired boy yells.

A petite woman with long auburn hair and huge boobs, who also appears to be significantly pregnant, drags her attention away from the giant of a man whose arm is draped protectively over her shoulder to address her son. "Honey, we don't broadcast that."

"But it's true!" he protests, little arms flailing.

"I know, sweetie, but we don't want to make the other mommies jealous."

I can't believe this is an actual conversation, happening right now, in public. I'd like to believe this mother is joking, but considering the statements are coming from a child and they're generally not adept at lying, I have to believe that what he's saying is true. I inappropriately wonder how that even works with a woman her size. And then, of course, because my brain is a messy place these days, I think about RJ and how . . . ample he was and how I'm close to the same size as that woman. I cut off that line of thinking right away, because it's unhelpful and embarrassing.

Heedless of his mother's warning, the little boy plasters himself against the glass, fascinated by what he's seeing, and yells, "Daddy! The dolphin has a big peepee just like you! Mine is gonna be just like that!"

"Robbie, buddy, we don't talk about that in public," the handsome man says, his eyes glued to his wife, or, more specifically, her cleavage.

Robbie's mother finally registers what's happening in the dolphin tank, and her eyes go wide. "Holy hell, that thing is freaking huge." She elbows her husband in the side. "Maybe you're part dolphin."

Her husband drags his attention away from her chest and follows her gaze to the spectacle behind me, eyes popping. "Wow. No wonder his girlfriend is trying to get away."

All hell breaks loose as a little blond boy starts crying. "Mommy! The boy dolphin is trying to stab that girl dolphin!"

His equally blonde mother tucks him into her side and pats his head reassuringly. "He's not trying to stab her, honey, he's trying to love her."

I really hope no one asks me to explain dolphin mating rituals, because I think I will likely burst into flames. "Okay, everyone! Let's give the dolphins some privacy and move on to the next exhibit! Who wants to see the sharks? Raise your hands!" I shout into my headset, causing feedback to echo through the cavernous room.

Thankfully it distracts everyone from the fornicating dolphins. As I usher a few of the most distraught kids and their parents on to the next exhibit, apologizing profusely for something beyond my control but still insanely embarrassing, a man at the back of the group catches my attention.

My heart stutters as I take in what I swear is the familiar set of RJ's shoulders and the distinct shape of his cut jaw. I took up sketching again just so I could try to capture the memory on paper. Yes, I'm that pathetic. No, I haven't gotten over him.

"Excuse me, can you tell me where the bathroom is?" The woman's shoulder is covered in spit-up, and the infant in her arms looks like he's about to cry.

I drag my eyes away from what very well may be a complete hallucination based on the lack of sleep I've had over the past several months and point the poor mother in the direction of the women's bathroom. When I look back to where my hallucination/fantasy was standing, all I see is a bunch of balloons.

I'm losing it today.

I rush to the front of the group and continue with the tour. Thankfully, the sharks are behaving themselves, and it's feeding time, which usually goes over well with the kids. But not this time: one little boy starts crying again when he realizes that they're feeding the sharks fish and calls them cannibals. Another boy asks if we'll get to see the shark's peepee too. His mother pulls him aside and gives him a stern talking-to.

I keep glancing at the back of the group, trying to figure out if I'm truly hallucinating. But then I get another glimpse of the man who came into my life over a year ago, turned it upside down, and kept it that way.

It's definitely RJ. I wonder if he's related to one of these hockey players. Maybe his brother relocated from LA or he has a cousin here. But as I take in the other men at this birthday party, I realize they're all wearing the same baseball caps and T-shirts with the same logo, like it's a uniform. And RJ is no different, his huge, bulky frame filling out the T-shirt that matches the rest of the men's, all rivaling each other in size.

Shaken and very much confused, I lead the party through the tour, stumbling over my words more than once. Of course the dolphins can't be the only ones acting up today. When we get to the sea otters, one of the males presses himself against the glass and rubs himself on it, licking the window. The kids think it's hilarious, and the parents all pull out their phones and take videos. At least the otters aren't trying to mate.

I'm relieved when the tour is finally over, because my mouth is dry and my stomach is in knots. I'd given up long ago on ever seeing RJ again or contacting him, and now here he is. Over the past year I called every alpaca farm in New York, but none of them linked to RJ, and without a last name it was like trying to find a needle in a haystack. I can't believe we didn't even exchange last names. I hoped I might hear from him once he found the note I left for him at the cabin with my contact information; instead there was nothing but painful silence. I'd be lying if I said I didn't hold my breath every time my phone rang the entire summer.

I stand there, wringing my hands, as he weaves through parents and avoids stepping on small children.

His eyes move over my face in a familiar, searching way. I'm sure I look like hell today. I was up several times last night and had trouble falling back to sleep, so no amount of concealer could cover up my dark circles this morning. Also, my entire uniform is beige, and the pants have pleats in the front, so neither the style nor the color is flattering on me—or anyone else, for that matter.

He stops just inside my personal-space bubble, which makes my palms sweatier than usual. I'm forced to tip my head back so I can look at his face. His perfect, gorgeous face. He looks exactly like I remember, except his hair is shorter, as if he's had it cut recently.

"God, I thought I'd never see you again, and here you are," he says in that deep baritone that makes the hairs on the back of my neck stand on end.

I just stare at him, incapable of ungluing my tongue from the roof of my mouth. He's so beautiful and real. At least I think he's real. I hope so—otherwise I need to see a doctor.

His brow furrows, eyes swimming with an emotion I can't quite identify. Hurt, maybe? Or worry? "Lainey? Do you remember me?"

"Of course I remember you, RJ," I whisper.

Relief softens his expression. "It's so good to see you." He wraps his thick, strong arms around me and pulls me against him.

I'm shocked stupid by the contact and the sudden wave of calm that accompanies his touch. I inhale deeply, breathing in the familiar smell of his cologne and the scent that is uniquely him. Emotions slam into me: sadness, longing, relief, and fear. His hold on me tightens enough that I let out a small squeak.

He loosens his grip and takes a cautious step back. "I'm sorry. It's just so good to see you after all this time." He runs his palms down my arms and takes my hands in his, squeezing gently. "You look amazing."

I glance down at my outfit, wondering if maybe he needs glasses or something.

He doesn't let go of my hands. "How are you? What are you doing in Chicago? I mean—obviously you're working, but what brought you here? Are you staying?"

"That's a lot of questions," I reply, like an idiot, because that's what I've become, apparently. I don't know how to handle him being here. That brief wave of calm has disappeared as quickly as it arrived, and in its wake is bewilderment.

He laughs a little. "You're right. It is a lot of questions. Let's start with one. How are you?"

"I'm . . ." *Exhausted, elated, terrified, confused.* "Good."

"Good. You look good." His thumb smooths back and forth over my knuckles. It feels nice, but it's also distracting. "What brought you to Chicago?"

It's closer to New York than Washington and a way to escape my parents' overprotectiveness. And a way to prove to them and myself that I could do this on my own. But I don't say any of that. "I was offered a job, and I thought I should take it."

"That's amazing, Lainey. Does that mean you finished your master's?"

"It does. Yes."

He hugs me again, not as vigorously or as long as the first time, but it still steals my breath and threatens what little composure I have. "Does that mean you're here permanently?"

"I have a temporary contract, but I should be here for another six months or so, as long as I don't mess it up. You know, scarring small children for life with fornicating dolphins and such."

"It's not like you can control those horny bastards. They can't help that they like to get it on for fun, right? And clearly they don't mind an audience." He smiles, but the awkwardness of this whole reunion makes it seem uncertain.

"Clearly not." I shift my gaze away from his, unable to erase the memories of RJ and me getting it on pretty much anywhere we could, anytime we wanted, during those brief weeks in Alaska. "What about you? What brings you to Chicago? Are you visiting friends?"

His expression shifts from excited to distressed between one blink and the next.

Before he can answer, another man dressed in a red shirt and ball cap approaches, giving me a curious once-over. "Hey, Rook, sorry to interrupt, but—uh, we need you for a minute."

"Just hold on." He doesn't even look at the man.

"We're taking a team picture—you'll only be a minute, then you can get back to your friend here." His gaze darts from RJ to our clasped hands.

"Team picture?" I glance back and forth between them.

"Lainey . . ." RJ says my name like an apology.

And it all clicks into place. All the hockey stuff in his cabin—how huge he is, and built—his stamina, the matching T-shirts and ball caps.

"I thought you said you were an alpaca farmer from New York."

CHAPTER 13
NOT-SO-LITTLE WHITE LIES

Rook

All the awesomeness that comes with finally seeing Lainey again disappears with that single statement. It's amazing what a person can forget in a year. Such as the way I built our entire brief relationship on a lie.

It doesn't matter that I had a plan all worked out to explain why I lied. Because the truth is, I had plenty of opportunities to tell her—and every time I was about to, something would happen or I'd find a reason to put it off. Until it was too late. I was too afraid that I would lose what we had, that it would change things, that she would see me differently. I lost her anyway, though, because she didn't answer when I called from LA. Even worse, she didn't leave me a way to contact her: no note, no number, nothing.

"RJ?" Lainey looks confused, and hurt, and nervous, and just so damn beautiful.

"I can explain."

She wrings her hands. "Are you a professional hockey player now?"

"Yeah, but—"

"For how long?"

I blow out a breath. There's no point in lying anymore. "This will be my seventh season with Chicago."

"Seventh?" Her lips flatten into a line, and that hurt shifts, turning into something that looks like betrayal. "You lied to me about your job?"

"I was going to tell you the truth, I swear." It's the worst cop-out.

Her brow furrows. "It was the two of us for weeks—you had plenty of time to tell me the truth. Why would you lie in the first place?"

"There's a logical explanation, Lainey. I promise, if you'll let me explain, it'll all make sense."

She continues to wring her hands. "How can I even believe you? What else did you lie about?"

"Rookie, Lance, you two comin'? We need you for the team picture," Alex calls from behind me.

Fuck. I forgot that Lance is still here, watching this train derail.

Lainey takes a step back. "I have to get back to work anyway."

"Just give me another minute," I call out.

Alex throws an arm over my shoulder, completely oblivious to the tension flaring or Lainey's anxiety, which I'm far too familiar with. "Sorry to interrupt, but I need to borrow this guy for a minute—can't take a team picture without the captain."

"Captain?" Lainey parrots, eyeing me like I'm a stranger and not the man she spent almost six weeks playing house with.

"You being all modest again, man?" Alex slaps me on the chest. "This guy is the best player in the league."

"Uh, Alex, I think—" Lance tries to interrupt.

"You're an excellent player too, Romero." He winks at Lainey. "You did a great job on the tour, especially dealing with the whole dolphin situation."

"Thank you. That usually doesn't happen during birthday parties. Typically Dillon waits until evening to get frisky with Daphne." Lainey takes another step back, muttering something under her breath as her cheeks flush.

"Do you think we can put a hold on the team photo? I need a minute with Lainey. We know each other." I pin them both with a meaningful look.

Alex's eyebrows pop, while Lance's pull down and then shoot up. It would be funny if things weren't so tense right now. Alex drops his arm and steps back, eyes darting between us. "Sorry, sorry. Sure thing. Liam and Lane are getting antsy to open their presents."

Lainey's still trying to back away slowly.

"Please. It's not what you think."

Her spine straightens, and she crosses her arms over her chest. "You don't know what I think."

"Can we go somewhere and talk?" I glance over at the information desk, where three girls are huddled together, watching us.

"I can't—I'm in the middle of a shift." She takes another step toward a door that reads **STAFF ONLY**.

"What about when you get off? We could meet for coffee somewhere close by?" I realize how inappropriate the first part sounds after it's out of my mouth.

Either she doesn't notice, or she pretends not to. "I can't. I'm busy."

"It's been a year, Lainey. I tried to call when I got to LA, but you never picked up. All I want is the chance to talk—at least give me that."

"There was a storm. A tree took out the phone lines and all the power. Even the generator didn't work." Her rigid stance wavers, and her bottom lip trembles.

That explains why the phone just kept ringing and ringing and eventually all I'd get was a click and a dial tone, but she could've left me with a way to get in touch with her. "I didn't know about the phones. Why didn't you leave me a way to contact you?" I take a step forward for every step she takes back.

She blinks, confused. "I did. I left a note with my phone number and email."

My stomach twists with this news. I'd considered going back to Alaska after LA, but things had been so difficult with Max's birth, there hadn't been time. "I didn't find one when I went back this summer."

"I left it in your bedroom. And maybe it was a good thing you didn't find it, considering you're a liar." Her chin trembles, and her hands flutter in the air before she clasps them together in front of her.

I was in such a rush that morning, worried about my brother and Joy and the baby, wishing I'd done things differently with Lainey. I didn't even think to leave her my cell. "I made a mistake—granted, it was a big one. I just . . . you didn't recognize me. I didn't think . . . can I give you my number now? I get that this is a lot to take in, and maybe you need time to think? I can give you that, but please, at least give me a chance to explain."

She shakes her head, but she pulls her phone out of her pocket, keys in the pass code, and hands it over to me. I quickly add myself as a contact before she can change her mind. Then I send myself a message to make sure I have her number before I hand it back.

I don't know what to do with my hands, so I shove them into my pockets. "Can I call you later so we can set up a coffee date?"

She holds her phone to her chest, eyes darting to the **STAFF ONLY** door and then to the group of women gathered by the information desk before coming back to me. There's no warmth, just wary mistrust. "I don't even know you. Why would I go on a date with you?"

"Don't say that. You know me, Lainey. The only thing you didn't know about was my job. That's it." I take another step toward her, but she shakes her head and backs away.

"That's it? It's not a little lie, RJ. You told me you were an alpaca farmer instead of telling me you were the captain of a professional hockey team. That's kind of a pretty huge detail to leave out, don't you think?" Her voice shakes, whether with anger or another emotion I can't be sure, but she looks as if she's on the verge of tears, and I hate that I'm the one who did that to her.

The door behind her opens. "Lainey? Sorry to interrupt, but I need your help with the otters. Ollie keeps trying to make moves on all the female otters, and you're the only one who seems to be able to control him when he's like this."

"Of course. I'll be right with you." I don't like how relieved she seems by the interruption. She spares me another wary glance. "I have to go. Take care of yourself, RJ, if that's even your name." She spins on her sneakered heel and speed walks away from me.

Even in the awful beige pants her ass looks fantastic, which is a terrible thing for me to notice or focus on.

I take my hat off and run my hand through my hair, cursing under my breath. What are the chances that I'd run into her here, of all places? That she would end up in my city? At least I know where she works, and I have her number. Now I just have to work on getting her to agree to talk to me.

I head back to the party, take part in the team photo, and watch fifteen kids from newborn to six years old turn a room upside down faster than a bunch of drunk frat guys on a bender.

Alex steps up beside me and sips out of a red cup. "You all right?"

"Yeah." I nod, even though I'm probably the furthest thing from all right. For a few minutes I was ecstatic. Now I'm confused, disappointed, and freaked out. I just want to sit Lainey down and make her hear me out. And I want to understand what the hell happened to the note she left and why it wasn't there when I went back this summer.

I was pretty sure I was falling in love with her, and I figured it was mutual. One minute she was the center of my world, and the next she was just gone.

"I'm gonna call bullshit, Rook. Wanna tell me what's going on with the tour guide?"

"Lainey. Her name is Lainey. And we had a . . . thing a while back." I'm being vague, mostly because explaining this sucks. I've never told anyone the full story about what happened with her.

"She doesn't really seem like your usual type, or what used to be your usual type, anyway."

I nod in agreement. "You're right about that."

Alex looks around and slips a flask out of his pocket. "You look like you could use a shot."

I lift a brow.

He motions to the screaming gaggle of children, players, and wives. "I know you're here because you're the team captain and you want to make a good impression on your teammates, not because you love spending your Saturday afternoon with a bunch of screaming kids. Add in whatever's going on between you and the tour guide, and you definitely deserve a drink. Besides, I figure this'll get you to talk. Can't keep it all bottled up forever, Rook. I know the last couple of years have been intense."

He has a point. I hold out my glass of lukewarm soda. I'll leave my car here and pick it up in the morning if I need to. And based on how things are going, I have a feeling a lot of alcohol will be involved in the rest of my evening.

"So, tell me what's going on with the tour guide."

I drain half the cup in one gulp. "I met her on Kodiak Island last summer."

He's in the middle of a sip and cough chokes. "That's the girl from Alaska? I thought you said she was from Washington. What's she doing here? Don't tell me you have another stalker." The year before I took over for Alex as captain of the team, we got pretty close, mostly because he took me under his wing and mentored me. At the time I didn't realize he was grooming me to take his place. Since then we've stayed pretty tight.

"Yes, she's the girl from Alaska. Yes, she's from Washington. She got offered a job here and took it, and I'm pretty sure she's not stalking me."

"How can you be sure? I mean, you're not that hard to find."

"She wasn't big on technology." I scrub a hand over my face. "And I never told her I played professional hockey."

"Too busy getting busy to be bothered with the chitchat?" Alex asks.

"No. Well, I mean yeah, there was lots of . . . sex, but that wasn't what it was all about."

"So how is it that you being a professional hockey player never came up?"

"I might've lied about where I lived and what I did for a living." I mumble it quickly and drain my cup. I could use another drink. Or just downing whatever is left in his flask.

"Why lie?"

"She didn't recognize me, and she wasn't into hockey. You know how it is with bunnies. They're just in for the fuck and the ride, right?"

"But she's not a bunny, so I'm not getting why it would matter then." He looks confused more than anything.

I sigh, aware explaining my rationale isn't going to be easy. "I wanted to be normal for a few weeks."

Violet squeezes her way between us, snatches Alex's cup, sniffs it, and raises an eyebrow. "Seriously, Alex? You better be careful how sauced you get. Your parents said they'd have a sleepover in the pool house with Robbie, and you know how I get in my second trimester."

Alex grins and bends to whisper something in her ear. She hands him back the cup, turning her attention to me. "I assume you're coming out for drinks after this shitshow." She motions to the table of children shoveling cake into their mouths.

I rub the back of my neck. "Uh, we'll see."

"Rook's trying to hook up with the tour guide," Alex supplies.

Violet grins knowingly. "You mean the poor woman who was trying to hide that huge dolphin dick?"

"That's the one," Alex replies.

She gives me a light punch on the arm. "My respect for you just went up a few notches. I had no idea you were into the nerdy chicks."

"She's not nerdy," I say defensively.

Violet gives me a look. "Uh, she knows an insane amount about aquatic animals and can rhyme off statistics like a Beat poet. Also, as a nerd, I can easily identify other nerds—and she is definitely one. It's too bad they can't put her in something other than beige, because she's also super gorgeous. You should invite her along. Introducing her to your friends will go a long way toward getting you into her pants—if that's your plan, anyway."

"I don't know if that's a good idea."

"Why not? When was the last time you went out with someone, Rook?" Violet looks like she's about to start in on me about dating. It wouldn't be the first time in the past year.

At one point Violet and the rest of the girls mentioned setting me up with one of Poppy's massage therapist friends I'd been interested in back when I first came to Chicago. But I wasn't in the right headspace, and I didn't want to make things awkward or mess up a friendship if things didn't work out.

"Nerdy tour guide is the Alaska girl from last summer." Alex passes me the flask behind her back.

"Wait, what? She's Alaska girl? That's so awesome!" Violet jumps up and down once with excitement. It quickly turns into a grimace, and she grabs on to her boobs. I look away because Violet, for being as small as she is, has a huge rack, and she's currently wearing a shirt that shows off a significant amount of cleavage, and all the jumping and self-groping only draws more attention to it. Also, I don't want Alex to catch me looking.

"Yeah, I don't know if awesome is how I would describe this situation."

"Why not? It's like fate." She grabs Alex by the shirt and tips her head back so she can look up at him. "Just like when you accidentally let your nerd hang out when you mentioned how I was reading Fielding at a hockey game. My beaver took the reins that night."

He gazes down at her, wearing a half smile, all the fucking love in the world oozing out of them like freaking rainbows. Actually, I think he might be looking down her top. "Best damn night of my life."

I'm about to ask them if they want some privacy, but Violet returns her attention to me. "You have to go talk to her."

"It's not that simple."

"Of course it's that simple. Why wouldn't it be?"

"Apparently he lied about his job," Alex tells her.

Violet frowns. "Why would you do that?"

I shrug. "Because I'm an idiot. She didn't know who I was, and it was kind of nice being a regular guy for a few weeks, you know what I mean?"

"So what kind of job did you tell her you have?"

"I told her I was an alpaca farmer, which would've been true if I didn't play professional hockey."

Her frown deepens. "That's an oddly specific lie."

"My parents were alpaca farmers."

Her nose wrinkles. "Really. How did I not know that?"

"It doesn't come up much in conversation, I guess?"

"Okay, so you lied about your job—no big deal, right? Unless you lied about something else?"

I scrub a hand over my mouth and mutter, "My name."

"I'm sorry, did you say your *name*? Why lie about that?"

"Well, like I said, she didn't recognize me, and it wasn't like I made up a fake one. I just gave her my nickname instead."

She blinks a few times. "You told her your name was Rookie?"

"No, I told her it was RJ, which is what my dad always called me and what my brother and sister still call me now. So it wasn't totally a lie. I mean, my name is pretty uncommon. Shit. I handled this all wrong, and now she's going to look me up and see all the bunny crap."

"So was it just that you didn't want her to know you used to let the puck bunnies use you like their personal dildo?"

"No. That wasn't it. I mean, now it's obviously going to be an issue, but I just wanted to be normal for a few weeks. And now she knows I lied to her about my job and my name, so I'm pretty sure she doesn't want anything to do with me. And even if she's willing to talk to me, once she realizes what else I've left out she'll probably never want to speak to me again."

This fuckup is on me. I kept putting off telling her the truth, maybe in part because I hoped that if she fell for me the way I fell for her, by the time I finally told her what I really did for a living, it wouldn't matter.

"Well, that's a complication, since you're still obviously hung up on her."

"Yeah. I have her number, though, so that's good, right?"

"If she'll answer your calls, sure," Alex says.

"And what happens when she finds out about my personal relationship history?"

"You mean that you used to be a manwhore?" Violet asks.

"Yeah. That."

Violet puts a hand on my shoulder, her expression serious. "If it's meant to be, she'll get over it—as long as you didn't give her some kind of lasting STD as a gift."

CHAPTER 14

WHAT YOU DON'T KNOW ...

Lainey

Eden's disembodied head appears in the doorway of the observation room. She's the reason I have this job. We grew up homeschooled in the same community, but when she became a teenager she went to a local school and then went on to attend regular college. We still stayed close and even managed to keep in contact when she moved to Chicago a couple of years ago, despite my not being on social media.

When things got a little crazy with my family after I returned from Alaska, Eden suggested I come out for a visit. Since I'd already braved a plane before, I decided I could do it again. Also, my parents were back to smothering me, especially since I came home brokenhearted. My mother never outright said *I told you so*, but it was implied. Often.

I went for a weeklong visit, fell in love with the aquarium, and a couple of months later returned, this time with a job and an apartment.

"Hey. I figured I'd find you in here." Eden lets the door close behind her.

"It's peaceful." I turn off the tablet clutched in my hands, almost glad for the break from yet another distressing article I've stumbled upon.

"Researching again?"

"Something like that. Am I needed up front?" Occasionally I'll have to work at the information desk. I don't mind talking to people one-on-one, especially when they're asking about the animals.

She leans against the door. "I'd stay put for right now."

"He's back again, isn't he?" I fold my hands in my lap to keep from wringing them.

"Yeah. He's back again."

It's been over a week. Nine days, actually. Nine long days since RJ—otherwise known as Rook Bowman, captain for Chicago's NHL hockey team and apparently quite the notorious playboy, according to the many, many accounts on the World Wide Web—dropped back into my life.

Since then he's stopped by the aquarium every single day. He's also called and texted daily and has taken to sending me rather extravagant gifts. Well, extravagant by my standards, but I've also discovered that his salary is a staggering eleven and a half million dollars a year, so the hundreds he's likely spending on ostentatious flower arrangements and gift baskets is similar to tossing a handful of dollar bills into the air and watching them fall like snow into a pit of lava—or the mouth of a shark.

"He seems really . . . apologetic," Eden offers.

I give her a hard look. "Not you too."

She crosses over to sit beside me on the bench. The seals swim by, unaffected by my anxiety or my slightly morose mood. "I understand that this is difficult, especially because he lied to you, but maybe he had a reason?"

"I can only imagine what that reason is."

"Wouldn't it be better to hear it from him instead of going on speculation?"

"I don't need to talk to him, because it's not speculation, it's sarcasm—which I know is the lowest form of wit, but I looked him up, Eden. The picture the media paints isn't very pretty." I open the article again and pass her the tablet.

Eden points to the date. "This article is old."

"There are more recent ones."

She arches a brow. "How recent?"

I focus on the happy seals. "From a couple of years ago. It doesn't matter. He lied."

"Probably because he was worried you'd react like this," Eden says softly. "I understand you're upset, but don't you think he deserves—"

"Do *not* say it, Eden."

She sighs and puts her arm around my shoulder. "All of these rumors you're so focused on are old news. I know you're scared, but you can't avoid him forever, and you know it. And you'll never know if he's really just a lying asshole with a pretty face and rock-star moves in bed if you don't at least sit down and hear what he has to say."

"I never thought I was going to see him again," I whisper, fighting tears. "And I just started seeing someone."

Eden makes a face. "You mean Walter? That guy in your building?"

"He's nice." And he is nice. He works in IT; he's quiet, likes Italian food, has a cat named Sam—and he's kind. He also knows about my circumstances and hasn't bailed, which is saying something, since I'm kind of a huge mess. The last time we went out he kissed me good night. Like him, it was nice. No fireworks or shooting stars, but it wasn't unpleasant either.

"So is the weather today—it doesn't mean he's right for you."

"And just because RJ keeps showing up here doesn't mean he's right for me either."

"Or maybe it's a sign. I mean, think about it. I get a job out here, and all of a sudden they need someone who specializes in dolphin reproduction behaviors? How many people are qualified for that specific job?"

"Anyone who specializes in aquatic mammals has the right background."

"But they hired you—after a phone interview, which never happens, by the way." She gives me an *I told you so* kind of look.

"They'd already met me in person, because I'd been here before."

"Okay, I can give you that one. But what about the fact that his teammate's wife funds the initiative you've been hired for, and then they throw a birthday party and *he* ends up here. It feels a lot like fate intervening to me, and I usually don't even believe in things like fate. You have to give him a chance, Lainey."

"I'll think about it."

The following day RJ shows up while I'm covering the information desk. It's a Tuesday, which is one of the slower days of the week. Not that it's ever slow per se, but there are fewer staff on days like this one. And it means I can't run away and hide in one of the anterooms of the exhibits.

He's dressed in a T-shirt and jeans. His hair is styled instead of covered with a ball cap. He looks just as gorgeous as he did a year ago, if not even more so. Today his arms are loaded with white flowers. Truce. Surrender. Peace.

I plaster my hands to the countertop so I don't give in to the urge to touch my hair. My heart stutters in my chest and then kicks into a full gallop as he approaches the desk.

"Hi." His voice is soft and warm, like marshmallows melting in hot chocolate.

"Hello." Mine is hard and sharp like knives.

"I brought these for you. I don't know if you've gotten all the other things I've left for you or not—"

"I got them all." Each one has been like twisting a knife in a wound, because they've all been attached to memories from Alaska—which is clearly the point.

He sets the bouquet of flowers on the desk; the fragrant scent of the blossoms surrounds me. I want to reach out and stroke the pretty petals, but instead I keep my hands on the counter. "Lainey, please, can we talk? I know I lied to you, and you have every right to be angry with me about that—but if you just give me a chance to explain, then maybe you'll understand that it wasn't my intention to ever hurt you."

"I can't right now."

"I understand that, but can we set something up?" His hand covers mine before I can pull it away and hide it under the counter. "Just— please, Lainey, all I want to do is talk."

My heart aches, and my skin burns where he touches it. "Fine. We can talk."

He clasps my hand between his, lids fluttering shut as he lifts it to his lips, brushing them over my knuckle. I can't breathe through the sudden emotional deluge. I pull my hand free from his grasp and take a step back, even though my head feels light.

"Tonight? Are you free? I can come to you if that works best."

"No!" I lace my fingers together to keep from fidgeting. "I mean— tonight won't work, and I would prefer if we did this in a public place."

"Uh, that might not be the best idea. Chicago is a hockey city—I get recognized a lot here, so it would be ideal if I either came to you or you come to me."

"Oh." I hadn't considered that. "It would be better if I came to you, then."

"Would tomorrow night work? Or—Thursday's your day off, right? That might be better for you."

"How do you know Thursday's my day off?"

"Uhhhh . . ." RJ taps on the counter nervously. "I might've asked about your schedule in exchange for tickets to the first game of the season. I can get you tickets too, if you want—for whatever game you want, really."

"I'll have to get back to you about Thursday." I also need to speak to Eden about taking bribes.

"You'll call me—or text?"

"Yes."

"Promise?"

I remain stone faced apart from my arched brow.

"Okay. I'll wait to hear from you."

On Thursday morning I'm standing on the curb waiting for a car to pick me up. Apparently RJ has sent a taxi for me—or something. I assume he didn't come to pick me up himself so as not to make me uncomfortable. I have a car, but I'm not sure driving is a good idea, considering how anxious I am.

I looked up his address on my computer. It's in a very nice neighborhood, from what I can tell. A black SUV with dark tinted windows pulls up to the curb. I step back, assuming someone is going to get out. I don't want to get hit with the door.

A man dressed in a black suit, wearing sunglasses, rounds the hood of the SUV. "Miss Carver?"

I look around, expecting someone with the same last name as me to breeze by, but there's no one there.

"Miss Lainey Carver?" The man looks at something in his hand.

"Yes?"

"I'm here to take you to Mr. Bowman's."

I glance at the nondescript black SUV and then back at the man in the suit. "Can you give me a minute, please?"

"Certainly, Miss Carver."

He folds his hands in front of him and stands beside the SUV while I pull up RJ's contact and hit the Call button.

It doesn't even finish ringing once. "Please tell me you haven't changed your mind."

"Welllll, that depends," I say slowly.

"On what?" His panic is frustratingly endearing.

"There's a black SUV and a man in a suit claiming he's here to take me to you, but I've watched enough crime shows to know better than to trust a man in a suit driving an SUV with tinted windows."

"You can ask him to tell you his name—it's George Oriole."

"That sounds like a fake name."

"It's not. I promise."

"And I should have faith in your promises? How do I even know RJ isn't something you made up?" It's a legitimate question. He's been dishonest with me before. In fact, everything I know about him is based on a lie.

He sighs. "RJ isn't a made-up name for me either—it's what my dad used to call me, and my brother and sister still do most of the time. It's only my teammates and non–family members who know me as Rook or Rookie. Please ask him his name, Lainey, so I can see you."

"Fine. Give me a second." I relent, because as angry as I still am, I want some answers. "Excuse me, sir, can you please tell me your name? First and last," I call to the suit. He's eerily still.

"George Oriole, Miss Carver. I'm in Mr. Bowman's employ as a driver. Please allow me to take you to him."

"Thank you." I hold up a finger and give him my back. "He gave me the right name."

"So you're on your way?"

"What if he's not actually George Oriole? What if he hijacked the SUV on the way here and he's posing as him? What if George's body is in the trunk?" I realize I sound like a lunatic, but this is the kind of thing that happens in crime shows all the time. Also, last night I couldn't sleep, so I stayed up too late watching TV, and I woke up on the couch after midnight to that exact scenario playing on the screen.

To his credit, RJ doesn't even question my sanity—he simply tells me to take a picture of the driver and message it to him, so I do, and he confirms that it is, indeed, George.

"I'm getting in the SUV now."

"Okay, great. I would've come to get you myself, but I wasn't sure how you'd feel about that."

"This is better, thanks. I'll see you soon." I end the call, and George opens the back door, holding out a hand to help me in.

I feel very much like I've entered the twilight zone. Bottles of water, both still and sparkling, sit in an ice bucket in the center console. There's also a take-out cup containing a hot beverage. I pick it up and give it a sniff.

"Mr. Bowman requested a hot chocolate for you, Miss Carver—I hope it's to your liking."

"Thank you—I'm sure it's perfect." I settle in and watch the scenery change as we leave the Loop and head toward the outskirts of the city. The farther we get from my apartment building, the bigger and nicer the houses are. We pass grand-looking estates with manicured front lawns and gorgeous landscaping.

I shouldn't be at all surprised when the SUV pulls down the driveway of one of the really nice, really big houses. It's a two-story Craftsman with a huge wraparound porch. In some ways the rustic-ness reminds me of his cabin in Alaska, except tailored to the city.

I pop a breath mint and crunch down on it as George pulls up to the front steps and puts the car in park. My palms are sweaty and my mouth is dry as I gather my purse and run my hands over my thighs. I'm wearing jeans and a sweater. I went light on the makeup, only covering up the dark circles under my eyes and throwing on a coat of mascara—and, okay, maybe a bit of eyeliner and a hint of shadow too. I want to look decent but not like I tried too hard for him.

George opens the door and extends a hand, helping me out of the car. "I'll be here to take you home when you're ready, Miss Carver."

"Thank you, George."

"It's been my pleasure."

As I climb the front steps, the door opens. I almost expect to be greeted by a butler, but it's RJ standing there, waiting for me. He has one hand shoved in the pocket of his jeans; his black T-shirt stretches across his broad chest.

"Thank you for agreeing to come." He moves back, allowing me to step inside.

"You're welcome." I'm both relieved and disappointed when he doesn't try to hug me.

I take in the spacious entrance, cataloging the decor. Despite the house being huge, probably twice the size of the cabin in Alaska, it still manages to have a homey, cozy feel to it. The floors are rough-hewn hardwood; the color palette is warm and light and the decor a combination of rustic country and modern elements.

I leave my shoes at the front door, a habit I've never been able to shake, having grown up on a farm. I follow RJ down a wide hallway to a state-of-the-art kitchen. I wonder if he cooks at all or if he has someone who does that for him. All the articles I've read about him and the horrible pictures I've seen chronicling his womanizing ways come to mind, and I have to wonder how many women he's paraded through this house—how many parties has he thrown?

"You have a nice house," I croak, feeling awkward and vulnerable.

"Thanks. I just moved in at the end of last season, in June." He stops in the middle of the kitchen. "Can I offer you something to drink?"

"Water would be good, please." I loathe how relieved I am about the short span of time he's lived here, which significantly reduces the number of women who are also intimate with this space and him.

"I have grapefruit juice."

My heart skips a stupid beat and takes off at a sprint. "Just the water, but thank you."

He nods, chewing on the inside of his lip as he turns away, retrieves a glass, and fills it with water. "We can sit outside, if you want."

"Sure." I hate how uncomfortable things are between us. I don't know how to deal with any of this. He feels like a stranger despite the fact that we lived together in a tiny little bubble a year ago. A bubble that's left me with no end of repercussions.

RJ's sprawling backyard is heavily landscaped, with a covered sitting area, an outdoor cooking space, an in-ground pool, and beyond that, an outdoor hockey rink. The amount of money it would cost to have all of this, especially in a place like Chicago, is mind boggling.

I'm fortunate my apartment is subsidized by my job at the aquarium, otherwise I'd never be able to afford it.

I take one of the single chairs, and RJ sits on the love seat perpendicular to me. "How are you?" he asks.

"Very confused and anxious," I say honestly.

He nods. "I'm sorry I lied about who I was."

"So am I. It feels like everything between us balanced on that lie, RJ—or should I just call you Rook?"

"I like it that you call me RJ."

"I'm sure that was purposeful, giving me a name that would be impossible to search." Before I found out who and what he is, I'd idealized him in my head, but now . . . I don't know.

"Not the way you think." He exhales a long, slow breath, his expression pained. "I had a reason for keeping the truth from you, Lainey, and I never meant for it to hurt you."

"Because you never planned to see me again after Alaska," I shoot back.

"That's not true."

I arch a brow. "We lived on different ends of the country—it wasn't like a long-distance relationship was an option after six weeks together. It was a summer fling." I say the words because it's what I've told myself in my head this past year. But my heart says something different, and hope beats like a hummingbird's wings against the fragile cage inside.

"Maybe it started out that way, but it was a lot more than that. At least for me, anyway." RJ keeps running his hands over his thighs. He props his elbows on his knees and leans forward. "I know we weren't together long. And maybe we never talked about it being anything beyond a fling, but I wanted it to be more. And then Joy went into labor, and I had to—"

"How is Joy? And the baby?" For the past year I've wondered if everything was okay—if they were okay or not.

"She's great, and so is Max."

"She had a boy."

"She did. He's growing like a weed. They're not planning on having any more children because it was such a high-risk pregnancy, but everyone is happy and healthy."

I nod. "That's good. I'm glad to hear it."

"I tried to call when I got to LA, Lainey, at least twenty times. Things were hectic and stressful, but I didn't want you to worry—and then I was worried because you weren't answering, and things were really touch and go with Joy and the baby. Kyle was beside himself. Stevie and I have never seen him like that before. I thought he was going to have a complete breakdown."

"I'm so sorry." And I am—for the pain he endured, for the fear he must have experienced, for the danger they might have been in.

"It was rough at the time, but everyone is doing well now. Would you like to see a picture of Max? He's a real bruiser." RJ slips his phone out of his pocket and waits for my nod before he pulls up his photo app. "Do you want to sit here? It'll be easier to see them." He pats the cushion beside him.

I stare at the empty space. He's a big man, taking up a lot of that love seat. He shifts to make more room for me, obviously sensing my hesitation.

"Or you can stay there. Whatever's more comfortable for you."

I relent again—partly because the way he's sitting will make it awkward if I don't move next to him. I shift to the spot beside him, and he moves the phone so it's between us. "This is Max in the hospital. Apparently babies are a lot bigger when the mom has gestational diabetes, which I didn't realize."

"Geez, how much did he weigh?" I cringe at the idea of pushing that head out of my vagina.

"Almost eleven pounds, I think?"

"Oh my goodness, that's *huge*! Some three-month-olds barely weigh that!"

"Yeah, Joy ended up having a C-section. He was breech, and there was something going on with the placenta. I don't know all the details, but it wasn't an easy pregnancy or birth for her—or anyone, really." He flips through pictures showing his nephew at various stages over the past year. There are pictures of RJ holding him as an infant, of Max in a tiny Chicago jersey, of him holding on to RJ's hands as he takes a wobbly step.

"It looks like you're a good uncle." My voice cracks, and I have to clear my throat as I fight to hold back tears.

"Being an uncle is easy. I get to spoil the shit out of him and then give him back to his mom when he gets cranky."

"Sounds about right." That's always the way with uncles, aunts, and grandparents.

"I don't get to see them as much as I'd like since they're so far away, but I try to make the most of my time when I'm with them. I'll get to spend time with them when I play in LA, which is good." RJ covers my hand with his. "I should have taken you with me—to LA. I should've booked two seats and brought you, but my brother was so panicked, and I didn't think it through."

"You couldn't bring me with you, though, because you'd lied about who you were." I slip my hand out from under his; he tightens his grip for a second before he lets me go.

RJ sets his phone on the table and scrubs a hand over his face, muttering a curse. "I wanted to tell you so many times, but I didn't want to ruin things between us. I figured if I told you the truth, you'd leave, so I kept putting it off—and the longer I did, the harder it got to tell you." His gaze meets mine, imploring me to understand. "After I left you, I realized I had so many things I still needed to tell you, including my truth. I had this plan in my head that, once I got to LA, I'd tell you everything."

"Why lie at all? Why taint everything with untruths?"

"You didn't recognize me."

It's a simple explanation that tells me nothing and everything. When he doesn't continue, I push. "And? That's supposed to explain why you built what we had on a lie? You had weeks to tell me the truth, but instead you layered on more lies to support the one you started with."

"I omitted more than anything, but I regret not saying anything. I just wanted to be normal for a while. You don't understand what it's like—"

"You mean all the parties and the women?" My stomach rolls as the images I've seen online come back to haunt me. I can't get them out of my head. "I looked you up, RJ, as soon as I realized you'd lied. What I found is nothing like the man I was with in Alaska. I don't even know who you are."

"Yes, you do, Lainey. I'm the man you met on the plane who comforted you, the one you spent all those weeks with, the one who taught you how to drive and held you through a thunderstorm. That's the *real* me."

He moves to touch me again, so I shoot up off the love seat and step out of reach. "I don't know what to believe."

"I get that it looks bad—I really do, Lainey—but if you check all the dates you'll see it was years ago. I came from a small town and was drafted young. I made some choices that weren't the best, and I live in a city where hockey players are on par with celebrities—in an era where everything that should be private is public fodder. My mom and my sister wouldn't speak to me for almost a year because of all the shit out there, so I know what the consequences of my actions are."

I scoff at that last part. He has no idea what kind of repercussions I've faced as a result—or the strain it's put on my relationship with my parents. If I thought they were protective before I went to Alaska, they were a million times worse when I came back.

"There had to have been a time in your life where you rebelled. Haven't you ever gone through a wild phase, Lainey?"

"Yes. You were my wild phase, and clearly that was a terrible mistake," I snap.

RJ pushes out of his chair and tries to corral me, but I slip between the chairs, out of reach once again.

"You said you planned to tell me the truth once you got to LA and we got in touch, but how was that ever going to work? I'd see all the same things, and I would've been on the other side of the country. How would you explain it then? How would you have been able to make me see whatever truth you want to feed me?" I move toward the house. "I tried to find you—I called every single alpaca farm in New York looking for you, but no one knew who you were, which makes sense, since I was asking for someone they'd never heard of."

RJ's expression is pained. "My mom sold the farm right after Max was born—to an investor. She wanted to be in LA with my sister and brother."

I shake my head, not wanting to hear how we missed each other by weeks. "I tried to find you, but how hard did you try to find me, RJ?

Really and truly?" I remember how devastated I was when I couldn't find him and how, recently, I began to wonder if it hadn't been a karmic blessing. "I need to go."

RJ's shoulders cave. "Please, Lainey."

"I can't be here right now. This is too much." I move toward the sliding door, needing to get away from him and all the memories and the conflict I'm feeling over him and everything I know now.

"Can't you give me a chance to prove you already know the real me?"

I can't look at him and see that his expression matches the sadness in his voice. I want to give him that chance, but I don't want to set myself up for more disappointment. "And put my heart on the line for you again? How will I trust you?"

He steps in front of the door before I can reach it. I stumble back, and he grips my biceps to keep me from falling—or maybe to keep me from running away. I long for the feel of his arms around me again. I want to sink into his warmth and the comfort I remember so vividly still.

"I was falling for you. I was halfway in l—"

"Don't!" I all but shout. "Don't play with my emotions. It's unfair."

"That's not what I'm doing. I'm trying to be honest."

"You had plenty of chances to be honest. Just let me go, *Rook*." I say his name like a curse.

"I already let you go once, Lainey, and it gutted me—I don't know if I can do it again."

"Well, you can't hold me captive, can you?"

"No. I can't." He releases me, and I spin around, yank the door open, and pad across the hardwood to the front entrance. Stupid, rogue tears start to fall as I shove my feet into my flats. I don't know how to reconcile the version of him I thought I knew with the one who lives in an almost mansion and has a reputation for being a colossal playboy.

I struggle to open the door, unable to figure out how the locks work with how blurry my vision is. I realize I'm on the verge of a full-blown panic attack—all of this is too much to handle. I struggle to breathe, to think. My vision swims with dots, and suddenly I find myself pulled into his solid embrace.

His lips find my temple. "Breathe, Lainey—just breathe."

I cling to his shirt, trying to force myself to let go when all I want to do is hold on tighter. He rubs soothing circles on my back, murmuring for me to breathe over and over, telling me he's sorry, that he never wanted to hurt me.

I count all the things I can feel, see, hear, taste, and smell. Eventually I calm down enough that I'm able to pry my fingers from his shirt. I press my palms against his chest, his heart beating hard under them.

He brushes away my tears. "I'm so sorry, Lainey. This wasn't what I wanted. I thought your silence was your way of telling me my feelings were one-sided."

"I have to go." It's nothing but a broken whisper.

He cups my face in his palms. "Please look at me."

I slowly lift my eyes, taking in his devastatingly handsome face.

"I messed this up once, Lainey, and I understand that I've blindsided you with all of this, but I promise I'm the man you met a year ago, and I'm going to do everything in my power to prove that to you." For a moment I think he's going to kiss me.

And he does—on the cheek.

My skin burns. My heart stutters.

I should tell him my own truth.

But for now we're tied: a lie for a lie.

CHAPTER 15

BACK IN THE GAME

Rook

Lainey asked for space, but considering how upset she was yesterday when she left my place—and how poorly I slept—I call her first thing the next morning and leave a voice mail asking how she's doing and letting her know I'm thinking about her before I hit the gym.

I still haven't heard from Lainey by the time I'm finished with my workout, so I fire off a message with basically the same content as the voice mail and then proceed to order her a bouquet of flowers. I'm just about to head home when my phone lights up. I check the screen, elated as fuck when I see Lainey's name pop up.

"Hey, hi. How are you?"

"Uh, hi. Is this RJ?" It's a female voice, but it's not Lainey.

"It is." I check the screen. It's definitely Lainey's number, which I memorized the night I acquired it. "Who is this?"

"Uh, it's Eden. I'm a friend of Lainey's, and I'm sort of staging an intervention."

"An intervention? Is Lainey in some sort of trouble?" I consider the dark circles under her eyes and her anxiety—which I was familiar with in Alaska, but it was always something she seemed to manage okay when she was comfortable and felt safe—but maybe I'm missing something.

"Not like an *intervention* intervention—more like I'm trying to give her a friendly nudge in the right direction. So I'm probably going to get myself in some trouble for telling you this, but she hasn't ever really gotten over you. I mean, she's been dealing with a lot of stuff, and she's only recently tried to start dating."

"She's dating someone?" This is not what I want to hear.

"Not really. I mean, they've gone on a couple of dates, and she thinks he's nice and stable or whatever, but she's not really into him."

"So it's not serious?"

"No. Not yet, anyway. Like I said, just a couple of dates, but I think he really likes her—and he lives in her building, so that's not ideal for you."

"Shit. No, it's not." I really need to step up my game.

"It's just that Lainey has a lot on her plate, most of which I'm pretty sure she hasn't mentioned to you but definitely should."

"Is there something I can do? Some way I can help?"

"We both get off at four. You should come by the aquarium."

"But I just saw her yesterday, and she said she needed time."

"Lainey's already had lots of time. More than a year. She's scared. If you're really serious about wanting her to give you a second chance, you should be here. She's leading a private tour until three forty-five. Shoot, gotta go." She hangs up before I can thank her.

I need to get my ass in gear and figure out how to make Lainey see I'm serious—and that I'm more than just lies and empty promises.

I stop at home, shower again, and change into black dress pants and a button-down. I don't know why I feel the compulsion to dress like I'm ready for a date, but on the off chance Lainey's interested in more than telling me to fuck off, I want to be adequately prepared.

I arrive at the aquarium at three thirty, just to be safe, and approach the front desk. A familiar-looking woman with brown hair, glasses, and a whole lot of curves gives me a once-over and a raised eyebrow. "No flowers this time?"

"Dammit." I can't believe I forgot to stop on the way over. "Is there a place close by where I can pick some up real quick?"

She holds up a hand. "Lainey left the last bouquet here because she doesn't have room in her apartment for more, so I think you're good on the flowers."

"What about chocolate or something?"

"She left the last box of chocolates here too. And while we all appreciate it, because they were delicious, I'm trying not to gain ten pounds *before* the holidays this year, so you can put a hold on the chocolate and flowers for a little while. Maybe for a week." She extends her hand. "I'm Eden."

I wipe my palm on my pants before I shake her hand. "Rook Bowman—I mean, RJ."

"Oh, I know who you are." She props an elbow on the counter and motions to a bench close to one of the many fish tanks. "Might as well take a seat—you've got a few minutes before she's done. You get bonus points for being early, though." She pushes her glasses up her nose and turns to the screen in front of her, dismissing me.

"Okay, thanks."

I manage to stay seated for about five minutes before I get antsy and start to pace. I end up standing in front of the dolphin exhibit while I wait for Lainey. Today the boy dolphin seems to be on his best behavior.

Eventually Lainey and a small group of very scholarly-looking people enter the lobby. Most of them disperse, but one guy stays behind to talk to her. I can tell by the way he keeps jamming his hand into his pocket and then rubbing the back of his neck that he's interested in her. Which isn't much of a surprise. Lainey's gorgeous, even in her drab beige uniform.

As if she can sense my presence, her gaze shifts to me. The guy she's talking to is in the middle of a sentence when she walks away from him, heading straight for me. I'd like to say getting her attention is a good thing, but based on her expression she's not all that happy to see me.

"Why are you here?" she snaps.

I jam my hands into my pockets, just like the guy she blew off. "I wanted to see how you're doing after yesterday."

She blinks a few times, maybe a little shocked, and wrings her hands. "I'm fine."

"You don't seem fine. You seem upset." The circles that I noticed under her eyes yesterday are even more pronounced, like my appearance in her life has caused her to lose sleep. I don't like that idea, but I guess I can understand. I haven't been sleeping all that great either.

"I didn't expect you to show up here after yesterday." She tugs at the end of her braid.

"Can I take you for coffee—or hot chocolate?"

"I can't, I have to . . . I-I have an obligation," she stammers; the hand-wringing ratchets up a notch.

Eden appears out of nowhere, laden down with jackets and purses. "Actually, I can handle your obligation for you."

Lainey gives her a meaningful look. "You really don't need to do that."

"It's no big deal. I can totally handle it." She hands Lainey her purse.

"I'd like to at least change first and check on . . . things."

"You look beautiful just the way you are, but if you want, I can drive you home. We could even pick up coffee and go to your place if that's easier for you."

"No!" she shouts and then lowers her voice. "I mean—I need to clean. And I live just across the street. There's a coffee shop next door. I can meet you there in twenty minutes."

"Okay, sure." I assume she's being all sketchy because she doesn't want to run into the guy she's dating in her building. A coffee shop isn't ideal, especially since I don't have a ball cap to hide under, but I'll take whatever I can get here.

CHAPTER 16

HEY, BABY

Lainey

I am going to kill Eden. Okay, that's untrue. I can barely manage killing a spider, but I'm going to be very annoyed with her for at least the rest of today. I take several deep breaths as the elevator counts down the floors to the lobby.

I would really like to be less anxious right now. My palms are insanely sweaty. Actually, a lot of parts of me are sweaty. I check my reflection in the surrounding mirrors, making sure the concealer I dabbed under my eyes is blended in properly. This morning I got into the elevator and realized it was still smeared in a line—like those black lines football players have, except it was flesh colored.

The elevator doors slide open, and I step into the lobby, murmuring hello to people getting on. And, of course, one of them happens to be Walter. Instead of getting on the elevator, he lets everyone else pile in and pulls me into a hug.

Through the window across the lobby I can see RJ, hands jammed into his pockets, watching the exchange with narrowed eyes. I release

Walter first and take a step back, which makes him take a step forward. He's weird about personal space.

"You look nice—are you going somewhere?" Walter fingers the end of my braid, which also puts his hand close to my boob.

I glance toward the window again. RJ's face is practically pressed up against it, and if he had superpowers, I would bet that laser beams would be shooting out of his eyes right now and Walter would be minus a hand.

"Just coffee with a friend."

"Lucky friend." He gives me an exaggerated wink. "Will you be around later? Maybe I could come by and we could watch an episode of *Jeopardy!* together."

"Oh, um, can I take a rain check? I'm not sure how long I'll be out, and I haven't been sleeping all that well the last few nights."

His smile drops. "Sure, of course. You can call if you change your mind. I have a bag of sweet-and-salty popcorn and some of that special mint hot chocolate you're always drinking."

"That sounds nice." I push the elevator button for him. "I'll call you later."

"Sounds great." He leans in and kisses me on the cheek before I can run away.

Thankfully, the elevator dings.

RJ is waiting outside the front doors for me. I glance over my shoulder, relieved to see that Walter is already in the elevator. He lifts his hand in a parting wave at the same time as RJ pulls me in for a brief hug. Walter's smile slides off his face like an egg off a nonstick pan as he disappears behind the elevator doors.

"Friend of yours?" RJ asks, obviously referring to Walter.

"Yes. He is." I adjust my purse. I want to tack on that it really isn't any of his business, but I refrain.

"Does he work in IT or something?"

I frown. "How did you know that?"

He smirks. "Lucky guess."

"Walter is nice. Not everyone is built like a Greek god and gets to be a celebrity." As if I need to stroke his ego. Based on everything I've seen in my internet searches—which is all I have to go on, since I have no idea where the lies end with him—he and a good percentage of the female population of Chicago know how amazing his body is. I push past him and head for the coffee shop next door. I know the baristas here, and there are always a lot of regulars, so it feels like a safe space.

RJ grabs my hand. "Sorry. I'm just . . . jealous and being petty."

I purse my lips and try not to let the butterflies in my stomach get the best of me.

RJ puts his hand on the small of my back, inciting another storm of butterflies. He also opens the door for me and pays for our coffees and pastries, although I order a decaf tea because I'm already having enough trouble sleeping these days without hopping myself up on caffeine at dinnertime.

He picks out a table in the corner, and we settle into our seats. I'm barely out of my jacket when two teenage boys approach us asking for autographs. For the next half hour RJ is bombarded every two minutes by another group of people asking to take pictures and wanting an autograph. Teenagers, college kids, adult men, and fawning women who rudely drool all over him with me sitting right there across the table. It's incredibly overwhelming. And enlightening.

This is his life. This is what happens to him every time he goes out in this city. It's what he knows, and I have to assume it's much worse depending on where he is and who's around him. I consider all the pictures I've found since I discovered his true identity, and a very small part of me can understand how difficult it would be to have a relationship that involves any kind of equity.

He would never know if he was wanted by someone because of his fame or because of who he really is. And isn't that another question I don't have an answer to? The man I was with in Alaska was kind and sweet and down-to-earth. But this . . . it's completely different. And this is what his life is *really* like.

I move aside, unable to handle the number of people clamoring to get close to him, and allow his fans to mob him while I observe from the sidelines. RJ is gracious and accommodating and charismatic, but I can sense his frustration by the tic in his cheek as more people gather for selfies. Finally, once everyone has had their picture taken and he's signed all the hats and random pieces of paper people shove at him—and even a couple of magazine spreads—he gives me a pained smile. "Is there somewhere we can go that's a little less openly public? I should've worn a ball cap—it helps make me less identifiable."

"There's a park not too far from here. We could go there?" I offer. He can't come up to my apartment. Not yet. Maybe not ever, depending.

I use the bathroom before we leave, and when I return RJ has fresh hot drinks for us in take-out cups. I don't know what to think about this entire situation. Walter is nice, he doesn't travel for work, and he doesn't make a scene or get mobbed when we go out in public. And he's been very accepting of my current situation and my obvious reluctance to get into a relationship.

I decide I need to just be honest with RJ—it's really the only way I'll know for sure what his real intentions are. If he can't handle the truth, then he'll disappear from my life again, and that will be that.

We find a secluded bench in the park down the street from my house. There are parents seated on the other side, near the play structure, but otherwise it's peaceful.

"I'm sorry about that. I probably should've suggested we just come to a park in the first place. It's not always this intense, but the season is starting soon, so we're getting a lot of promo. I've been trying to stay off the media radar, but being team captain makes it tough." He stretches his arm across the back of the bench, fingers brushing my shoulder.

"Can I ask you something?" I fidget with the sleeve on my cup, picking at the edge so I don't have to look at him. He's just so disarmingly beautiful.

"Yeah, of course."

"I don't understand why you're so intent on pursuing me when you could have anyone you want. What am I to you, other than the woman you pretended to be someone else with for a handful of weeks?"

"That's the thing, though, Lainey. I wasn't pretending to be someone else. Yes, I lied about my job, but everything else was me—you got the *real* me."

"But did I really? Because what I saw back there, isn't that the real you? Is that what happens to you whenever you go somewhere and people recognize you?"

"I just wanted someone to see me, *authentically* see *me*, and I felt like you did. I never felt more like myself than I did when I was with you."

I consider that—and how, for those weeks I was with him, I'd felt like the best version of myself. He made me feel safe and special and important. "I have to tell you something." I clutch my tea, trying to find the resolve to spit the words out. I can't decide anymore if I want him to still be the man I spent those weeks with or the lying jerk who recently dropped back into my life. Both are complicated for very different reasons.

"Okay. I'm listening."

I shift, turning toward him, knowing I need to see his reaction when I tell him this, because for better or worse, it will change everything.

"I have a son."

CHAPTER 17

DO THE MATH

Rook

"I—what?" I don't know what I expected her to say—maybe something along the lines of *I'm still in love with you.* Or *I missed you,* or *I used to be a fucking circus clown,* but *I have a son* was definitely not on my list of possibilities.

"His name is Kody, with a *K.*" She sets her tea down and pulls her phone out of her pocket. Her hands shake as she keys in the pass code. "He was born on April fourth, about ten days earlier than expected. The pregnancy was good—I was very healthy, and I had a wonderful doctor and lots of support. Although my family was not happy about it, there was really nothing they could do." She's still looking down at her phone as she continues to talk, like she just wants to get it all out. "It took me a couple of months to realize I was pregnant when I came home. I'd thought I was lovesick, but then I missed my period two months in a row, and I went to see a doctor, and well . . ." She cradles the phone to her chest. "He's four months old now."

I suddenly feel like I'm choking. It's also like being hit with the most extreme case of déjà vu in the universe. It's like Sissy part two—except worse, because I spent six weeks with Lainey, screwing on every available surface. We'd used protection. Well, except that once. And it was only for a stroke—one delicious, amazingly memorable stroke. But she got her period the next day, so everything was fine. And it lasted all of three days, so it didn't slow us down much, if at all. I'm so shocked, and frankly really freaked out, that the first words out of my mouth are "You're fucking with me, right?"

A little kid runs by, followed by his mother, who shoots me a dirty look. I mutter, "Sorry," and turn back to Lainey, lowering my voice. "Is this your idea of a joke? If that Walter guy is actually your boyfriend—or, worse, your damn husband—then the last place you should be is with me." She's not wearing a ring, and if that baby is four months old, then she—what, moved right the hell on the day I left?

Lainey looks at me like I've lost my mind. "Kody is yours."

"How is that even possible? We used condoms every single damn time." I have to fight to keep my voice down.

"Yes." She nods in agreement. "Except—"

I railroad right over her. "So how the fuck can it be mine, unless you fished a used condom out of a wastebasket and turkey basted yourself?"

She raises a hand right in my face. "Okay, that is just . . . absolutely disgusting and appalling. It's also disturbing that you could come up with something so ludicrous without even having to think about it."

She has a point. Also, it's something I could see Sissy doing, because she was a certifiable lunatic. And now the woman I thought might be my soul mate is clearly one as well. I should take a vow of celibacy. "What other explanation do you have? Unless I magically inseminated you from across the country," I snap.

Lainey's lips thin into a line, and she pins me with a look that makes me feel about two feet tall—which is pretty impressive, considering my mother is the only person who has the power to do that.

"Because we used protection every time *except* the last time."

I shake my head. "That's not—" I filter through the foggy memories from that morning. The phone call that came at 3:00 a.m., my brother's panic, setting up my flight to LA, and throwing all my stuff in my duffel and starting the truck.

Only when I was ready to leave did I go back upstairs and do the thing I desperately didn't want to: say goodbye to Lainey. I remember how frantic we were when we realized we'd reached the end sooner than we'd meant to, how intense the sex had been, how it ended far too soon . . . because I hadn't even thought about a condom.

"But it was only that one time." I scrub a hand over my face.

"That's really all it takes. I was fertile, and you're apparently virile." Her tone is matter-of-fact, but her voice shakes with anger. "I tried to contact you as soon as I realized. I called every alpaca farm in New York but couldn't track you down. I even called the cabin, but of course no one ever answered. I had no other way to get in touch with you. Well, I guess if I'd bothered watching anything other than Netflix and documentaries, I might have figured it out." Lainey grips her phone tightly in her hands, lips pursed as if she's waiting for another accusation.

If I hadn't been in such a rush that morning, I would have given her my cell number. Hell, I would've given her the whole truth if I'd had the chance. I look at her, really look *at her*. She's scared and sad and angry and guarded. My stomach twists and drops. "I have a son?"

She nods, and her chin trembles as she asks, "Would you like to see a picture of him?"

"Yeah. Yes. Please."

With shaking hands, she punches a code into her phone again. It's old—a smartphone, but it's been around for a while. She scrolls through some pictures until she finds one she likes and holds it out so I can see. "Go ahead, take it." She wraps my hands around the device and slides a little closer, her cheek brushing my arm. "He's so beautiful."

I stare at the two-dimensional little face in the screen, looking for . . . I don't know. Something that reminds me of myself? He's laughing at the camera, the end of Lainey's braid clutched in his chubby little fist. He has Lainey's dark hair and her nose, but that smile is all mine, and so is the little dimple popping in his right cheek.

I swallow thickly, reality finally setting in. I consider all the things I missed: her entire pregnancy, his birth, the first four months of his life. She's been doing this all on her own.

And she's always been close to her family—even when she was staying with me in Alaska, she called her parents at least twice a week and spent a good hour on the phone with them. So what had happened to make her come all the way here and raise a baby alone? There are so many questions that don't have answers. Except one: this baby is definitely mine.

"Can I meet him?" I ask.

Lainey bites her lip. "I don't know if that's a good idea right now."

"You don't know if it's a good idea for me to meet my four-month-old son who I didn't know existed until now?"

"Don't you want a paternity test or something?" Her fingers go to her lips.

"Well, I might if he didn't look like me, and yeah, it's probably a good idea regardless just to make it all official—and I'm pretty sure my agent will insist on it, so we'll have to set something up—but for now I'd like to meet him."

Lainey's eyes are wide, and she's practically eating her fingernails. I set the phone down and take her hands in mine. "Please, Lainey. Put yourself in my shoes—I've already missed out on so much."

She exhales in a heavy rush. "Let me message Eden." She quickly types out a text. It only takes a few moments before she gets a response. She holds up the phone. On the screen is a picture of Kody, swaddled in a blanket in a crib, a stuffed teddy bear beside him. "He's sleeping."

"That's okay. I don't mind if you don't."

"I'll let her know we're on our way."

Lainey's quiet on the way back to her apartment building. I don't push conversation, even though I have questions. It's clear she's already overwhelmed, and I don't want to make it worse, since it'll only make her more anxious. When we were in Alaska together, I'd distract her with sex whenever she got nervous. Everything is different, though—she's different—and now I know why.

I follow her into the apartment building. Thankfully we don't have to wait long for the elevator. When we get to the eleventh floor, Lainey holds up a hand and peeks out into the hallway. She brings her finger to her lips, signaling that I should be quiet. Then she grabs me by the wrist and pulls me out of the elevator and down the hall. I don't know why we're trying to be all stealth like we're pulling a heist, not going back to her apartment so I can meet my son.

Jesus. *I have a son.* I'm not sure when that thought alone is going to stop feeling completely surreal.

She roots around in her jacket pocket and quietly retrieves the key. She eases it into the lock and slowly, carefully turns it, grimacing as it clicks. She sucks in a sharp breath and pushes the door open, ushering me in. Her palm lands on my back, urging me forward as she closes the door.

"You wanna—" She slaps her palm over my mouth and makes a shushing motion.

I hold my hands up like I'm being held at gunpoint. After a few breaths she drops her hand and drags me away from the door.

Eden appears in the hallway. The two of them make random hand gestures I don't understand.

"Can some—" Lainey smacks me on the chest and shushes me again, then drags me across the open living room and pushes me into the galley kitchen. There's barely enough room for me, let alone Lainey and her friend, in the cramped space.

"Do you think it's safe for you to leave?" Lainey asks Eden.

"That's dicey. He already knocked on the door once, and you know he'll probably be waiting for it to open again, since you just got in."

"Once you leave, he'll think the coast is clear."

"Exactly."

"Someone wanna fill me in on what's going on?"

Lainey says, "Nothing," and Eden says, "Walter." I'm inclined to believe Eden over Lainey in this case, especially with the look she shoots at Eden.

Eden shrugs and mouths, "Sorry."

"Is this the guy you were talking to in the lobby?"

Lainey blows out a breath. "Yes."

"He lives right across the hall from you?" This is not good. Not for me, anyway. As much as he might not *look* like competition, he clearly has designs on Lainey.

"Yes."

"What does he do, stand at his door with his eye pressed against the peephole, waiting for you to come home every night? Am I the only one who finds this a little fucking creepy?"

"His living room is right by the door, and the walls are thin."

"Or maybe he's just a creepy-ass stalker. I don't like this."

Lainey crosses her arms over her chest. "Walter is not creepy or a stalker. He's nice, and helpful, and kind."

"So why are you worried about him hearing Eden leave?"

Lainey rubs her temple and gives me a pointed look. "Because he saw me with you, and I'm sure he has questions. I think I have enough going on without having to deal with Walter tonight."

I arch a brow. "I can deal with Walter."

"Absolutely not," Lainey snaps.

"I thought it wasn't serious." It better not be serious. The idea incites panic, because if she's actually into Walter, that means I'm going to have to share my son with some other guy—and I'm not sure I'm cool with that. At all.

Lainey shoots Eden a look. "It's not . . . it's complicated, especially with you being here. I don't want to hurt his feelings, and I'm going to have to explain what's going on, and I'd like to do that without an audience."

"Should I go? Or . . ." Eden thumbs over her shoulder toward the door and looks between me and Lainey.

Lainey sighs and nods. "Sorry. Yes—thank you so much for watching Kody."

She hugs her friend, who gives me a look I can't decipher. I hang back, half in the kitchen, half in the living room, while they whisper talk and Eden puts her shoes on.

The apartment is small but cozy and functional. The walls are a generic cream color and bare, but there are framed photos on the side table beside the gray couch. A basket of baby toys is tucked under it, and a blue blanket is spread out on the floor in front of it. I wonder how long she's lived here.

Lainey's expression is set in a cringe as she carefully unlocks and opens the door, ushering Eden out. She doesn't even have the door closed all the way before there's a soft knock. She looks over her shoulder at me and makes a waving motion.

I mouth, "Really?" Because clearly she wants me to hide.

I don't see the point, because he probably already knows I'm here, but she mouths, "Please," so I do what she wants. For now.

I can hear the low tones of a male voice and Lainey's soft responses but not the content of their brief conversation. Less than a minute later, the door clicks shut. I step out from my hiding place to find Lainey standing there with her hand still on the doorknob and her fingers at her mouth.

"You okay?" I ask.

She closes her eyes and exhales an unsteady breath, but she nods all the same.

I'm at a loss as to what I should do. I want to offer her some kind of comfort, but I don't know if it's at all welcome—or if it's even appropriate. I decide the situation warrants more than me being silent on the other side of the room.

I cross over to her. "Do you need some safety cuddles?"

She looks up at me, eyes watery, chin trembling.

I open my arms, and after a few uncertain seconds she steps into me, gripping my shirt while she buries her face against my chest. I wrap her up in a hug and absorb the feeling of being close to her like this again, of the way she still seems to fit with me. I drop my head, breathing in the scent of her shampoo. Everything about us just got a shit-ton more complicated, and I'm sure she's feeling the hard truth of this new reality.

"Is he upset?" I almost choke on the words but manage to get them out without sounding like a dick.

She releases my shirt and steps out of my embrace, smoothing out the fabric with her palms. "He's confused and concerned. He's been a good friend."

I have to remind myself that while I've been living the single, mostly celibate life, she's been raising a baby alone.

She sniffles and pats my chest. "Come. Let me introduce you to Kody."

She brushes by me, and I follow her down the hall.

"I just moved him to the nursery a few weeks ago, because he got too big for his bassinet." She pushes open the door and steps into the room.

Unlike the rest of the apartment, the walls have been painted a pale, buttery yellow, and there are decals of mountains and cartoon animals on the wall beside his crib. A mobile of airplanes hangs above it, and in the middle of the airplane-themed sheets, lips parted and eyes closed, is a bundle of baby.

Lainey reaches into the crib and brushes her finger along his cheek. He smacks his little lips, and his hands open and curl back into fists. I stare down at him, so small and new and very clearly mine. I can see it in the shape of his face, the set of his mouth.

"Isn't he beautiful?" Lainey asks on a whisper.

I nod, unable to find words. I want to ask if I can hold him, but I don't want to wake him, especially based on how tired she looks. "Does he sleep through the night?"

"Occasionally." Her smile is soft.

My mind is spinning in a million different directions. "I can help. I'll help. I know we'll need the paternity test, but we can have that done right away, and I'll talk to my agent, and we can figure out exactly how to manage this. My schedule is about to get really busy, but when I'm not traveling for away games, I'll be here to do this with you. I'll take care of both of you. I'll get a nursery set up in my house."

"No!" Lainey growls in a tone I've never heard before.

A hot feeling creeps up my spine. One I'm not sure what to do with. I may not be prepared to be a parent, but if he's my son, damn right I'm going to do what I can to support and raise him. "I'm his father. I'm responsible for him, just like you are. I take care of what's mine."

Lainey moves to stand in front of the crib, protective and possessive. "We don't need to be taken care of. We've made it this far on our own, and I don't need you coming back into my life and turning it upside down. You've already done that once—I won't let you do it again!"

I open my mouth to argue, but I'm cut off by a shrill, angry cry.

CHAPTER 18

MINE

Lainey

I scoop Kody up and cradle him to my chest. My heart is pounding; anxiety makes my mouth dry and my hands sweaty. "Shhh." I bounce him gently and pat his bottom while he continues to wail.

"You need to leave," I tell RJ.

"Come on, Lainey. You can't keep me out of his life." I can both see and hear his panic.

It's echoed in me, likely for very different reasons. "And you can't come barreling back into mine and think you can take over. That's not how this works."

He runs a hand through his hair. "I'm not trying to take over. I just want to be part of his life and yours, if you'll let me."

The screaming ratchets up a couple more notches, and I worry I won't be able to get him to settle—and then it'll be another night of too little sleep. "Can't you see you're making us both upset? Please, just go."

"We need to talk about this. You can't tell me I'm a father, let me see my son once, and then ask me to walk away."

He's right, but I also don't know how to deal with everything that's been thrown at me since RJ came slamming back into my universe. He has fame and money—lots of money. Enough that he could fight for Kody. Anxious tears slide down my cheeks, and Kody's cries get even louder. "Please, you're only making it worse." I turn my back on him and shush Kody, whispering brokenly that it's going to be okay. "Mommy's right here. I'm right here, shhhh. I'm not going anywhere." I take deep breaths, willing myself to calm down, to find some perspective.

I should be glad he wants to be part of Kody's life, but all I have is fear—because I'm struggling in this tiny apartment, and he has a huge house and all kinds of resources that I don't. I don't really know him, and he doesn't know me. We only have six weeks in a bubble, which is nothing like real life. Especially not one filled with diapers and baby vomit and sleepless nights.

Kody's cries quiet down, and he bumps his nose along my collarbone. I stroke his silky black hair as he hiccups and whimpers. I turn to face RJ, but he's gone.

At midnight I wake up in Kody's room. I'm sitting in the glider, one boob hanging out, Kody nestled in my arms. I slowly, carefully adjust my hold on him. My arms have fallen asleep, so I have to wait several minutes before I can transfer him back to the crib.

I tuck his blankets around him, make sure his teddy bear is close, and tiptoe out of the room. I breathe a sigh of relief when he doesn't wake up. I use the bathroom, pour myself a glass of water, and make sure all the lights are turned off before I head for my bedroom. I pause and root around in my purse for my phone. I could hear it buzzing from Kody's room when I was feeding him—and apparently fell asleep.

I touch the screen and see I have messages from Eden, Walter, and of course RJ. Eden's message came through at nine, asking for an update on how things went with the daddy-and-son meet and greet. Walter wants to talk, and RJ . . . well, he's sent a slew of messages, all of them asking if we're okay, if Kody has stopped crying, if I have, if I'm ignoring him, and to please, for the love of God, answer this message before he goes insane. That one was sent less than ten minutes ago.

I start and stop composing a message about twenty times. I'm in the middle of typing that we're both fine and that Kody is asleep when another message pops up from RJ.

RJ: I've been watching the little dots for 15 min. RU ok?

Lainey: Yes. Kody is asleep.

RJ: I didn't mean to upset you.

I stare at the message for a minute before I finally compose a response.

Lainey: I'm just overwhelmed.

RJ: Me too, but we'll figure it out.

I don't know how to interpret that, so I end the conversation with good night.

Setting an alarm has become a pointless practice, since Kody wakes up every morning at five fifteen to let me know he's hungry.

I roll out of bed, more exhausted than I was yesterday, if that's even possible, and stumble down the hall to his room. "Morning, little man. I have breakfast right here for you." I already have my boob out and ready to go.

His little fists wave in the air, his mouth opening and closing as I bring him to my breast and settle in the glider. I fall back asleep for as long as he feeds on the right breast. He squawks when he's ready for the other side. I burp him first, then set the left boob free. I'm already leaking, so he splutters when he first latches, the milk coming too fast.

Once the initial gush and rush slows, he settles in, punctuating sucks with happy grunts. I stroke his hair, and he looks up at me, his blue eyes locked on my face. "Oh, sweet boy, what am I going to do? All these months I've been wishing I had some help, and now I'm afraid I have to share you."

He pops off my breast and makes a loud gurgling sound before he latches back on. I fall asleep again for another fifteen minutes before he lets me know he's done with breakfast and needs his diaper changed.

The wonderful thing about working at the aquarium is that they help subsidize the cost of day care, and there's one right inside my building. I'm extra quiet as I leave my apartment, not in the mood to deal with Walter yet, mostly because I have no idea what to say to him.

He's a good friend, and he's been so supportive since I moved into the building, but the progression from friends to dating hasn't been natural. I like him, he's nice and pleasant to be around, but I don't crave his affection.

RJ, on the other hand . . . I can't stop thinking about how good it felt to just be held by him. Which is yet another complication. And another reason why he's right that we need to talk. Maybe he wanted to relive our time together in Alaska when he first ran into me, but now . . . Kody changes everything, for both of us.

I drop Kody off at his day care and head to work. Today is a research day with no interruptions, which I'm grateful for since I don't have the energy required to deal with the general public.

I head to the lab and find Eden already set up at her computer. Like me, part of her job is to research and help manage the animals, so we often work together. She pushes a take-out cup in my direction and gives me a raised eyebrow. "Can I be optimistic and assume that the bags under your eyes are because you and the hockey hottie spent the night getting biblical with each other?"

"You're welcome to be optimistic, even if it also makes you very wrong."

"Uh-oh. What happened?"

I drop down in the chair beside her. "He wants to be involved in Kody's life."

Eden pushes her glasses up her nose. "Isn't that a good thing?"

"Yes. No. I don't know. It's just . . . what if he wants partial custody? He has bags of money. He can hire a nanny, have someone take care of everything for him if he wants to, and what do I have? This job and a tiny apartment. I'm just . . . scared."

"But isn't he, like, still way into you? And you've been pining for him for the past year. I mean, you named your son Kodiak, Lainey. I think that pretty much tells everyone where you're at with this guy."

"But that was before I knew he was a professional hockey player. You should've seen it last night at the coffee shop. There was a swarm of people waiting to take pictures with him and get his autograph. And the women were the worst! It didn't matter if they were teenagers or grandmothers, they practically dry humped him!"

"Can you blame them, though?"

I give her an exasperated look. "How am I supposed to deal with that? He used to be this huge playboy, and I'm sure women are constantly throwing themselves at him. It's nothing like I thought it would be, and now I'm connected to him for the rest of my life because of Kody. I just wanted a normal life."

"You had a normal life, Lainey. It was making you miserable."

"Being homeschooled and getting my degrees by correspondence isn't normal."

"What is normal these days? I know this is hard, but he's going to be part of your life no matter what. You know what I think the real issue is?"

"What?" I mutter into my coffee.

"It's not that he's a hockey player—it's not the lie, which I think you can probably get over. I think it has more to do with being afraid that he's going to come swooping in and try to take care of you, and you're going to equate that with losing your independence again."

"That's not—"

"True? Are you sure about that, Lainey? We drove across the country when you were seven months pregnant because your parents were smothering you. I'm going to go ahead and say you're really not keen on anyone trying to take over your life like they tend to."

"It was pretty extreme, wasn't it?"

"We can always blame the hormones."

"And now what do I blame?"

"Hormones and protective mothering instinct. And fear of having your heart broken, because let's face it, Lainey, even though he didn't mean to, that's exactly what he did the first time."

CHAPTER 19

WOO THE BABY MAMA

Rook

Leaving Lainey's apartment last night wasn't easy, but it was necessary. First and foremost, my experience with babies has been limited to my nephew and my teammates' kids. Sure, I'm good with them. I can make them giggle and smile, but the second they start to cry, I pass them back to their mother and I'm on my way.

Kody is mine.

I made him.

And I've had sweet fuck all to do with his mother or him since his conception. So I'm a little out of my depth here.

Also, I know Lainey. As much as she's changed, I'm aware that she's the woman I rescued from a thunderstorm. The same one who had never been on a plane before her trip to Alaska. And the woman who's been through some pretty traumatic stuff and still manages to be sweet, innocent, and a touch naive. But she's also fierce, strong, and determined. And whatever happened to bring her to Chicago has brought out that strength, which is both sexy and, frankly, really fucking inconvenient.

A year ago she would've welcomed me back into her life without batting an eyelash. One heroic rescue attempt would've been all that she needed, but now she's different.

I hit the gym, as one does when there's stress and preseason training coming up. It's ten by the time I'm done with my workout. I consider calling my brother, but it's early on the West Coast, and if there's half a chance Max is still sleeping, I don't want to be the reason he wakes up—so I message my sister instead, since she's an early riser, to see if she's around to talk. She's been in LA for her master's program. She might be younger than me, but she's female, and she can usually provide perspective I don't have. Thankfully, she's awake, so I video chat her.

"Hey, big brother!" Her smile turns into a grimace as my image fills her phone screen. "Whoa, you're looking rough."

"Last night wasn't great," I admit. The part where I met my son was, but the part where I made both Lainey and Kody cry overshadows that.

"I can tell. You look like a bag of shit, which is saying something, because you could probably go on a four-week bender and not shower once during that time and still manage to look decent—but right now you look like you've taken a beatdown by a gaggle of puck bunnies and you did not, in fact, come out on top."

"Your brain is a weird place, Stevie."

"You don't know the half of it." She props her phone up and leans back in her chair. "So? What happened last night? Oh, wait, weren't you supposed to try to see Lainey? I'm taking it that didn't go as well as you hoped."

I've already filled Stevie in on reconnecting with Lainey, my lie, and her response to finding out what I used to be like. "So she agreed to talk to me, but we went to a coffee shop, and I got mobbed."

Stevie groans and rolls her eyes. "You can't go to coffee shops when preseason is starting up."

"I didn't have a lot of options, and I didn't think it was going to be as bad as it was. I haven't been going out much, but the season promo has started, so people are all hyped up, you know? It was worse than usual, but eventually we got out of there . . . anyway, things are a lot more complicated than I expected them to be." I pour myself a glass of water because my mouth is dry. I'm drained and wound up.

"Complicated how? Why are you so freaking fidgety? Does she have a boyfriend or something?"

"No. Well, she's been seeing this guy, but I don't think it's serious, and I sorta trump him now."

"Trump him how? Because you're ridiculously good looking? Spit it out, RJ. You're antsier than me after a freaking accidental energy drink."

"So, last night I found out that Lainey has a baby."

Stevie jerks up, and the phone clatters onto the table, giving me a view of the ceiling fan. Suddenly her face is three inches from the screen and out of focus. "What?" she yells.

"Lainey has a four-month-old baby, and he's mine."

Stevie flops back down in the chair, her face a mask of shock. I wonder if that's what I looked like last night when Lainey told me.

"Holy shit. Are you sure it's yours?"

"I'm sure. I met him last night, and he looks like me."

"But . . . what if this is like that crazy chick who pretended to be pregnant with your baby and tagged you on social media for months?" I open my mouth to interrupt, but Stevie's eyes are wide, and she's on one of her tangents. "What if this Lainey woman has a type, and you're it? What if it's someone else's baby and she's trying to pass it off as yours because you're rolling in money? God, this is like a freaking soap opera. Actually, it's more like one of those scripted reality shows."

I level her with an unimpressed glare. "This is super unhelpful—you do realize that?"

"Sorry, sorry." She raises her hands in the air. "I'm just . . . shocked, I guess? You're *sure* the baby is yours?"

"Pretty damn sure, yeah. He has my mouth—and my dimple. There are some very strong family resemblances."

"Okay. Wow. So I'm an aunt again? Does this mean you two are going to try to make this thing work between you?"

"That's the thing—she freaked out last night and told me to leave."

Stevie narrows her eyes. "Why? What did you do?"

"Why do you automatically think it's something I did?"

"Because you're a guy, and you've never incubated a human life inside your body."

"Neither have you."

"Yeah, but I have the ability to, unlike you with your silly dangly parts. So, what happened to make her freak out on you?"

"I don't really know. She let me see Kody—"

"His name is Kody?"

"Yeah."

"I love it. Okay, continue." She crosses her legs and motions for me to go on.

I'm thinking I probably should've waited to call my brother for advice, but I continue anyway. "So, she let me come up to her apartment to meet Kody, and when I realized that he's really mine, I told her I would set up a nursery in my house and that I would take care of them."

Stevie arches a brow. "I'm sorry, you said what?"

"That I would take care of them. He's mine as much as he is hers. I've already missed out on the first four months of his life. I'm not going to miss out on any more of it."

"Did you happen to say that to her as well?"

"Yeah, of course. I have every right to be part of his life. I have all the resources to take care of him. Of both of them."

Stevie gives me her *you're an idiot* face.

"Why are you looking at me like that?"

She sighs and shakes her head. It's annoying that I can't force her to explain faster. "Listen to what you're saying, RJ. This woman has gone through an entire pregnancy on her own. She's spent the last four months raising a baby—*on her own*. You come swooping back into her life, she finds out that you lied about who you are and *also* finds out that you have ass loads of money. The second you find out that you made a baby with her, you essentially try to take over her entire world."

"I'm not trying to take over anything. I know I fucked up. I shouldn't have lied, and it's my fault that I've missed out, but I don't think it's unreasonable for me to want to be part of their lives."

"It's not unreasonable at all, but what you're saying and what she's hearing are probably two very different things."

"I don't get it."

Stevie nods, like she expected as much. "So, you know how after Max was born no one could hold him for more than like five seconds before Joy wanted him back?"

"Uh, yeah, but I don't see what—"

"The mothering instinct is strong. She barely put him down for the first week, and even Kyle could only hold him for a few minutes. I'm guessing—and this is just a guess, but I think it's a pretty solid one—that Lainey's terrified that you're going to try to take her baby away from her."

"Why would she think that?"

"Because you have an insane amount of money and you're planning to put a nursery in your house. It's all in the delivery, RJ."

"But I want to take care of both of them."

Stevie props her chin on her fist. "Does she know that?"

"Yes. Maybe. I don't know." I run a hand through my hair. "What am I supposed to do? Yesterday I was trying to get back into her life, and now I'm a dad with no rights to my own kid. I don't know how to handle any of this."

"Now you have to woo them. Show her that you want them both."

"How do I do that?"

"The same way you went about softening her up after you lied about being a millionaire NHL player—do nice things for them. She's a single mother living on a single income. Don't you remember how tired Joy and Kyle were at the beginning? Even now, it's a miracle if they're still up after ten. From what I've seen, being a parent is freaking exhausting, so I can only imagine that being a single parent is like signing on to be a zombie for a good three years."

She definitely has a point, one I hadn't really had time to consider. "This is why I want to help take care of them."

"Yeah, but Lainey needs help without feeling like she's being railroaded. Get her groceries delivered so she doesn't have to waste time shopping, get her a housekeeper, send her to the spa so she can get a freaking pedicure. Joy loved it when Mom and I did that for her. She couldn't see her damn feet for the better part of half a year, and I'm betting now she doesn't have the time, energy, or money to indulge in things like that. Give her a reason to trust that you're going to be there for both of them and that you're not just a playboy and a liar."

"It was one lie."

"Unfortunately, it was a pretty damn big one. She needs to know she can rely on you, so be reliable."

"Okay. I can do that. I can be reliable."

Less than twenty-four hours ago I was thinking about all the ways I wanted to get back into Lainey's pants and her bed, and now all I can think about is how I'm going to find a way to cement myself back in her life so I don't miss out on any more time with my son—because I sure don't want him to grow up without a dad.

CHAPTER 20

SHOW ME YOU MEAN IT

Lainey

I glance at Walter's closed door as I back out of the elevator. I don't want to hurt him, but I need to give RJ a chance with Kody—and possibly give us a chance too, depending on what he wants out of this. It isn't until I spin Kody's stroller around that I notice the pile of boxes stacked beside my apartment door. "What the heck is all this?" I ask Kody, who babbles and shakes his teddy bear rattle.

The door across the hall opens, and Walter appears, arms crossed over his chest. "Most of them have been here since I got home from work. Except the two on the top—they arrived a few minutes ago." He's still dressed in his work wear, a pair of khaki pants and a white short-sleeved button-down complete with pocket protector and striped tie.

"Oh, hi, Walter." I slip my key into the lock, aware we need to have a conversation, one I'm not excited about.

Walter is right there to help me, rushing over to hold open the door while I get Kody inside. He assists with all the boxes—some of which are heavy, based on the way the veins in his neck bulge and his face goes red with exertion.

Once we're done bringing everything in, he stuffs his hands in his pockets. "I didn't realize you were seeing other people."

I unbuckle Kody from his stroller and pick him up, half using him as a shield for this conversation. "It's not like that, Walter."

"Really? Because last night you went on a date while Eden watched Kody, and then you brought him back here and flaunted him right under my nose."

I realize how it all must look to him—and how I would feel if I were in his shoes. "I wasn't flaunting him. He's Kody's father."

The anger shifts to confusion. "I thought you said his father wasn't interested in being part of his life."

I rub my temple. "I thought he wasn't. We recently reconnected."

"Reconnected how? Are you planning to get back together with him? He hasn't been a part of Kody's life at all, and now you're going to let him jump back in like he's been here the entire time? Is this stuff all from him?"

"Maybe?" I glance at the stack of boxes. Logically they must all be from RJ, but I'd have to open them to be sure. "It's a complicated situation, Walter. I don't really know what's going on myself right now."

"What about you and me?" He motions between us.

"I don't know about that either," I say honestly.

His shoulders curl forward, and he nods at the floor.

Before he can say anything else, the buzzer for my door goes off. My phone also pings in my purse. "Just give me a second." I shift Kody to my hip and hit the intercom button. "Hello?"

"Delivery for Lainey Carver."

"Okay. Come on up." I buzz the person through.

"I guess I should probably go," Walter says dejectedly.

"I'm really sorry, Walter. I don't want to mislead you, but this whole situation is just . . . confusing."

"I understand." He bops Kody on the end of the nose. "See you later, little guy."

He leaves my apartment as a deliveryman steps out of the elevator rolling a cart of boxes. I recognize the name of the company on the side of the box; it's one of those high-end grocery delivery services.

Walter disappears inside his apartment without another word. I feel bad, but there's nothing I can do about it right now. I allow the deliveryman to come in and unload the cart in the kitchen. The boxes take up all the space on the counter. Once he's gone, I put Kody in his activity center to play while I unpack everything. Fresh produce and ready-to-cook meals, as well as a variety of types of baby food, fill my cupboards and my fridge.

I have to assume that all of this is from RJ. I can't even begin to guess how much this cost. Everything is name brand or high-end organic produce. I expected to have to make time for grocery shopping this evening, and now I'm set for at least the next week, if not longer. It's thoughtful and kind, which is more in line with the RJ I knew in Alaska.

Groceries unpacked and put away, I feed Kody, then sift through my now-stuffed fridge and debate what I'd like for dinner. I settle on a pasta dish. It's supposed to serve three to four people, which means I'll have plenty of leftovers for lunch tomorrow.

The muffled ping of my phone reminds me that I have unchecked messages. I leave the package on the counter and bend to kiss a happy Kody on the top of the head as I retrieve my phone. I have two voice mails, one from my mother and another from RJ.

I listen to the one from my mother first; it's a request for a call back. She left the message less than twenty minutes ago, but if I know my mother, she'll call again before an hour has passed. She knows I'm home from work, and she calls at least three times a week to check in on me and Kody. She wants me to come back to Washington, but I like it here. I also like not being smothered. And now I may have another reason to stay.

I skip to the next message, and RJ's deep voice fills my ear and makes all sorts of warm tingles happen in my body. "Hi, Lainey, it's Rook, RJ. It's . . . hi. I'm sorry about last night. I'm sure this isn't easy for you, and it's not for me either. I don't want to take Kody away from you. I just want to help and be a part of his life and yours, however I can. I sent you a bunch of stuff today, things I thought you could use. When you have time, can you call or message to let me know if everything arrived? I hope I hear from you soon."

He's obviously trying to show me he wants to be involved. Buying these things is . . . helpful, but it's not the same as getting up in the middle of the night for feedings or dealing with Kody when he's fussy for hours. The only way I'm going to know if he's really serious about wanting to be part of his life, and maybe mine, is by allowing him to spend time with us.

I listen to the message three more times before I finally call him back.

It doesn't even finish ringing once. "Hey."

"Hi." I chew on the inside of my lip, trying to summon some courage.

"Did you get my message? And all the stuff I sent?"

"I did. Thank you. Um . . . I was wondering if you want to come over? I have all this food and these boxes to open . . . maybe we could have dinner?"

"I'd love that, but I don't want you to feel obligated to invite me over. I sent all that stuff because I want to help however I can, and I figured this was a good start," he says softly, sounding hopeful.

"It was. It is a good start, I mean. And I don't feel obligated. Not really. Not in the way I think you're thinking."

"I can be there in less than half an hour."

"Okay. Great."

I realize I'm still in my stupid uniform, and I likely smell fishy. I take Kody with me into the bathroom and sing to him while I shower away the eau de aquarium.

I decide to go with leggings and a long, loose shirt. I don't want to look like I'm trying too hard, but I also don't want to look like I'm not trying at all. I'm back to my prepregnancy weight, but my boobs are twice as big because I'm breastfeeding, and my stomach is a little less toned thanks to how big Kody got while he was in there. I have a few stretch marks left behind as an extra reminder that I'm a giver of life, and I don't mind them one bit.

I brush out my hair, braid it while it's still wet, and finish up by applying a little concealer under my eyes to manage the dark circles. I exhale a long breath as I stand in front of the bathroom mirror and inspect my reflection. This isn't a date, but in a lot of ways it feels like one.

My stomach growls, reminding me that I haven't eaten since lunch, at the same time as my buzzer goes off. Kody lets out an aggravated wail, and I pluck him from his activity center, rushing down the hall to buzz RJ in.

I wait by the door, bouncing Kody on my hip while I listen for the elevator. I usher him in quickly, feeling a pang of guilt as I glance at Walter's door.

I need to find out what exactly RJ wants out of this. I don't want to open my heart back up to him just to have it broken all over again. It was one thing when we were both single and looking to enjoy each other's company, but now my life is completely different. And so is his.

I close the door in time to see Walter's start to open. I lock it and slide the chain latch home. Kody gives me another annoyed squawk and rubs his eyes. "Is someone getting tired?" I coo and kiss his cheek.

RJ holds up a bouquet of flowers, a bottle of wine, and a little gift bag and gives me a chagrined smile as he glances around my apartment. Since he appeared at the aquarium, he's been sending me flowers regularly, so there's a bouquet on almost every available surface. It's a good thing most of them came in their own vases, since I only had one of my own.

I glance pointedly at the stack of boxes still sitting just inside the door. "As if all of this wasn't enough?"

"I didn't want to come over empty handed." He rocks back on his heels and smiles, making that little dimple that matches Kody's pop.

Kody wails again, head bumping against my collarbone as he pats my boob and grabs on to my shirt. "I think I'm going to have to feed him again before I do anything else. This is his witching hour. He's tired, but he's hungry."

"What can I do to help? Can I feed him?"

"I've got the feeding part covered." I motion to my boobs.

"Oh, right." RJ's gaze drops and his eyes flare, cheeks flushing. "Should I start on dinner, then?"

"Sure. It's on the counter. Let me show you where the pots are. I was thinking the pasta puttanesca would be nice."

He follows me to the kitchen, and I show him where the pots and pans are. I check the recipe—the meals come with directions—and then I leave him to get started while I settle in the chair in the living room to feed Kody.

He latches on quickly, always extra hungry in the evenings, like he's been waiting all day for my boob because a bottle just isn't the same. I smooth out his dark, thick hair, trying to settle the cowlick, which keeps curling back up.

"Hey, Lainey, can I get you something to—oh shit, sorry!"

I look up to find RJ standing in the middle of the living room, eyes comically wide and focused on where Kody is latched on to my breast, one hand splayed protectively over the swell.

"I, uh . . . I wanted to see if I could get you something to drink, but you're booby, I mean busy. I mean—sorry." RJ blinks a bunch of times and averts his gaze, but he doesn't seem to be able to help the way his eyes keep darting back to me and my exposed breast.

"Water would be nice, actually."

"Okay. I can get you that. I'll be right back." He returns a minute later, setting the glass on the table beside me while trying to keep his eyes anywhere but me and failing completely.

I touch the back of his hand. "There's a privacy blanket over there, if it would make you more comfortable."

He looks at me and then down again and back up. "What?"

"I can cover up if it makes you uncomfortable. For now, anyway," I amend.

He licks his lips. "It doesn't make me uncomfortable. I just don't want to make you uncomfortable."

"I'm not uncomfortable."

"Then don't cover up for my sake." His eyes stay on mine, and a wry grin pulls at the corner of his mouth. "It's more envy than discomfort at this point, anyway."

I blush, not knowing what to say, but pleased he's still attracted to me.

He heads back to the kitchen.

Kody snuffles, and his hand flexes on my breast. "Don't worry, little man, they're all yours for at least another six months." Although it's nice to be reminded that I won't be a feed bag forever.

Dinner is almost ready by the time Kody's done feeding. He's sleepy and sated, at least for now, so I settle him in his swing, turn on the lullaby track, and join RJ for dinner at the dining room table, which I rarely use. I get two bites in before Kody starts fussing.

"Sorry, he gets cranky around this time in the evening. He doesn't really like to be put down until he's ready for bed." I pick him up and cradle him in one arm so I can soothe and eat at the same time.

"I could hold him while you eat," RJ offers.

"It's okay. I'm used to doing most things one handed these days. The fact that I'm eating something that's still warm is actually a treat."

RJ sets his fork down. "I get to eat hot food all the time, with both hands. I really wouldn't mind holding him. Please?"

I realize then that he hasn't even had a chance to hold him once yet. Yesterday I was scared of what I stand to lose by bringing RJ into our lives. But I can see that he's trying, and I can also see that despite the lies he told me, he's still kind and considerate and trying his best—so I need to try my best too, even if I'm still afraid.

Besides, this isn't about just me anymore. It's about Kody growing up with a father he knows and who loves him, and I need to give RJ the chance to be that, if it's what he truly wants. I can't freeze him out because of my own fears, even if in some ways they're valid. His lies make sense now that I've seen what his life is like, and I might not like what he did, but at least he's not making excuses. And he's not running the other way or throwing money at me to keep me quiet. He wouldn't be sitting across from me at my dining room table, after cooking dinner he bought, if he weren't trying to show he's invested.

"Of course." I kiss Kody's forehead as I push back my chair and stand. "I'm sorry I didn't think to let you hold him before now—it's just that I'm so used to having him all to myself. It's been him and me against the world."

"I can understand that." RJ smiles up at me.

I return the grin, directing him how to position his arms and cradle Kody's head.

He looks so tiny in RJ's arms. I stand back and press my fingers to my lips, fighting tears as I watch RJ's face light up with wonder. Kody makes a plaintive little noise, eyes darting to me. I stroke his warm cheek. "It's okay, baby," I coo. "This is your daddy."

I grab my phone from the side table where I left it and snap a few pictures of RJ and Kody before I sit down and resume eating. RJ's full attention is on our son, who has discovered his finger and keeps trying to eat it. Once I'm finished, RJ reluctantly passes him back. Kody snuggles right into my neck, one hand resting possessively on my boob. I sniff his head, taking in his baby scent and now the faint smell of RJ's cologne.

After we're finished with dinner, I pass Kody back to RJ and clean up the kitchen while he cuddles him. It's sweet and wonderful and confusing—because it makes me hopeful.

Once the kitchen is tidied and the leftovers are put away, I open the bottle of wine and pour us each a glass, although mine is modest since I'll need to feed Kody again around midnight. Usually I'd put him in his crib at this point in the evening, but I don't want to take him from RJ, especially when they're so enthralled with each other. Kody can't seem to take his eyes off RJ, and he giggles every time RJ makes a face or tickles his little feet. While Walter seems to enjoy Kody, he never really settles with him, not like this.

Once RJ is seated, I help make him more comfortable by propping his arm up with a cushion. "Is that better?"

"Yeah, much. Thanks." He smiles. "You're great at this—you know that, right?"

"Not really. I'm just figuring things out as I go."

"That's kind of how parenting is, though, isn't it?"

"Seems that way."

I spend the next half hour opening the various boxes RJ sent. There are clothes—most of which won't fit Kody for a few more months—toys, a new top-of-the-line stroller I drooled over when I was pregnant but knew I'd never be able to afford. There's even a sweet little hockey jersey with "Bowman" and RJ's number on the back—and a teddy bear with a matching jersey that's almost the same size as Kody.

"You went a little overboard," I say as I survey the empty boxes and the pile of new clothes and toys.

"I'm making up for all the missed time. And I want to reassure you that I have no intention of trying to take Kody away from you—I just don't want to miss out on any more of his life than I already have. Does that make sense?"

"It does. And I don't want you to think I don't want you in our lives. I've just spent all this time doing it on my own. He's just been mine, so the thought of having to share him is scary."

"I get it, but won't it be a lot easier if we're in this together instead of you on your own?" he asks softly.

"Is that what you want? For us to be in this together?"

RJ swallows thickly. "I had sort of hoped we could see if we still fit. I know I have to work to earn back your trust, Lainey. I get that I messed this up—and that's on me—but I'll be honest: it gutted me when I realized I had no way to contact you and I'd left you with no way to find me either. I wanted so badly to seek you out, but I figured your not answering the phone and not leaving a note was clearly telling me you weren't interested in an 'us' outside of Alaska. I should've tried to find you, but I didn't think I could handle hearing that kind of truth. I wish I could go back and do things differently."

I clasp my hands in my lap, trying to keep myself from wringing them out of nervousness. I fell so hard and fast for him last time, and the aftermath was more painful than I ever could have imagined, but it can't be by chance that we've found our way back to each other. I owe it to myself and to Kody to see if we still feel the same way. "I think, for Kody's sake, it's worth trying." I still need to be careful with my heart, though.

"Really?"

"We worked well together before, but everything was so different, so we'll have to see. One day at a time and all that, right?"

RJ nods. "I can handle one day at a time."

I don't mention my fears: that this reality is too different from the one we lived in a year ago. This one has responsibilities and obligations that Alaska didn't. And all the attention RJ seems to thrive on terrifies me. But for Kody I'll try—and, selfishly, for me, because the other option is shared custody, and I don't want to give up 50 percent of my time with my son.

"Um, I don't know how to broach this without it being awkward, but I spoke to the team doctor about a formal DNA test. It's pretty obvious that Kody is mine, but I figured we'll need it moving forward, and it'll avoid a lot of red tape—so whenever you have time, he can make a house call."

Kody starts fussing, as if he can suddenly sense my anxiety. Without my having to say a word, RJ carefully transfers him to my arms. I shush him, patting his bottom as he cuddles into my neck and snuffles quietly. "Any day is fine with me. I have tomorrow off, but I'm not sure if that's too short notice or not."

"We can make it work. I have practice in the morning, but after that I'm free. You could come, if you want—both of you. I could have a car pick you up?"

"I have a car."

"You got your license." He smiles—it's a statement, not a question.

At some point I should tell RJ the truth: that I knew how to drive in Alaska but I just never got my license. It was one of the first things I did when I returned to Washington, wanting that piece of independence. "I did, and I drove all the way here from Washington."

RJ's eyes bug out. "That's one hell of a drive."

"You should try it when you're seven months pregnant. It probably took twice as long with all the bathroom stops."

"What made you come all the way to Chicago?" RJ props his cheek on his fist.

I shrug and look away. "There was a job opportunity, and I took it." I press my lips to Kody's forehead. He's finally asleep. "I'm going to put him in his crib."

"Okay. Sure. Can I help?"

"Of course."

I teach RJ in whispers how to put Kody to bed. It's not particularly difficult, but we have a routine we follow. Once he's settled in his crib and sleeping soundly, RJ and I head back to the living room.

I pull out two photo albums, the first chronicling my pregnancy—including the ultrasound pictures, my progress from tiny bump to full-on baby belly, the drive from Washington to Chicago, setting up his nursery in this apartment, and the trip to the hospital with Eden.

One of RJ's arms is stretched out across the back of the couch, the album open between us. He's shifted until our thighs are touching. I'm hyperaware of our proximity, of every place where our bodies touch, of the way he keeps fiddling with the end of my braid. The closeness is easy—but not, because it reminds me of those weeks when we were together and of the way we couldn't keep our hands off each other.

"Eden was with you for the birth?" RJ asks, pulling me out of my head and my spiral of inappropriate thoughts.

"She was. She's been a good friend."

"I'm glad you have her. I'd hate to think of you completely alone out here. I can't imagine your parents were all that happy that you moved across the country."

"They're the reason I'm here."

"Can I ask what happened?" RJ shifts so he's facing me.

I focus on the picture in front of me, the last one I took before my entire life changed all over again. "My parents were happy to have me home when I returned from Alaska, but I was . . . not as happy to be there. I missed Kodiak Island—I missed you—and you were just . . . gone. It didn't take long before my mother started with the whole over-protective routine. It got old fast, and things went downhill quickly when I realized I was pregnant. I tried to find a way to reach you, but when I'd exhausted all my options . . . well, it all seemed pretty hopeless."

"I'm so sorry, Lainey."

"Me too." I reach for my glass of wine and take an unsteady sip. "I actually moved in with my oldest sister and her family for a little while because of the tension with my parents. I needed space, and I couldn't get any. I finished my master's thesis, and then Eden suggested I come out for a visit. I took a plane that time because I wasn't too far along to fly. I fell in love with the aquarium and the independence. I didn't want to go back to Washington, but at the time I didn't have a choice. Until the position came available at the aquarium."

"So you took it and drove out here on your own."

"Eden flew out, and we drove back together. My parents weren't happy, obviously, but I needed the space and the ability to prove not just to them but to myself that I could do this."

"You know you're amazing, right? After everything you've been through—and then handling a pregnancy on your own, coming here, raising a baby alone."

"I've had lots of support. And my job is fantastic. I have flexible hours. It's right across the street. I can even do research at home when I need to. The medical and other benefits are excellent. As far as moves go, this one has been great—for me, at least."

"Have your parents at least met Kody?"

"Oh yes. They came out to visit as soon as he was born. Tried to convince me to come home, but I was settled and determined, so I stayed." I flip the first album closed and open the second one, setting it between us. The first picture is the birth announcement.

"Kodiak RJ Carver," RJ murmurs, tracing the edge of the photo. "Kody. I can't believe I didn't put it together."

I look up at him, a little embarrassed but more nostalgic than anything. "We made a lot of special memories there. Well, they were special for me."

"It was the same for me, Lainey." His eyes are soft, his tone earnest. "I want to make more of those with you. With both of you."

CHAPTER 21

THE FALL BACK IN

Lainey

RJ left an hour ago—he kissed me on the cheek, which was very respectable and sweet. I'm disappointed, and then again I'm not, because I don't think I'm ready to explore the chemistry that's still very much present between us yet, and maybe he could sense that.

I'm about to give Kody his midnight feeding when my phone rings. I check the caller and see that it's my mother. "Mom, why are you calling me at midnight?"

"Because I just got off the phone with Walter, and he informed me that a male visitor just left your apartment, that's why I'm calling. Lainey Patricia Carver, you have a four-month-old baby—you can't be entertaining men at midnight!" she shrieks in my ear. "I don't know what in the devil has gotten into you, but Walter is absolutely devastated. *Devastated.* I raised you better than this. You are not some kind of hussy who spreads your legs for a man just because he's attractive. Have you learned nothing from your mistakes?"

I grit my teeth, annoyed that Walter had the audacity to tell my mother about RJ. "First of all, Walter has no business calling you to tattle on me—"

"He didn't call me. I called him because you hadn't returned my call from over six hours ago. Six hours, Lainey! I'm a wreck over here!"

I take a deep breath and try to find some calm. "I'm sorry I didn't call you right back. I was busy—"

"Being a floozy!" she shouts.

"First of all, you have no idea what was going on here. You're making false assumptions, and the name-calling is unnecessary. I have not ever been, nor will I ever tolerate being called, a floozy—especially by my own mother. Secondly, I will not allow you to make me feel bad for allegedly engaging in a healthy physical relationship with someone I cared very deeply for."

She scoffs. "He left you there—"

"Don't," I snap. "Don't try to spin it in a way that makes it seem less than it was. We cared about each other, and unforeseen circumstances separated us. And while I agree that my falling pregnant was not ideal, I do not regret a moment of the time I spent with RJ or that I now have Kody." The only thing I regretted was waiting until it was too late to tell him how I felt about him.

"That doesn't explain why you're tromping all over poor Walter's feelings."

My parents met Walter when they came out to meet Kody after he was born, and my mother instantly took a liking to him—so when I told her we'd become friends she was ecstatic, and she was even happier when I told her we'd gone on a date. Now I wish I'd kept that information to myself. "If you'd stop interrupting, I'd be able to explain that by some great karmic chance, RJ and I have reconnected. He lives here in Chicago, and he was here tonight, not some random male visitor I was flaunting in a bid to hurt poor Walter. And while I feel badly about the situation—and Walter—under the circumstances, I think it's quite reasonable that RJ and I at least attempt to see if we can make this work between us, for the good of our child."

"But I thought you said he was an alpaca farmer in New York—how can he live in Chicago?"

I cringe, because this is the part that's not so easy to explain and the most difficult to get over. "His family owned an alpaca farm in New York but have since sold it. RJ plays professional hockey, here, in Chicago."

"Professional meaning what?"

"He plays for the NHL."

I get several long seconds of silence. "Doesn't that mean he has to travel a lot? How can he provide any kind of emotional stability for you? For Kody? I don't like this. Not one bit, Lainey."

And this, right here, is the exact reason I'm in Chicago instead of Washington. I may have asked myself the same questions, but I don't need my mother making this harder for me. "You can not like it all you want, but this is my life, not yours—and I get to make my own choices, whether you approve or not. It's late—I'm tired. I have to feed Kody, and then I'd like to go to bed."

"Lainey, please. I'm your mother. I know what's good for you."

"I love you, Mom, I really do, but you know what's good for *you*, and that's not necessarily what's good for *me*. I'm going to try with RJ, for Kody's sake and my own. You can support me or not, but either way, this is the choice I'm making."

"Well, I think it's another mistake."

"You're welcome to that opinion. I still love you, whether you choose to support my decision or not. Good night, Mom." I end the call, expecting anxiety to take over. But it doesn't. Instead I feel good about standing up for myself, even though it wasn't easy.

◆ ◆ ◆

Over the next couple of weeks, RJ—I can't get in the habit of calling him Rook no matter how hard I try, which isn't all that hard, to be quite honest—infuses himself into my and Kody's lives. After the team doctor confirmed what we already knew to be the truth—RJ is Kody's father—we've been spending as much time as possible together.

I now have a housekeeper who comes by not once but twice a week to tidy the apartment. A layer of dust doesn't even have a chance to form before she's back again. She also does all the laundry, and I'll be honest— baby laundry is a giant pain in the butt. Baby clothes are adorable. And tiny. And babies go through clothes like they're modeling for a runway fashion show. Except they're often covered in spit-up—or, now that we've begun trying solids, explosive bowel movements. It's the opposite of glamorous, and I'm pretty okay with not having to scrub out stains.

RJ has taken to coming to my place most nights of the week, unless he has early practice or he has to meet up with his teammates for evening meetings—which sometimes take place at the pub. He invites me to tag along or come to his practices, but I'm still trying to get used to him before I get used to all the other craziness that comes with his life and my being in it. The idea of sitting in an arena with all those people is enough to make my heart race and my palms sweat. I'm just not ready for that yet.

It's bath night for Kody, which is his favorite. He loves splashing in the water and playing with his toys, so it's kind of a production, but I don't mind because he always sleeps so well afterward.

RJ picks him up from the play mat on the floor and gives him a raspberry on the tummy, which elicits a shriek and a giggle out of Kody. "Come on, little man, it's bath time! You want to smell good for Stella at day care tomorrow. I saw you trying to steal her soother today, and I gotta tell you, that's not the best way to make a good impression. If you don't watch it, that little punk Hunter is going to move in on your territory. I saw him sharing his giraffe teether with her the other day. Now that's how you get the girl." Kody coos at his father, enthralled by everything he says like he's actually mentally taking notes from him. RJ winks at me, and I follow him down the hall, shaking my head with a smile.

I've already set up the baby bath and all of Kody's toys. While RJ undresses him, I put lavender-scented bubbles and warm water in his tub. I turn to see how RJ is managing and smile even wider as he leans down and gives him another raspberry, then removes his diaper and gives him a tickle.

I'm about to warn RJ that naked tickles aren't the best idea—at least not where Kody is concerned—but I'm too late. Kody giggles loudly, which also prompts him to pee, and RJ is right in the line of fire.

"Oh shit!" RJ tries to use his hand as a shield, but Kody kicks his legs, which has a loose fire hose effect. RJ looks down at his now-wet shirt and hands. "Not cool, little man, not cool."

I clap a palm over my mouth to muffle my laugh and nudge RJ out of the way so I can get to Kody. "Did you pee all over Daddy? You got him real good, didn't you? Yes, you did! Daddy needs a bath too, just like you!" Kody babbles and smiles as I set him in the tub, immediately slapping at the bubbles and sending a spray of water my way. At least it's just soapy water and not pee.

At the sound of metal hitting metal, I glance over my shoulder—and suck in a breath when I catch RJ unbuckling his belt. I lift my gaze, eyes raking over six-pack abs, defined pecs, and heavy shoulders. I can't seem to command myself to look away as he unbuttons his jeans and drags the zipper down.

In the weeks since he's come back into my life, I've been hesitant to fully acknowledge the chemistry between us, to give it room to breathe, because once I do there's no going back. But I can't ignore the way my body heats up at the sight of him undressing in Kody's bathroom.

"What're you doing?" My voice is high, almost panicked.

He gives me a saucy grin. "You said I need a bath too."

"But—"

He shoves his jeans down his thighs, and I look away, focusing on Kody in the bath and not how almost naked RJ is, or how close to me he is, or how long it's been since I've had sex . . . the last time being the night—or rather morning—I conceived Kody.

RJ removes the showerhead and lets it hang, then steps over the edge of the tub and lowers himself in, one muscular leg on either side of Kody's baby bathtub. The tub itself has less than three inches of sudsy water in it, and I'm both relieved and disappointed that RJ is still wearing boxer briefs.

I pass RJ a cloth and the baby wash. "Might as well do the honors, huh, Daddy?"

His grin grows wider as I stare in blatant appreciation at his mostly naked body taking up the vast majority of the tub. "If I wash Kody, does that mean you wash me?"

"I think you can take care of yourself just fine." I have my doubts I'll be able to keep things safely platonic if I help RJ out. I use the edge of the tub to pull myself up.

"Where are you going?"

"I'll be right back."

I nab his pee-covered T-shirt and Kody's dirty clothes and throw them in the wash. On the way back to the bathroom, I grab my phone from the living room and pad quietly down the hall. RJ is busy splashing around in the shallow water, making Kody smile and giggle, so I quickly take a bunch of pictures, thinking that these would all be perfect with the caption *ovaries exploding*.

I watch the muscles in his back flex as he zooms one of the bath toys around over Kody's head. In the year since we've been together, he seems like he's in even better shape, if that's possible. My body has changed too—and it's definitely not more defined or toned. I don't want him to look at me differently, see me differently, although I'm aware he probably already does. I'm the mother of his child. We have a baby together. It changes everything. Which is part of the reason I'm holding on so hard to the things I know.

Also, the second I let him into my pants, I'll inevitably let him back into my heart. With RJ, there isn't one without the other.

I tune back in to their one-sided conversation. "You know what, little man? I think I'm making some progress with Mommy."

Kody babbles and smacks the water, splashing him in the face.

"I know. It's only been a couple of weeks, and I have a lot of work to do still . . . but dude, I gotta tell you, your mom's a MILF—and if you ever tell her I said that, I'll straight-up deny it. But God, she's beautiful."

Kody shrieks and kicks at the water.

"You're handsome, no doubt about that, little man. Can I tell you something important?" Kody giggles when RJ tickles the bottoms of his feet. RJ smiles, then turns serious. "I think if it wasn't for you, your mom wouldn't be giving me a second chance. So thank you. I love you, buddy, and I'm hoping I get to say that to you every day for the rest of my life. Even when you're a teenager and it embarrasses the shit out of you."

My heart squeezes as I take in this giant of a man telling his son he loves him.

"You know who would have loved to meet you and your mom?"

Kody babbles, as if he's answering his dad's question.

"Your grandpa Steven James, my dad. You and me both have his dimple." RJ touches his cheek and leans in to kiss Kody. "God, I miss him. He was such an awesome dad. We had the farm, and he was always so busy, but he still managed to make time to come to all my hockey games. I really don't know how he did it. Farms are hell to run. Long hours, hard work, but he did it with a smile and cheered me on. I wish he was still here." RJ squeezes shampoo into his palm and starts washing Kody's hair.

"Your grandpa worried about me a lot. I'll be honest, little man, I didn't always make the best choices, especially when I first made the NHL—and I'm going to try my best to help you make better ones than I did. But your mom was definitely the best thing that ever happened to me, and so are you, and I think your grandpa would've loved you both so much, just like I do."

CHAPTER 22

CAN YOU HANDLE IT?

Rook

Hours at the gym have become an absolute necessity these days, because otherwise, I have no way of exorcising the pent-up, restless energy that comes from being around a gorgeous, sexy woman who is also the mother of my child. Lainey is effortlessly beautiful, and she's an incredible, patient mother—which wouldn't have been a turn-on less than a month ago.

To be fair, I've seen a lot of boob recently. Seen but haven't been able to touch. It's an odd kind of torture. There's been a lot of hugs and kisses on the cheek and flirty touches, but I don't want to push too far too fast.

Then there was last night. Kody has been fussy the past few days because he's teething, and Lainey was wiped from lack of sleep. I offered to stay over and take the middle-of-the-night feeding so Lainey could get more than a couple hours in a row. I was prepared to spend the night on the couch, and in hindsight that likely would have been a hell of a lot smarter.

She lay down with Kody on her chest, and I waited until they both fell asleep before I transferred him back to his crib. I figured it would only be a couple hours before he woke for a feeding, and her bed is so much more comfortable than the couch, so I stretched out beside her.

The middle-of-the-night feeding never came, though, so I didn't relocate to the couch. Instead I woke up spooning Lainey, with my morning wood pressing into her back and one hand very close to cupping her boob. Thankfully it didn't make things too awkward, which I'm taking as a good sign.

Regardless, the mounting sexual tension is the reason I'm on set number six of chest presses.

"What rock have you been hidin' under the past couple o' weeks? The only time I see you is practice or workouts." Lance is my spotter.

"I'm a little busy these days," I grunt through the eighth rep.

"When you gonna stop hiding yer tour guide?"

"I'm not hiding Lainey—I just don't want to subject her to my shitstorm. And we're kind of figuring out how we work together. The last time we went out, I got mobbed, and it freaked her out."

"She can't get used to it without exposure." Lance racks the bar for me. "You can't hide her from the world, and it doesn't do her any good if you're trying to protect her from the media. Rip the bandage off, Rook. Bring her to a practice—and when she's ready, bring her and Kody to a game so she can meet the wives. She needs to know she's not alone. Your team is your family."

"She hates big crowds."

"The boxes are safe. And Poppy and Sunny are like the Zen team— they'll make her feel right at home." He slaps me on the shoulder. "I'm hitting the sauna, and you should too, if you don't want to be crying like yer baby later."

He has a point. I've asked Lainey if she wants to come to practice pretty much every time we have one. And it would be great if she could attend before an actual game when it's total mayhem. I decide I'll bring it up again tonight, once Kody is in bed.

I fire off a message to see if Lainey wants to have lunch. Most of the time I'll pick something up and bring it to the aquarium, but today I'm thinking we could try a café. Baby steps and all.

I don't hear from her before I reach the aquarium, but that's not all that surprising. She doesn't respond to messages when she's leading a tour or with the animals. I find out from Eden that she left work about an hour ago and that she was feverish, with the chills, feeling nauseous.

I try calling her again, but there's still no response. "What about Kody?" I ask Eden.

"He's still at day care, as far as I know. At least I hope he is. I don't think Lainey's in any state to take care of him right now. She really didn't look good when she left."

"I'm going to check on her. See what she needs." I'm halfway across the lobby when I realize I don't have a key, and if she's not answering her phone, I can't be sure she's going to answer her door either.

I turn to find Eden dangling a key chain from her finger.

"Can I borrow those?"

"No. I thought I'd taunt you with them." She shows me which one gets me into the building and the one for Lainey's apartment.

I rush across the street and take the elevator to her floor. I knock first, so I don't scare the crap out of her, but when she doesn't answer after about thirty seconds, I use the key to let myself in. "Lainey?" I call out as I close the door and lock it behind me.

I slip the keys into my pocket; anxiety makes my heart beat faster as I walk down the hall. I peek in Kody's room but keep going when I see it's empty. I pass the open, unoccupied bathroom and head for Lainey's bedroom. The comforter is turned down; there's a bowl on the floor and a half-full glass of water on the nightstand.

"Lainey? You here?"

"RJ?" It's more of a croak than my name, and it's coming from the bathroom.

"Eden said you weren't feeling well."

"I'm okay. Just give me a minute." That declaration is followed by a horrible retching sound, a splash, and the flush of the toilet.

I find her hugging the bowl, her cheek resting on the edge. She's wearing a loose nightshirt, legs bare and mostly exposed. Her hair hangs in a haphazard braid down her back, flyaways poking out, strands stuck to her neck and forehead. Her normally tanned skin is pasty white, and a fine sheen of sweat covers her face and neck despite the fact that she's covered in goose bumps.

"You don't look okay."

Her eyes are glassy and slow to track. "You shouldn't see me like this. I look awful."

I ignore her as I crouch down, and she tries to wave me away. I press the back of my hand to her forehead, then lean in and follow with my lips, like I remember my mom used to do.

She makes a little noise, sort of like a hum combined with a groan.

"You're burning up. Do you have a thermometer around here?"

"There's one in the medicine cabinet in the bathroom across from Kody's room, but I'm fine. It's just a bug. I need to sleep for a few hours."

"I don't know that sleeping wrapped around a toilet is a great option, Lainey."

"The bath mat is pretty soft." She shivers and looks over her shoulder at the floor.

"Let me help you back into the bed."

"I can't yet. The nausea is ge—" Her face pales further, eyes going wide, and then she pulls herself up, arms shaking, fingertips going white as she clutches the seat and heaves violently. She tries to tell me to leave, but she can barely get words out before she heaves again; this time nothing comes up. She flushes the toilet, but spasms continue to rack her for a good two minutes until she finally sags again, cheek resting on the seat.

I grab a washcloth and wet it so I can clean her up. She's so weak and spent that she doesn't put up a fight. "How many times has that happened?"

"I don't know. It comes in these awful waves. I've been in here since I came home, and that was before lunchtime."

"I'm going to get the thermometer so I can check your temperature and get you a glass of water so the dry heaves aren't as painful." I smooth her hair away from her forehead. "I'll be right back."

I fill a glass with water first, then search the bathroom for the thermometer. By the time I get back she's dry heaving again. Once she's done with that round I take her temperature, which is over 103 degrees. It's another hour before she finally stops heaving. She's pale and sweaty and exhausted. I pick her up off the floor and carry her back to bed.

Lainey struggles to sit up, shivering, eyes bloodshot and glassy with fever. "I need to get dressed and pick Kody up from day care."

"You're not going anywhere. I'll pick up Kody—you lie here and get some rest."

"But I—"

"Lainey." I put a gentle hand on her shoulder to keep her from sitting up. "You need to let me help you. You don't want to risk Kody catching what you have."

Lainey's eyes flare. "Oh God, I didn't think of that."

"I'm here, and I want to be involved. Let me show you I can do this with you."

She settles back on her pillows with a groan, teeth still chattering even though she has ten blankets piled on top of her.

"Do you want me to get you something warmer to wear?"

She pulls the covers up to her chin. "N-no. I'll get the s-sweats, and then I'll have to t-take it off anyway. I'll s-stop s-shivering eventually."

There's no way I'm leaving her here alone when her teeth are chattering like she's in a freezer. I round the other side of the bed and strip off my shirt.

"What're you d-doing?" Lainey asks.

"I'm gonna make you warm." I fold back the covers and slide under them.

"B-but I'll make you sick."

"I'll be fine unless you try to make out with me." I scoop her up and settle her in my lap, wrapping my arms around her.

She's too tired to resist or even consider fighting me on it, so she snuggles right in, tucking her frozen feet between my thighs. Her clammy forehead rests against the side of my neck, and she settles her palms against my chest. "You're s-so warm."

"Big teddy bear, remember?"

"Mmm. I remember."

Her hair tickles my arm, and I run my hand gently up and down her leg, waiting for the shivers to subside.

She keeps shifting in my lap, and despite that fact that she's sick as a dog, my body starts to react inconveniently to her proximity, the feel of her hands on my chest, and the inadvertent friction.

"RJ?"

"Yeah, baby?"

"Is your phone in your pocket?"

"No. Why? You need me to call someone?"

She wriggles around some more in my lap. "No, but there's something hard—oh." She lifts her head, bloodshot eyes meeting mine. She covers her mouth with her palm, and for a moment I worry she's going to be sick again, until she asks, "Are you . . . do you have a *hard-on*?"

I don't bother fighting my grin as I lift a shoulder and let it fall. "You're doing a lot of moving around. Some parts of my body are inconsiderate and don't really care that you're sick."

"I look like hell, and I probably smell terrible." She drops her hand, giving me a quick glimpse of her smile before she snuggles back into me. Eventually the shivering subsides and her breathing evens out. Once I'm sure she's asleep, I move her off my lap and cover her in blankets.

I make sure she has everything she needs before I put my shirt back on.

I wash my hands in the bathroom down the hall, making a mental note to call Lainey's housekeeper so she can come in and disinfect. The last thing any of us needs is for this to be passed along.

I grab Lainey's keys so I can return Eden's to her, then rush back to pick up Kody. I'm grateful Lainey had me added to her very short list of approved adults who can pick him up. Currently it's Lainey herself, Eden, and me. I'm happy to note Walter has never been given that privilege.

"Lainey working late tonight?" Kristen, one of the day care providers, asks as she leads me over to where Kody and the other infants sit in their activity centers, playing with the light-up buttons or squeezy, crinkly things. One of the other staff is sitting cross-legged on the floor, keeping them entertained.

"She's not feeling well, so I thought it would be a good idea for me to come pick up Kody. How's he been today?"

"He's been great—slept well this afternoon, and he's really loving the cereal Lainey's been sending with him. There's a flu bug going around, so we've been watching all the kids closely and, of course, making sure everyone is washing their hands."

"I don't think working at an aquarium with thousands of people going through on a daily basis helps much with the germ exposure." I crouch down so I'm at Kody's level. "How's my little man?" I lean in and give him a kiss on the forehead, checking to make sure he's not hot too. He smiles and makes a happy sound, holding out his arms like he's asking to be picked up. I lift him out of the activity center, and Kristen helps me gather his things. I didn't think to bring the stroller with me, which Lainey usually does, so it's a bit of a juggling act, but I manage to shoulder the bags and keep my hold on Kody with a little assistance.

We head back up to Lainey's apartment, the elevator half-full with people returning home from work.

"Mommy's not feeling all that hot, buddy, so we're going to take care of her, and you and me are going to have a boys' night. Sound good?" He squawks at me, like he's in agreement with this plan, so I keep talking. "We can watch some hockey, and I'll even let you drink all the mommy milk you want, as long as you don't rat me out." Kody makes more baby sounds at me and reaches up to smack uncoordinatedly at my face. "You high-fivin' me?"

The elevator dings and I glance up, checking to see if it's my stop, which is when I notice that every woman on the elevator is staring at me. Thankfully, it's my floor, so I excuse myself, and they all clamber to either move out of the way or hold the door open, since I'm laden down with baby things and a baby.

"I think my ovaries just exploded," says one woman as the doors start to shut.

"He's like the poster boy for DILFs," says another one.

I don't get to hear any more commentary, because the doors slide closed. I have to set all the bags down and root around in my pocket to find the keys.

The door across the hall opens, and Walter appears. I'm loath to admit it, but he's not a bad-looking guy. Lean, almost wiry build, still has all of his hair—but there's a hint of recession flirting at the temples, which means in about ten years he'll have a horseshoe. Solidly average, maybe, but that doesn't make up for the fact that he's an asshole. "You look like you're struggling."

"I got it," I mutter, finally snagging the keys.

"Just so you know, I'll be right here, waiting for the day when all the fun of playing house wears off and you abandon Lainey again."

I glance over my shoulder and find him leaning against the door-jamb, arms crossed over his chest. He's got balls, I'll give him that. "Look, I know my showing up threw a wrench in your plans, Walt, and I appreciate the fact that you were here to help Lainey when she needed it, but you should probably move on. I'm not going anywhere."

"I'll believe that when you're still here six months from now. You're on the road all the time, aren't you? Professional hockey player and all that. Must be hard on relationships, being away that much. Lainey's bound to need some help when you're not around, and me being right across the hall makes it easy for me to step in." He smiles wryly. "Have a good night, RJ." He turns his attention to Kody and gives him a little tickle under the chin, his tough-guy facade turning into wistful sadness. "Be good for your mom."

He disappears back into his apartment, and for a few seconds I feel bad for him. He was here when I wasn't. He wanted Lainey despite the fact that she came with a brand-new baby that wasn't his. He knows how special she is. But he's wrong about being around to help out, because as soon as she's ready, I'll be moving them into my house, so Walter will effectively be removed from any and all equations.

I might feel bad for him, but I sure as hell don't want him as my competition.

I put Kody in his activity center in the living room before I grab the fifty million bags Lainey sends with him to day care. I drop them all on the couch, lock the door, pick Kody back up, and head down the hall to check on Lainey.

I peek in the room and find her sleeping, which is good. She obviously needs some rest. I mentally scroll through the list of things Lainey typically does when she gets home from work. Usually she feeds Kody right away, and considering how he's bumping his nose on my shoulder, I have a feeling he's not going to be quiet about how hungry he is soon. And there's no way I'm going to wake Lainey up to take care of him right now.

"Come on, little man, let's get you some dinner."

Lainey keeps bottles in the fridge, and there's a box of baby cereal on the counter, probably from this morning. I put Kody in his saucer to bounce around while I follow the directions to make him dinner and heat up a bottle to go with it.

Word to the wise: feeding a baby cereal the consistency of . . . things I'd rather not compare it to is messy business. By the time I'm done, Kody has food in his hair and all over his neck, his bib, and his hands.

I somehow have managed to get it all over my shirt as well. I don't have a change of clothes, so I'm forced to use a dishcloth to clean off the spots. Then I take Kody to the bathroom, run him a tepid bath, and wash all the cereal off him before I give him his bottle.

It's well after six by the time we're done with dinner and the bath, and I still haven't eaten. I don't want to make unnecessary noise on the off chance it'll wake Lainey up, plus the smell might not go well with nausea.

I take stock of what's in her pantry and the fridge and decide a shopping trip is necessary. There's a small grocery store down the street where I can pick up a few things for her and something for me. I leave a note on her night table and get Kody dressed in his going-out gear.

Getting him into the stroller is another epic feat, but I figure it out. Lainey has one of those baby carrier things where I can strap him to my body, but there's about seven hundred yards of fabric that I don't know what to do with, so I leave that for another time.

I don't take into account that this is Kody's fussy time of day, or the fact that I can't see him as he squawks his irritation, probably at still being awake and not in his mother's arms. I manage to pick up the necessities, such as ginger ale, soda crackers, chicken soup, sports drinks, and some bread and cold cuts so I can make myself some sandwiches when we get back to the apartment. I also pick up a pizza slice and devour it while I'm loading things on the belt.

Kody's turned into a banshee by the time I finish paying. People give me looks ranging from pity to something like disdain and judgment. His face is beet red, mouth wide open as he screams, tears streaming down his cheeks. "Okay, little man, I hear you. We're going home now." I unbuckle him from the restraints, wondering if maybe they're too tight, but as soon as I lean in close enough, I know that's not it.

"Oh sh—" I manage to censor myself just as a woman with a kid probably a few years older than Kody passes me. "Smells like you're up to no good," I tell Kody.

Of course, I didn't have the foresight to bring his diaper bag, so I'm forced to buy a pack of diapers, cream, and wipes so I can take care of the situation before we head home. I'm grateful that there's an extra sleeper in the stroller, because he's demolished the one he's currently wearing.

I use half the package of wipes, aware that bath time round two is going to take place as soon as we're home. The smell rivals the inside of a hockey bag combined with an outhouse.

By the time we get back it's after seven, and by the time I'm done with the bath routine it's almost eight, which is way past Kody's usual bedtime, so it makes sense that he's cranky as hell. I at least have the foresight to get a bottle ready before his bath so I can feed him again as soon as he's clean, dry, and dressed in his jammies. I pick the hockey-themed ones, for obvious reasons. It doesn't take much to get him to fall asleep, and I have a feeling I won't be far behind him.

Once he's in bed I check on Lainey again; she's still sleeping. Her phone buzzes, so I snatch it up as I pull the door closed behind me, not wanting to disturb her. The name on the screen reads *MOM*. I let it go to voice mail.

I'm aware her mother knows that I'm back in her life. I haven't pushed for a lot of details on the situation there, but this distance she's created has been purposeful. I'm also aware that she speaks to her mother several times a week, which tells me that—as much as Lainey wants to prove she can do this on her own—there's still a lot of love there.

Her mom calls again less than fifteen minutes later, so I answer this time. "Hello."

"I'm sorry—I must have dialed the wrong number."

"You're looking for Lainey?"

That makes her pause. "I . . . yes. Who is this?"

"It's RJ. Rook, Lainey's . . . friend." I cringe a little at that. I don't think I'd classify myself as her friend at this point, but she's not referring to me as her boyfriend, and it's not like there have been a lot of opportunities for dating. Middle-of-the-night accidental spooning doesn't really count.

Her mother scoffs. "Is that what you're calling yourself, now? You get my daughter pregnant, lie to her about who you are, and then it's a year before you show your face again. Some *friend* you are. I suppose you think that just because you're some big-time hockey player none of the usual rules apply to you."

As much as getting chewed out by Lainey's mom sucks, I get where she's coming from. And I tell her as much. "With all due respect, Mrs. Carver, I understand why you're unhappy with me. If I had a daughter and this happened to her, I would do everything in my power to protect her—and I sure as heck wouldn't have any kind of warm feelings toward that guy, which I realize is me in this case."

"Well, I can't say you're wrong about my feelings toward you. Lainey's always been a special girl—she's delicate—"

"Maybe not as delicate as you think, though."

"You don't know what she's been through."

"You mean the shooting at her college?"

"She told you about that?" She seems shocked.

"She did. Alaska has some pretty bad storms in the summer, which is an understandable trigger for her."

"She never talks about that with anyone," her mother says softly. "I'd like to speak with her now, please."

"I'm sorry, Mrs. Carver. As much as I'd like to be able to get her for you, she's not well, and she's sleeping right now. I'm sure you can understand why I wouldn't want to wake her up."

"Unwell? What's wrong?"

"I think she has the flu."

"The flu? You better not have gotten my daughter pregnant again."

There's real threat behind her words. "I'm sure it's the flu and that she's definitely not pregnant. That's not . . . that would be impossible." And that, right there, has to be the most awkward of awkward first conversations with the woman I'm assuming will one day be my mother-in-law.

"Well, that's a relief." I think that's sarcasm, but I can't be sure. "How sick is she? Should you take her to the hospital? Do I need to come out there? I kept telling her working at an aquarium wouldn't be good for her. It's a cesspool of germs and disease. It's actually amazing that she hasn't gotten sick before now. She really just needs to be done with this and come home so she can have the help she needs to raise that child."

"Lainey has me."

"Is that right? And for how long is that going to be the case? Do you know anything about raising children? Who's going to be there when you're traveling all over the place and she's taking care of that baby alone?"

"She has friends here, and so do I. There are other wives—"

"Other wives?" she screeches in my ear. "Oh my God, did you elope? Did you marry my daughter without even asking permission first?"

I can see now why Lainey ended up moving halfway across the country. "No, that's not . . . I meant the other players' wives. We didn't elope. I've made a lot of mistakes with Lainey . . ."

"Oh, you think so?" Her sarcasm is on point.

"I should've told Lainey the truth about my job from the start. My life is complicated—and that's not an excuse, but know that I never wanted to lose contact with Lainey. If I'm completely honest, I was gutted when I couldn't reach her after I left Alaska, and when I found her again and realized what had happened, I was devastated all over again. I missed her entire pregnancy—I missed the birth of my son and the first four months of his life. I can't go back in time and change how things happened, but I'm trying to make up for it. So I'm here, taking care of her the best I know how—which right now is to let her sleep so she can get well."

She's silent for a few long, drawn-out moments. "How's Kody?"

"He's asleep as well, for now. But as soon as Lainey wakes up, I can have her call you."

"Yes. Okay. I'd like you to do that. But also, I'd like updates every couple of hours. When Lainey gets the flu, she can sometimes be down for days. She spikes high fevers. We had to take her to the hospital more than once when she was young. And make sure you keep Kody away from her until her fever breaks. She'll want to feed him, but that's too much of a risk. And you should make sure you have ginger ale and soda crackers for when she can stomach food again."

"I have all those things. And I'll definitely message with updates every couple of hours."

"I just wish she was home so I can take care of her."

I decide the best way to win them over is to offer them the opportunity to see her. "Would you like to come for a visit?"

"It's a long drive."

"I can arrange flights for you."

"Oh . . . I don't fly." I can almost see her wringing her hands, like Lainey when she's anxious. I see where it comes from now.

"You could do it for Lainey, though, couldn't you? When was the last time you saw Kody?"

"Not since he was born . . . but the farm . . ."

"You have lots of help there, don't you? Lainey would love to see you. And Kody's sitting up now. You can think about it."

"Let me just ask her father, see if he thinks it's something we can do." I wait while she has a muffled conversation with Lainey's dad. "Okay. Yes. Simon thinks a visit is a good idea."

"I'll book your flights and arrange accommodations for you."

"You don't need to do that. Simon can take care of it."

"Please, it would mean a lot to me if you'd let me handle it. I'll just need information for the tickets and an email to forward them to."

She hesitates for a minute but finally relents. I take down all the information I need, grab Lainey's laptop, and bring up flights, finding the first one out tomorrow morning from Washington to Chicago. Once everything is booked, I forward the email.

I end the call and toss Lainey's phone on the couch. I'm beat. I don't know how Lainey has done this on her own all these months. And now I've invited her parents out for a visit. Winning over her mom is one thing, but her dad . . . well, let's just hope I still have my balls by the time they leave.

CHAPTER 23

METTLE

Lainey

I wake up around one o'clock in the morning, breasts aching, but I don't feel feverish anymore or like I'm going to throw up, which is a relief. Dry heaves are the worst.

I roll out of bed. Every muscle in my body hurts, like I tried to run a marathon or lift weights for several hours in a row. My stomach is raw and tender from all the throwing up.

I take a few tentative sips of water, cringing at how sore even my throat is. And my mouth tastes awful. I use the bathroom and brush my teeth, catching my reflection in the mirror. My hair is a wild mess, random strands having freed themselves from the braid.

I have dark circles under my eyes, and my skin is the color of paper. I consider going right back to bed, but I need to pump. Or feed Kody. I'm light-headed and weak, but at least the worst of the sickness seems to have passed.

I peek into Kody's room and immediately go into panic mode when I don't find him in his crib. I rush down the hall and come to an abrupt, dizzy stop. RJ's huge body is sprawled out in the glider, my breastfeeding pillow secured around his waist, head lolled to the side, Kody cradled in his arms, both asleep. An empty bottle sits on the table beside them. They look so sweet together.

I sneak into the kitchen and try, as quietly as I can, to find my breast pump. It takes me less than fifteen minutes to fill two six-ounce bottles. Once I'm finished, I clean everything in the bathroom sink and also manage my own horrid appearance—although RJ's seen me barf, twice, so I'm not sure why I feel the need. And unless I dreamed it, he cuddled with me and managed to get hard with me looking like yesterday's strung-out lady of the night.

I change my pajamas and wipe myself down with a warm cloth, aware I've had the fever sweats for most of the night. The whole process is exhausting, and by the time I'm done I need to lie down again. Which of course means I also need to close my eyes. And fall asleep thinking about how I'm glad I made the choice to give RJ a second chance—and that he's proving to be worth it.

I wake up at five thirty to the sound of a hungry baby. I throw off the covers and shrug into my fuzziest robe. If I'm quick enough, I can catch Kody before he's fully awake, and often it means he'll fall back asleep for another hour or so once he's done feeding.

I'm still a little clammy and warm, and my entire body feels like I've been hit by a transport truck, but it's a significant improvement over yesterday. The fact that my stomach rumbles is also a good sign.

I find RJ in the kitchen, Kody propped on one hip. His hair is all over the place—both boys—and since RJ slept in his clothes, he's a wrinkled mess. There's also a spit-up stain on his shoulder. And yet I don't think I've ever seen him look as sexy as he does right now, in this moment. "Let's see if there's any more mommy milk in here, little man."

"Morning."

"Oh, hey. Sorry if we woke you up. How ya feeling?" He gives me a once-over. "You look better."

"I feel better." Kody lets out a shriek and lurches toward me. "I can take him."

I hold out my arms, but RJ cups the back of his head protectively and turns his body slightly away from me. "I don't know if that's a good idea, Lainey. We don't want him to catch what you had."

I'm both irritated and impressed, considering he looks like he needs six more hours of sleep and a shower yet still manages to be gorgeous and concerned. "I'm sanitized and changed. He can get his milk right from the source, no bottle necessary."

"Your mom said it would be better—"

"My mom? When did you talk to her?"

"She called last night. She was worried when you didn't call her back."

Kody screams again, louder this time, insistent. I step forward and put a palm on RJ's chest. Giving him this second chance hasn't been easy. I haven't wanted to put my heart on the line, afraid it'll just end up broken again, but I'm beginning to see just how much RJ wants this. He fielded a call from my mother, and that says a lot, all on its own. "It's okay. I'm okay, and he needs to be fed—and I need to feed him, because I'm running like a leaky faucet."

With a little reluctance and a whole lot of wide eyes, he passes Kody over. As soon as Kody's in my arms he's bumping around, pecking at me almost like a bird, mouth open and waiting for food. I'm on auto-pilot, not really thinking about what I'm doing as I shift my robe aside and undo the snap on my nightshirt, which is designed specifically for middle-of-the-night feedings.

Kody roots around almost frantically. "It's okay. Mommy's here. Breakfast is on its way." He latches on, and after a few seconds he coughs, so I tuck my pinkie between his mouth and my nipple, forcing him to let go. Even though I pumped, I'm still way overdue for a feed, so I'm like a fire hose, shooting everywhere.

Unfortunately, RJ seems to be the main target, as I spray him across the shirt. I try to cover up, but all I end up doing is diverting the spray and hitting him in the face. I pull my robe closed, much to Kody's displeasure. I maneuver around RJ, who's clearly shocked, and lean over the sink, giving my boob a good squeeze before I attempt feeding Kody again. I wait until he's latched on and there's no sign of him choking before I turn around.

"So, that actually happened." RJ wears an amused grin. "I feel like I can add and cross getting sprayed with breast milk off my bucket list, which is right up there with getting peed on by my son."

I laugh—and then groan, because my stomach still hurts from all the hurling I did yesterday. "Sorry about that. I'm a bit of a gusher."

His smile quickly becomes a smirk. "I remember."

I poke him in the chest. "Our child can hear you."

He grabs my finger. "The one we made, together." Lacing our hands, he presses his lips to my knuckle. "You should sit down—you look better, but you're still pale. Can I get you something? Water, juice, ginger ale, something with electrolytes?"

"I don't think I have ginger ale or anything with electrolytes in the house, so water would be good, thank you."

"Kody and I went grocery shopping last night—you have both of those things, so if you want something other than water, let me know."

"I'll take electrolytes, please. What flavor do you have?"

"Lemon-lime—that was your favorite kind, right?"

"It still is."

He sends me off to the living room while he gets me a sports drink and a plate of saltines slathered in butter. I eat them slowly, dropping crumbs all over poor Kody, but he's so intent on eating he doesn't notice or care.

RJ makes sure I'm okay with the smell of coffee before he makes himself a cup, then sits on the couch across from me, fidgeting, eyes bouncing from Kody to my face and back down. I think it's sweet that he's so concerned. "He's going to be okay. The worst is over, and I'm on the mend."

"I believe you. I'm just trying to reconcile my semi and the fact that your boobs aren't my toys and they're meant for Kody. It's a weird thing to try to wrap my head around."

I laugh again and groan. "Please don't be funny—my stomach hurts too much for that."

"I'm sorry. I'll be serious from here on out." His phone buzzes, and he checks it, thumb typing a message in response.

"Who's messaging you at six in the morning?" A sudden spike of irrational jealousy hits me. He's been here almost every night since I introduced him to Kody, and we woke up spooning the other day. Sure, he might be ogling my boob—but he's a man, and they don't have boobs, so of course they're fascinated by them. Just like women are fascinated by the penis and all the interesting things it does.

"Your mom. She and I have been messaging back and forth all night."

"Oh my God. Did you tell her I was sick?"

RJ looks up from his phone. "Well, yeah, I wasn't going to lie to her. She wanted me to wake you so she could talk to you, and there was no way in hell I was going to do that, so I told her you were sick."

"She must have flipped her lid." I can't even begin to imagine how she would've reacted to him denying her.

"She was concerned about your well-being, like any mother would be."

His tone tells me more than his words. "So you—what? Told her you'd text her hourly updates?"

"Every couple of hours," he mutters.

I almost want to laugh. I can just picture my mom bargaining with him for updates. "It's the middle of the night there—why is she still up? Maybe you should give me the phone. I should call her."

"She's packing right now." RJ makes a weird face, sort of a cringe and an *oh shit* look.

"Packing? Are they going somewhere?"

He rubs the back of his neck. "Uh, well—"

Of course this is the exact moment Kody decides he wants to switch boobs. I set him on my shoulder and pat his back, waiting until he burps before I go ahead and make the switch.

Once he's latched and I'm sure he's not doing a keg stand on my boob, I refocus my attention on RJ. "Uh, well, what?"

"I might have invited your parents to come for a visit."

I scoff and wave that off. "My mother will never get on a plane."

"She's planning to, for you."

"Are you serious?" My high pitch startles Kody, and I shush him, stroking his hair, which helps tone down the anxiety a little.

"I wanted to reassure her that I wasn't some douchebag looking to screw her daughter over. I figured the best way to do that was to show them exactly how much I care about you and Kody."

"So you decided to fly them out here?"

"Yes."

"Where are they going to stay? I don't even have a spare room or a pullout couch."

"I can set them up in a hotel if you'd like, or we can make alternate arrangements."

"Alternate arrangements?"

"I have lots of space in my house. You could all stay there. I can even stay in a hotel if that would make you more comfortable."

I can't believe he's managed to convince my mother to come out here—on a plane. Once again my heart does that fluttery thing, and this time I allow that feeling to spread instead of trying to keep it contained. I can see in his expression and actions that he's serious about making this work. He wouldn't have spent the night taking care of us or offered to fly my parents out to visit if he wasn't. Since he's come back into my life, our lives, he's proven time and time again that he sincerely wants both of us. Last night was a true testament to how committed he is. Little by little he's erasing his lie and earning my trust with everything he does.

"I would never kick you out of your own house—that's just silly. It would actually be great for my parents to see us together."

"Like a family?" RJ looks so hopeful.

I nod as I smooth my palm over Kody's silky hair. "Thank you for taking care of us last night. It means a lot, RJ—and for convincing my parents to get on a plane and come visit. I'm warning you, though, they can be a lot to handle."

"I think I've got your mom covered."

"Yeah, well, she's the easier of the two to win over." But I'm hoping that when they see the way he cares for me and Kody—and how much I care about him—they'll come around. That he's willing to face them and the choices that have brought us to this point tells me everything I need to know.

CHAPTER 24

HOUSEGUESTS

Rook

It's been a very, very long time since I met the parents of a woman I was dating. Like, all the way back to high school. And this isn't just a regular meet-the-parents scenario, because the reality is I'm not a regular guy. Being a professional hockey player in Chicago is like being Britney Spears in Vegas. It's not the low-key image I painted of myself when I first met Lainey, and that lie is going to be a huge issue with her parents. Which I can understand.

Lainey seems to want to pack the entire contents of Kody's bedroom, so I finally admit that I've already converted one of my bedrooms into a nursery and she just needs the basics.

Lainey stops stuffing a bag with clothes and diaper cream and gives me an incredulous look. "When would you have time to set up a nursery? You've been here more than you've been home the past couple of weeks."

I shove my hands into my pockets. "I ordered a bunch of stuff and had painters and a decorator come in."

She sits down on the edge of the bed, looking tired again. "It's not easy to get used to the fact that you can afford to hire people to do all these things for you."

"I'll work on conditioning you slowly. In the meantime, can you let me take care of this? We don't have to pick your parents up for another five hours. You spent a good part of yesterday reenacting that scene from *The Exorcist* into the toilet bowl. You might feel better, but you're not really in any kind of shape to be doing much other than lying around, getting better."

"We'll pack Kody's bag. Then I'll lie down."

I'd like to argue with her, but I can see that she's not going to be able to relax until his bag is packed too. And I know without her having to say another word that she doesn't trust me to pack it without her supervision.

I force her to take a seat in the rocking chair, from which she calls out all the things he'll need. I don't bother to tell her I have almost all the same things at my place already.

After a few minutes she stops calling out items. I look over to find her passed out in the chair. I leave her there while I change her sheets, then carry her back to her bedroom. Since we're all underslept, I use one of her nursing pillows to surround Kody and set him in the middle so he's flanked on either side, and the three of us have a nice long nap.

When Lainey wakes, I run her a bath filled with Epsom salts for the aches and pains while she nurses Kody. Lainey looks significantly better than she did twenty-four hours ago, and she's ready for a trip to the airport.

I'm a bit of a mess, still wearing my shirt Lainey sprayed with breast milk and Kody spit up on earlier. I'm also still unshaven and unshowered. At least I have a jacket to cover the shirt stains, and my ball cap covers my hair.

We head down to my SUV, which already has a baby seat installed, and load all the bags. I park at the airport, and Lainey straps Kody to my body with the straitjacket carrier. She wanted to wear him, but I thought the extra weight and exertion wouldn't be good for her. It's impressive how quickly she can manage to get four hundred yards of fabric wrapped around me.

I've learned that just because we won't be at the airport long doesn't mean we should leave the baby bag in the car, so I shoulder that too. At least it's blue with little airplanes, so it's sort of manly-ish.

My palms are sweaty as we walk from the parking garage to the arrivals area. Lainey slips her hand in mine and gives it a squeeze. "They're going to love you as soon as they see how hard you're trying."

"Fingers crossed." I squeeze her hand back. "Should I get you a wheelchair? Do you feel well enough for this? Maybe you should've stayed in the car."

"I'm fine. Just a little tired, and this won't take long."

As soon as we're at arrivals, I make Lainey sit down. Then I find the closest airport café and grab her a bottle of water, a mint tea, and a buttered bagel to nibble on while we wait.

I take the seat beside her, adjusting Kody's legs so he's comfortable. He's also managed to pass out again. Lainey eats half the bagel before her parents arrive. Her mother and father pull her into a group hug, murmuring how much they missed her and how happy they are to be here.

I can see, in just that one hug, how much they truly do care, even if sometimes that love has been stifling for her. And I get it, because Lainey comes across as delicate at times, when in reality her innocence and sense of adventure are exactly the things that make her stronger and more resilient than people give her credit for. And if that's not convincing enough, then the fact that she came to Chicago to raise a baby on her own should do it.

Having Kody strapped to my body functions a lot like a shield.

"Oh! Isn't this a picture? All this handsomeness is almost too much to handle!" Lainey's mom pinches Kody's cheek with one hand and pats mine with the other. "And you're not bad looking either."

Her father stands behind her mother, mouth set in a grim line—at least until his gaze shifts from me to Kody, and then his eyes light right up. Lainey unstraps Kody from my body and passes him to her dad. He's not allowed to hold him very long before her mom swoops in and steals him away.

I shake her dad's hand and introduce myself, not at all surprised by his wary expression and the very tight grip.

"How was the flight?" I take both suitcases off their hands, and we head back to the parking garage.

"Well, it was just lovely. My doctor gave me something that was supposed to help with the anxiety, and it worked like magic! I wasn't nervous much at all, and I slept most of the flight because the seats were so comfy. And they served us the nicest breakfast. If I'd known flying would be like that, I would've gotten on a plane a long time ago!"

"We flew first class, Elaine. For most people it's not that nice," Lainey's dad, Simon, says.

"Well, then, I guess first class is the only way to go, then, isn't it?"

Lainey and her mom sit in the back seat. Her mom fusses over her, telling her how she looks pale, and asks if she's taking care of herself. Meanwhile, I try to drag conversation out of Simon. I would liken it to a tooth extraction, without freezing, done with a set of rusty pliers.

I ask him about his farm, which gets little more than grunts in response. I can feel the confrontation brewing.

My nerves ratchet up a few notches once we arrive at my house. I wonder if this is how Lainey often feels—and if it is, I'm even more amazed by her, because it's exhausting to be this amped up.

My house isn't ostentatious, but it's big. I've seen pictures of Lainey's family home, and while it's bigger than average—to accommodate all her brothers and sisters when they were growing up—it's a traditional farmhouse.

"Oh wow! This is just . . . a lot of house. Is it just you here?" Elaine asks as I show them through to the living room.

"For now, yes. I have a brother who lives in LA, and he often comes to visit with his wife and son during the holidays. My mom and sister will come visit as well."

"You could lose a person in here!" I'm not sure if Elaine is joking or not.

I turn to Lainey, who's propped herself up against the wall. I press my lips to her forehead. She's not warm like she was yesterday, but we've had a lot of excitement for someone who was tossing her cookies less than twenty-four hours ago. "You should lie down—you must be wiped."

"Maybe just for a bit." She gives me a grateful smile.

"Why don't I show you the bedrooms, and everyone can get settled?"

I carry both suitcases to the second floor and bring Lainey's parents to one of the guest rooms, taking Kody from Elaine. We leave them to unpack, and I shift Kody to one hip so I can take Lainey by the hand, guiding her farther down the hall. "I have something to show you."

"Okay."

I open the second door on the left and flip on the light. Lainey's palm covers her mouth, and her eyes go wide. "Oh, RJ, this is just . . . amazing."

The nursery is decorated in a hockey theme, because, well, it's my life. The crib is designed to look like a hockey rink, an idea I got from Alex and Violet, and the bedding boasts our team logo.

I set Kody in the new crib. He reaches up, as if he's trying to grab the mobile hanging over his head. "I figured it would be good to introduce Kody to hockey at an early age. Maybe he'll have the same love for it as I do. But he might be more like you, so I figured it was good to have a bit of both of us in here." I turn on the sea creature mobile and motion to the mural of Kodiak Island. It's a decal, rather than painted, so we can switch it up whenever we feel like it.

Lainey wanders around the room. She takes a seat in the glider and rocks back and forth a few times before she moves on to the dresser and changing table. Eventually she comes back to stand in front of me, eyes bright with unshed tears.

"I didn't do this because I want to take him away from you, Lainey—you understand that, don't you? I did it because I wanted you to see that I care about both of you and I want to be part of raising him. Together or apart, he'll always be ours."

She smiles, a little sad, a little wistful. "You were right, you know."

"About what?"

"You're exactly the man I thought you were."

"Is that a good or a bad thing?"

"Good. It's good." She wraps her arms around my waist and rests her cheek against my chest.

I fold her into an embrace, relieved that she's here and that she seems to understand and believe that I genuinely want to right my wrong. "I made some big mistakes, Lainey, but I'm trying my best to make up for them."

"You're doing a great job." Lainey pulls back and tips her chin up. She settles a palm against my cheek and smiles softly. "I understand it better now, why you omitted the truth at first."

"I'm still sorry I didn't tell you when I had the chance." That I missed all this time with them is a punishment I'm not sure I'll ever really get over.

"I know you are, but I can also understand how it became harder to tell me the longer we were together. And I'll be honest with you—I don't know how the version of me you knew then would've handled all of that, because so much has changed." She exhales a shaky breath. "And I'm sorry I didn't tell you about Kody right away."

"I understand why you waited. I blindsided you with the truth."

"And telling you had the potential to change my entire life, and at the time, I wasn't sure if it was going to be a good or a bad change—so thank you for being patient with me while I figured all of this out."

"Thank you for giving me a chance to prove I'm the same man I was a year ago." I press my lips to her temple and hold her, grateful for this second chance.

Since Kody seems content in his crib—for now—we leave him there while I show Lainey the bathroom connected to the nursery. There's another door leading to a bedroom on the other side, so all three rooms are connected.

"If you want to stay in here, you can." I don't want to push Lainey for more than she's prepared to give.

Lainey nods and bites her bottom lip. "Where's your bedroom?"

"I'm actually connected to Kody's room too, through the closet." It was a design feature I didn't understand at first. But I realized later that the guest bedroom I'd planned for Lainey to stay in was actually meant to be a nanny suite. I take Lainey through the walk-in closet full of new clothes for Kody to the door on the other side, which takes us to my bedroom.

She crosses over to the bed, which is exactly like the one from the cabin in Alaska. Even the comforter is the same. She runs her hand along the edge of the footboard. "What if . . . I want to stay in here instead?"

"I can take the other room if this is what you prefer."

She glances over her shoulder, lip caught between her teeth, looking shy and nervous. "No. I mean, what if I want to stay in here with you?"

I bridge the gap between us and wrap her up in my arms. "I missed you every day for more than a year. I missed the smell of your shampoo, the way you feel in my arms, the sound of your voice, the softness of your skin—and even though your dad might kill me if you stay in here with me, I'm willing to take that risk."

Lainey chuckles. "I'm a twenty-six-year-old woman—and a mother. I think we all know I'm not the innocent little girl he would like to pretend I still am. And I've missed the way my heart feels when you're close to me—so please, be careful with it this time around."

Despite the fact that Lainey might still be a little on the right side of fluish, when she tips her head back and her gaze settles on my mouth, I dip down with the intention of kissing her.

She turns her head a few inches so I make contact with the corner of her mouth. "I don't want to make you sick."

"My immune system is stacked—I'll chug a bottle of vitamin C and chase it with hand sanitizer if I need to."

Before I can make a move to kiss her properly, Kody lets out a loud cry.

Figures I end up cockblocked by my own son. "I'll get him—you lie down."

"What about my parents?"

"I can handle entertaining them. You need rest, and they'll want to visit with Kody." I make an adjustment in my pants on the way to Kody's room. I close the door behind me so Lainey has some quiet and enter the nursery at the same time as her dad. He reaches the crib before I can and picks up Kody. "Where's Lainey?"

"Taking a nap. The flu took a lot out of her."

He nods and looks around the room. "This is, uh . . . an expensive-looking room for an infant."

Kody keeps crying—not loudly, but still squawking all the same. I want to take him, but I don't want to deprive his grandfather of the opportunity to soothe him either. It's definitely not an easy situation to navigate. "Maybe we should take Kody downstairs. I don't want to disturb Lainey."

Simon follows me to the main floor. I'm not 100 percent on what all of Kody's different cries mean, like Lainey seems to be, but I can tell by the way he's bopping his face on Simon's shoulder that he's probably hungry. I root around in the baby bag until I find one of the bottles packed in the separate cooler space and put the spare in the fridge.

Simon frowns. "I thought Lainey was breastfeeding."

"She is, but she pumps so he can have bottles when he's at his day care. It also means I can be involved in feeding him and she can have a break when she needs it."

I offer him the bottle, but he shakes his head. "I never really got the hang of that."

"Doesn't hurt to give it a shot, though, does it?"

After a short stare down, he allows me to show him how to hold Kody so he can feed him. I'm a little annoyed when he takes the bottle without a problem, mostly because I want an opportunity to show Simon I'm good for more than just my bank account and my sperm donation.

"I can't believe Lainey's already working again. She should be raising Kody, not some day care provider." He adjusts his hold on Kody and shoots me a pointed glare.

I maintain eye contact, aware that looking away would be like backing down with a bear. "She likes her job." At least that's the impression I've gotten from her. I don't see why she'd move across the country and take a position like this if she didn't want to. Or maybe she felt it was the only option.

"If she came back to Washington, she could just stay at home and she'd have our help. She wouldn't need to work." He scans the living room, eyes bouncing over the expensive electronics, the leather furniture, and the hockey-themed art before they settle on me again, cold and accusatory. "I did a little research on you, son—you're making more than enough to support them both, so the question is, why aren't you?"

I knew this conversation was imminent, and I tried to prepare myself for it, but I'm not sure I quite understood the wrath of an angry father until now. "We're just getting reacquainted, and if I know anything about your daughter, it's that she's not very fond of feeling like she's being taken care of or like she's being forced into situations that are out of her control. So I'm doing everything I can, and everything she'll allow, to involve myself in raising Kody." I fight to keep my hands at my sides and not give away my nervousness by jamming them into my pockets.

Simon doesn't respond right away—processing, digesting, maybe trying to decide how sincere I'm being. "What are your intentions with my daughter?"

I have to give it to him. He's meeting me head-on, like any protective father would. I'm having second thoughts about the whole "Lainey staying in my bedroom with me" thing while Simon is in the house. He's a dairy farmer. He's had to put animals down, which means he knows how to use a gun. Not a comforting thought, really. "Well, sir, I plan to take care of Lainey and Kody in whatever capacity she'll allow me to. I've already missed Lainey's entire pregnancy and the first few months of Kody's life—I don't want to miss out on any more time with them."

He arches one unimpressed eyebrow. "You're still going to miss a lot of time, though, with how much you have to travel. Your career isn't very conducive for family life."

"I have plenty of teammates who are happily married with families."

He frowns, eyes narrowed and still fixed on me. "Is that part of your plan? To marry my daughter?"

I feel a lot like I'm standing at the edge of a cliff, waiting to be pushed over the edge. I swallow down the horrible anxiety. "If I'm going to be one hundred percent honest with you, then yes, eventually, with your permission I'd like to ask Lainey to marry me, if we get to a place where that's something she wants."

"And if she doesn't get to a place like that, then what?"

I don't like these questions, because they bring up fears that already plague me. "I'm not sure I understand what you're asking."

"What if Lainey finds someone else? What if she wants to move back to Washington and she meets someone better for her? How will you handle that?"

I blow out a breath and rub the back of my neck, my stomach twisting at just the mention of this—or the idea that there's someone better for her than me. "Honestly? I'll be devastated. Sir, I fell in love with your daughter, and I've spent the last year wishing I'd made different choices when it came to her and our relationship. But if she decides I'm not the right person for her and she meets someone else, I won't stand in the way of her happiness, and we'll figure out a way to raise Kody so he knows we both love him. Until that happens or she tells me she's not interested in trying to make this work between us, I'm going to do everything in my power to win back her heart."

He seems to relax the tiniest bit, but his face remains a stony mask. "You're going to have to do a lot more than throw money at her if you want that to happen."

"I'm aware, sir. Money can certainly make things easier in a lot of ways, but it isn't a replacement for time and love—and I plan to give Lainey and Kody as much of both as I can, in spite of the fact that my career means I can't be with them all the time."

He nods, but his posture remains guarded. "I hope you mean that, son, because I've never seen Lainey as devastated as she was when she came back from that trip, and I never want to see her go through that again. She might be strong in a lot of ways, but she has a soft heart. I won't watch it get stomped on by you or anyone else—I don't care how much money and flash you throw my way."

"I understand your reservations, and I respect that you want to protect Lainey, but I flew you out here so you could spend time with her and see for yourself that I'm head over heels in love with your daughter—and our son."

CHAPTER 25

HOCKEY HAZING

Rook

Based on Lainey's recent bout of flu and the fact that her parents are visiting, the aquarium gives her the rest of the week off. Apart from ice time and training, I spend every spare moment I have with Lainey and Kody and her parents.

They see, maybe in a way they haven't before, how incredibly competent and independent Lainey has become. I also get to see the overprotectiveness in action, and I understand better why Lainey came to Chicago.

Once Lainey's back to herself, I decide a good way to help make her parents see that Lainey will have support when I'm on the road is to invite my teammates and their families over for a dinner party. In theory it seems like a great idea—the reality is a little different.

I'm currently standing between the kitchen and the living room, trying to figure out how nearly four thousand feet of living space suddenly feels cramped. The living room looks more like a ransacked toy store than a place we can relax in.

Some of the wives and Lainey are sitting in a circle in an area that's been cordoned off with an extensive series of adjustable baby gates and fences meant to corral the toddlers and infants who are too young to go wandering around the house. It's a friendly version of baby prison.

The older ones, who are less at risk of falling down stairs or putting dangerous objects in their mouths, are in the backyard with Alex and Miller—playing hockey, of course.

Lainey's mom is in the kitchen ordering around Lance and Randy, who are currently wearing aprons and seem either too scared or too bewildered to do anything but follow her directions. I see where Lainey gets her kitchen bossiness from.

Violet is standing just outside the cordoned-off area where the infants are, talking animatedly to Simon and the wives. That could be a good or a bad thing, since pretty much whatever Violet's thinking comes out of her mouth unfiltered.

Kody has learned how to roll over, but only in one direction, so he barrel-rolls across the floor until he bumps into the barrier of the gate by Violet's and Simon's feet.

I grab a nonalcoholic mimosa, which is essentially orange juice and fizzy white grape juice, from the counter and a bottle of beer from the fridge and make my way over to them.

"Alex was so enamored with Robbie the second he popped out." Violet's eyes are wide, and she leans in. "I mean, babies are all kinda funky looking, though, right? At least at first. Robbie looked like an alien. His head was shaped like a damn cone, and he had these crazy puffy eyes. He looked like he'd been smoking all kinds of the green demon while he was waiting to ruin my damn vagina." She pats her belly. "I'm hoping this one looks a little more like a regular human than a distant relative of E.T. when he comes down the chute."

I expect Simon to look scandalized, but instead he throws his head back and laughs. "The first one always looks the strangest. After that they start coming out looking a little less squished up." He leans in and drops his voice. "Lainey came out looking just perfect right from the start. We knew we weren't going to have any more kids after Lainey, so Elaine asked the midwife to fix things up a little." He makes a hand motion below his waist.

"Oh my God, Dad! Are you serious?" Lainey looks mortified.

In Simon's defense, people have been handing him beers steadily for the past three hours, and I'm about to offer him one more.

Violet doesn't seem bothered in the least by this discussion. "Did it work? Alex wants us to have a hockey lineup, thanks to that one." Violet thumbs over her shoulder at Sunny, who is also Alex's younger sister. "I told him three is my max, because after that point I think they just kind of slide right out on a sneeze, you know?"

Simon chuckles. "It was like we were newlyweds again."

And that, right there, is far more information than I ever needed about my future father- and mother-in-law. "Anyone need a refill?" I ask, sounding a lot like a prepubescent teenager.

Simon and Violet startle a little, possibly at my squeaky voice. Violet takes the glass from me and drains it in two long gulps. "I'm so freaking thirsty all the time, but this kid is trying to use my bladder like it's a trampoline." Violet pats Simon on the shoulder and then gestures below her waist. To Simon's credit, he keeps his eyes on her face. "Thanks for the reassurance that my lady bits won't be permanently ruined, but if you could avoid sharing that story with Alex, that'd be great. I'd rather he not know I can have six kids and still be a size extra small." Violet waddles off toward the main-floor bathroom.

"She's a lot of fun, isn't she?" Simon tips the bottle back and takes a swig.

"She certainly can be. Pretty much always says exactly what's on her mind." Kody bumps up against the gated barrier, but when Lainey tries to move him back to the center of the circle, he squawks his irritation and reaches for me.

"You want to hang out with me and your gramps, little man?" I take him from Lainey, lifting him high in the air before I bring him in for a raspberry on the tummy. He giggles loudly and flails. Another, less adorable sound comes out of the back end.

Lainey glances at the clock. "I should feed him soon, or he's going to get fussy."

"How about I give him a bottle, and you can have a real mimosa and enjoy your time with the girls instead?" I offer.

"Are you sure?"

"Positive." I kiss her on the cheek, get her a mimosa, and warm up one of the bottles from the fridge so I can feed Kody. At first he used to balk when I'd try to give him a bottle, but now he's used to it. Lainey being sick, while not great for her, has been helpful in getting Kody to take a bottle easily from me. I get comfy in one of the lounge chairs, and Kody settles right in, sucking loudly.

Simon drops into the chair beside mine.

"You know, Lainey never really used to speak her mind, not until last summer. And I have to say, I think it's a good change, even if it was hard to get used to at first." Simon taps the arm of his chair and surveys the living room. "Your friends tell me a lot about who you are as a person, RJ."

"They're like a second family. Lainey won't ever be alone—even when I have to travel, she'll have people she can rely on."

Simon nods, his attention shifting from Elaine in the kitchen, trying to help Randy take the hairnet off his beard—that he let her put it on in the first place is a miracle—to Lainey and the wives laughing with each other while they take turns tickling babies. "I can see that, and as hard as it's been giving her space and independence, it's clear that it's been good for her. You're good for her." He says it almost reluctantly but with a smile that tells me I'm finally winning him over.

"She and Kody are the best thing to happen to me."

The dinner party seems to be a turning point for me and Simon. After that he loosens up and lets his guard down. We talk baseball and farming, and I take him and Kody to the arena one afternoon while Lainey and her mom are at the spa getting pedicures together.

Two days before Lainey's parents are scheduled to fly home, Elaine announces that Lainey and I need to go out on a date. "It's wonderful that the two of you are so involved with Kody, but give us grandparents a night with him and go enjoy yourselves. Take Lainey for a nice dinner and a movie."

"Are you sure? Kody can get fussy around seven, and sometimes he'll cry for an hour."

Elaine gives Lainey a look. "I raised eight children. I'm practically immune to the sound of crying. Go have fun, enjoy each other's company."

Since the get-together, Simon has lightened up a bit, so I feel a lot less like I'm walking on eggshells.

I make a reservation at one of my favorite exclusive restaurants where I won't get mobbed by fans.

One of the biggest challenges so far is finding time to be adults without an interruption. So we take the opportunity that's offered. I throw on a pair of black pants, a button-down, and a tie while Lainey gives her parents an outline of Kody's every need and want—including a rundown of possible atypical scenarios—until Elaine holds up a hand and tells her that she's pretty sure she can handle one night with her infant grandson and not to rush back.

And with that, she ushers us out the door.

We stop at Lainey's apartment so she can change into dinner-appropriate attire, since she didn't have anything formal to wear at my place. While I wait, she offers me a glass of white wine, the only alcohol she has, apologizing for the lack of options since breastfeeding and booze don't really go well together.

"You have nothing to apologize for. I'm just happy to have time with you—I don't care about your wine selection."

She disappears down the hall into her bedroom. I'd like to follow. The time with her parents has been good, but I've felt a lot like I'm back in high school being monitored. Beyond that, there really haven't been any opportunities for actual privacy, and by the time everyone is in bed, we're both exhausted.

So when Lainey appears in the hallway in a slinky black dress, asking me if I can help her zip it up, all the blood in my head rushes to the one south of my navel. The prospect of having to sit through dinner with a raging, potentially embarrassing erection is rather unappealing. And peeling her out of that dress and worshiping every inch of her becomes the only thought I can entertain.

"Rook?" Lainey snaps her fingers a couple of times.

"Huh?" She never uses my given name, so I must have missed something.

"Never mind. I'll change into something else."

"Wait. What? No. I don't want you to change. You look stunning."

She scoffs and self-consciously runs her hands over her stomach. "My body is different."

"The only difference I see is up here." I pat my pecs. "And I'm sure as hell not going to complain about that."

"You might when I'm not breastfeeding anymore and they resemble sad mud flaps."

I push out of the glider—they're ridiculously comfy and soothing to sit in—and cross over to where she's standing. "Enough with the self-deprecation. You're gorgeous. End of story. My body doesn't lie." I motion to where my pants are snug at the crotch.

Lainey's eyes dart down, and that blush I've missed so much colors her cheeks. She ducks her head. "You haven't seen me naked in a while. Nothing is the same under here."

"Is that an invitation, a challenge, or a statement of fact?"

She settles her palms on my chest, and for a moment I think she's keeping me at bay, until she says, "Can it be all three?"

"I'll accept the invitation and the challenge, but I don't think it's a statement of fact. Maybe you see yourself differently than I do." I brush her hair over her shoulders, appreciating the slight tremor and her sharp inhalation as I move into her personal space.

"You're blinded by the boobs."

"They're pretty incredible." I ease a hand up her side. "But then, so is the rest of you."

She steps into me and tips her head up. I don't need more encouragement than that. I've kissed her on the cheek countless times in the past few weeks, but this isn't the same. This is the first time I get to kiss her—*really kiss her*—since we said goodbye in Alaska.

I caress the edge of her jaw and sweep my thumb along the contour of her bottom lip, enjoying the anticipation before I drop my head and touch my lips to hers. A million memories come flooding back at her soft whimper and the bite of her nails against the back of my neck. And just like every single other kiss that's had the intention of becoming more—and even the ones that didn't—it starts out sweet. She tastes the same, feels the same—but better. She feels like *mine* and *home* and *love*.

I'm acutely aware that Kody isn't here to act as an adorable cockblocker—that we're very, very much alone—and all the tension that's been driving me crazy seems to funnel right down into my pants.

Lainey pushes her hips into mine and moans softly. Her fingers slide into my hair and latch on, and her tongue sweeps out to tangle with mine. Two or three velvety swirls quickly devolve into no-holds-barred making out. Like we're teenagers who dropped Ecstasy and can't get enough of each other.

Lainey pulls at my shirt, freeing it from my dress pants, and her hands slide up and under, roaming over my back. Then she tugs at my belt buckle, freeing the clasp.

I break the kiss, and she freezes, fingers dipping into the waistband of my pants, close to my insanely hard erection. We stare at each other for a few seconds, panting.

"Bedroom?" I ask.

"Floor, couch, kitchen counter. I don't really care."

I pick her up and wrap her legs around my waist, and we resume kissing. I'd like to say there's some finesse once we get to the bedroom, but that would be a lie. I drop her on the edge of the mattress and follow behind her as she scoots back.

Lainey's skirt bunches up, exposing the satin-and-lace panties underneath. Ones I'd like to take off with my teeth. Which then becomes part of my master plan, if I can get us to slow down from Mach 4 million to somewhere along the lines of Mach 2 or 3.

Lainey fumbles with the button on my pants while I loosen my tie and yank it gracelessly over my head. I unfasten the first few buttons on my shirt, and she drags the zipper down, the metallic vibrations making my cock twitch.

There's zero teasing involved as Lainey reaches into my boxer briefs, wraps her gorgeous, soft hand around the shaft, and sets me free. She's not even finished the first stroke before she leans in and wraps her lips around the head, sucking gently.

I groan several filthy expletives, which makes her both blush and smile around my cock. And then she takes me deeper, stroking with her hand and her mouth. She pops off for a second—likely to pull the freaking move that always makes my balls feel like they're going to explode. The one I haven't experienced in more than a year but remember so vividly it's often the image-sensation combo I pull up when I'm in self-gratification mode—so I take the opportunity to pull her dress over her head.

And then she's back to sucking me off.

I fumble with the clasp of her bra, highly distracted but very intent on getting her as naked as I am. It slides down her arms and drops to the bed between us. "God, I missed everything about you."

She pops off long enough to say, "Same," and then she's right back at it.

Once her boobs are free, my stamina takes a terrible nosedive—and I issue a warning that I'm about to come. And as soon as I do, it's like I've finally jumped off the sex speed train, able to focus again.

"Thank you. That was amazing." I lay her out on the bed, taking my time now that 90 percent of my blood flow is no longer pooled below my waist. I cup her boobs, so full and lush, and pepper them with kisses.

"Just don't squeeze too hard unless you want a shot in the face," Lainey says, somewhat breathlessly.

I laugh into her cleavage. "Can I kiss and lick?"

"Yes—everything is supersensitive, though, so just be careful."

I devote attention to her breasts, 100 percent enthralled with them and the fact that most of the time I'm not really allowed anywhere near them. Lainey writhes under me, legs wrapped around my waist, fingers in my hair.

Eventually I go lower, kissing my way over her stomach. And just like I planned, I tug her panties down with my teeth and kiss her until she comes.

She reaches over to the nightstand and opens the top drawer, rustling around until she produces a box of condoms. A spike of jealousy hits me.

Lainey puts her hand on my cheek and forces my gaze back to hers. "I bought them after you started coming over here every night. I wanted to be prepared, just in case all my restraint evaporated and something like this happened."

Relief that I don't deserve hits me, and I settle between her thighs and roll my hips. "I missed you. I missed us."

"Me too."

I open the box and tear a condom free. Lainey plucks it from my fingers and pushes on my chest. She rolls it on, and instead of pulling me over her, she settles in my lap, slowly taking me inside.

And when we're together like this, connected in the most intimate way we can be, it's like we've never been apart, like the year that separated us has been erased. We find a slow rhythm that allows us to kiss and touch and breathe each other in. Lainey comes first, and I get to watch her tumble over into bliss. I missed this with her—I missed everything in her absence, but this feeling, like my world has been tipped back into alignment, tells me what I knew then but failed to acknowledge: that she was and always will be my balance.

I don't look away from her as my own orgasm hits, and afterward we stay wrapped in each other, kissing, hands roaming, relearning each other through touch.

I cup her face in my hand and meet her stunning chocolate gaze. "I love you, Lainey."

She smiles softly. "I love you too."

"I wanted to tell you that when we were in Alaska, but I ran out of time," I admit.

"Well, you can tell me as much as you want now, can't you?"

By the time we leave her bed we're cutting it close for dinner—not that it matters, since they'll hold my table regardless. Lainey checks her reflection in the hall mirror while we wait for the elevator. "Oh my God, did you leave a mark on my neck?" She tips her head to the side and inspects the right side of her throat.

I wrap an arm around her waist and press my chest against her back. "I don't see anything, but if you want a mark I'm more than happy to put one there."

I nuzzle into her neck and nibble on the spot just as the elevator doors slide open. Lainey elbows me in the side, and I take a step back—which is when I notice Walter standing in the elevator.

229

Lainey covers the side of her neck like she's hiding something. "Walter! Hi!"

This should be fun.

"Lainey." He gives me a curt nod as he reaches out for something beside him. Which turns out to be a *someone* in the form of a petite brunette. He pulls her into his side and awkwardly throws his arm over her shoulder. "This is my cou—date, Ursula."

His "date" Ursula's eyes widen, and she looks up at him, maybe a little confused. He squeezes her shoulder, and she grimaces. "We went out for dinner, and now we're going to watch *Jeopardy!*" He turns his head to look at her. "Isn't that right, Ursula?"

"Uh, yes?" Her eyes bounce back and forth between me and Lainey, and then her brows raise. "Oh my God, is this your neighbor? The one that lives across the hall?"

"We have to go! *Jeopardy!* is starting, and we don't want to miss the first round! It was nice to see you again, Lainey." He shoots dagger eyes at me as he drags Ursula out of the elevator. "RJ."

"Bye, Walter—it was nice to meet you, Ursula." Lainey gives me raised eyebrows.

We step into the elevator, and the doors start to close, but not before we hear Ursula ask, "Isn't that Rook Bowman? The hockey player? Oh my God! I would have gotten his autograph! And is that the Lainey woman you were dating? God, she's really pretty—no wonder you're such a mess. Good thing you didn't tell your mom about her, right?"

The doors slide closed, and I hit the button for the lobby, waiting until we're moving before I speak. "Sooo . . ."

Lainey cringes. "Well, that was super awkward."

"I think more for Ursula than anyone else. I'm guessing, based on the family resemblance, she's not really his girlfriend." I tap my nose to signal what I mean, then wrap my arms around Lainey's waist and pull her against me. "Did you two watch *Jeopardy!* together?"

"Why? Does it make you jealous?"

I shrug. Truthfully, maybe a little, but mostly because I know that show is on when Lainey gives Kody his before-bed booby snacks. "Smart is sexy, Lainey—even Walter knows that."

"Do you know what I think is sexy?"

"What's that?"

"You. Especially when you're showing me how much you love our son."

I dip down and kiss her until the elevator dings.

We end up being late for our dinner reservations, but Lainey is the best appetizer—and later, when we get home, we steal quietly up to my bedroom so I can make her dessert too.

CHAPTER 26
ANXIOUS NEW BEGINNINGS

Lainey

My parents' visit is both a good and a bad thing. Good in that they see exactly how hard RJ is trying and how sincere he is in wanting to prove that he's really in this with me. But the bad comes with my parents leaving, because as much as they drive me crazy with their overprotectiveness, I miss them.

I don't miss living under their roof or having them fuss over me like I'm a helpless infant, but I miss having them close. There really isn't an easy solution either. Not when RJ plays for Chicago. He'll be on the road a lot very soon, but this is still his home base.

My dad might have asked, more than once, what I plan to do when my contract expires with the aquarium. It's only supposed to be a temporary research position, and in all honesty, I should be able to complete the research in the allotted time. Even if I take reduced hours like RJ has suggested and manage to negotiate a slightly longer contract, once it's complete, I'll need to start looking for a new job. Unless they happen to need more research on aquatic animals' mating habits that specifically relate to dolphins and whales. Which is unlikely.

Finding a new job shouldn't be difficult in a city like Chicago, especially with three master's degrees. But I don't interview all that well, since I get so nervous, and I can't be guaranteed that any other place of employment is going to be quite as accommodating as they continue to be at the aquarium. For the time being, I try not to worry too much about the things I can't control. Instead, I focus on research when I'm at work, loving Kody when I'm not, and falling in love all over again with RJ whenever we're together—which, for the time being, is often.

In the week since my parents went home, I've slept at RJ's house three times. In his bed, with him. We've had sex all three of those times.

We're currently cuddled up in his bed, Kody's asleep in the room next door, and RJ is reading hockey-related articles while I brush up on dolphin seduction techniques. Like humans, a male dolphin will present the female with a gift—but substitute a sea sponge for flowers or chocolate—in order to gain her sexual favor.

So far, when RJ tries to explain hockey to me, I feel very much like I'm being taught a foreign language. I've never really understood sports, so it's all a little over my head.

"How far are your parents from Seattle?"

I look up from the article I'm reading. "About two and a half hours, depending on weather conditions. Why?"

"Just wondering." He sets down his phone and props himself up on an elbow. "I think we need to talk about the start of the season."

"You mean the hockey season?"

RJ nods. "Yeah. Exhibition games start soon. I'd really like you to bring Kody to a practice game. A lot of the other wives and girlfriends come, and they'll bring their kids."

"Will there be a lot of people there?" My fingers are already at my lips. I've come a long way in the past year, learned how to cope with the anxiousness that results from being in places with a significant crowd.

But an arena crammed with thousands of people is not the same as the aquarium, or a full bus, or even the inside of a shopping mall—the latter of which I generally avoid if at all possible. Actually, I'd still rather avoid two out of the three most days.

"Practices are pretty chill, which is why I want you to come. I know the idea of the arena freaks you out, but it won't be crazy like it is during the regular season. Even exhibition games aren't as heavily attended. I just . . . I want you to see what it's like, so you can get used to it. And I promise it'll be fun." He looks so nervous and hopeful.

We can't just live in the tiny bubble of his house and my apartment, with the occasional dinner out or gathering with friends and a grocery shopping trip thrown in here and there. Most of our relationship has been built in a cosmos of domestic compatibility.

Hockey is his passion, his job, and the thing that drives him. It's a huge part of his life, and while I've watched games with him on TV and seen footage of him playing, it's not the same as seeing him on the ice in real life. I love the man I met in Alaska and the father of my son, but I want to be able to love all of him, even the parts that scare me—and that includes the NHL star that women drool over.

In order to do that, I need to learn how to handle the other very significant part of his life. And I'm not going to do that by limiting our lives together to the inside of a house. "I think it would be a great idea for Kody and me to come to a practice."

"Yeah?" RJ's smile is radiant.

I return his grin, although I'm sure mine is nervous instead of breathtaking, and nod. I had a great time with the girls when they came over while my parents were visiting.

RJ lifts my hand and kisses my knuckles. "I can talk to Lance and Miller—you seemed to really get along with their wives when they were over."

"You mean Poppy and Sunny? They're sweet, and you don't need to talk to Lance and Miller. I can just message the girls—we're already in a group chat. We can organize something. They've already been asking when I'm coming to a practice, so they'll be happy when I tell them the next one."

"That's perfect." He tugs on my waist, pulling me closer. "There's something else I want to talk to you about."

I sit up a little straighter, and so does he. "What's that?"

He shifts around, patting his thighs. "Come here."

I give him a look. "We had sex two hours ago."

"It's not about sex. I just want you close to me."

I'm not sure if I believe him or not, but I move to straddle his lap. He smooths his hands up the outside of my thighs and licks his lips. It's not sexual, though; it's all about nerves.

"What's going on?"

"So, I know everything is pretty new, and there's been a lot of change in a short time—maybe more for me than you—but I don't know . . . it's just . . . I'll be on the road a lot soon, which means I won't have as much time with you and Kody."

"We'll all adjust to the schedule."

He nods. "I know. So I was thinking . . . I looked into hiring a part-time nanny, someone who could take care of Kody when you're at work and I'm playing away games."

"I already have day care, and Kody does well there."

"Yeah, I know." RJ's chewing on the inside of his lip. "Kristen is fantastic with him."

"She really is." As much as I don't like being away from him, I do love that there's someone I feel comfortable with taking care of him.

"Which is why I offered to pay her double what they do if she's willing to take care of just Kody."

"You what?"

RJ holds up his hands. "Hear me out—those women don't get paid enough for what they do, and Kristen is great with Kody."

"But I like that he has interaction with other kids. That part is really important, RJ. I spent most of my time with my siblings, apart from the homeschool community events. I want Kody to have a full social life with lots of friends. I don't want him to struggle like I did, like I still do sometimes. A lot of the time," I amend.

"I totally agree, although I think you're better than you realize with people. But I also figured you would say that. Miller and Lance both live in this neighborhood. Their nannies can coordinate playdates with Kristen and Kody. He'll have lots of friends."

"But I'll have to get him here every day before I go to work. How efficient is that?" I've been spending a lot more time at his place, but we haven't really had the relationship talk. Our entire situation is unconventional, and nothing really seems to fit into a neat box where we're concerned.

"Well, that's the other thing I wanted to bring up." He keeps running his hands over my thighs. "What if you moved in? Then it would be easier all the way around, right? Especially if you'll be able to work from home sometimes and the aquarium is being flexible about your hours."

"You want us to move in with you?" Now it's my turn to be nervous. The only people I've ever lived with, aside from when RJ and I were in Alaska, are my family.

"It's a big step, but it makes the most sense, don't you think? I'm already going to miss you and Kody when I'm on the road, and when I'm home I want to be with you. I was kind of hoping you wanted the same."

Moving in with him means that slice of complete independence is gone, but at the same time, he makes a good point. We can't be partners, not the way I think we both want, if I'm living under a different roof. He wants to be part of our lives, and I want the same. And that's what love is—learning how to lean on someone else, doing it together.

"It'll be just like Alaska, except you already have friends here, and once you come to practice you'll get to know the girls better. You don't have to decide right now. I just want to make it easier for us to spend time together, as a family and as a couple. Think about it, okay?"

"Okay. I can do that."

"Good." His hands settle on my waist. "Now bring those lips here—I need a hit of your love before bed."

I lean in for a kiss that turns into sweet, slow lovemaking. It's as much a distraction from all the things RJ is asking as it is a way to show me that he loves me and needs me just as much as I'm starting to accept that I need him.

Three days later, Kody and I accompany RJ to practice. I changed my outfit an unreasonable number of times, until RJ finally told me jeans and a team shirt with his name emblazoned on the back are perfect. He's right: the arena isn't crowded with people like I've seen when I watch game reruns with him. Instead there's a smattering of observers spread out in the seats. RJ shows me around and introduces me to the players I haven't met before, which makes me nervous since it means I have a whole bunch of new names to remember. Typically I have a great memory, but when I'm nervous it can be a challenge.

I'm relieved when I start to recognize a few of the guys who came over to RJ's while my parents were visiting, and as soon as I see Sunny's blonde hair, Poppy's wavy red mane, and Violet's auburn ponytail I'm totally at ease. I'm learning, slowly, that I can't control all the things that happen in my life—but I can control how I react to them. The only way to conquer my fears is to face them with as many safety nets in place as possible.

"It's so great to see you again." Sunny gives me a side hug, since we're both holding babies. And when we try to separate, we have to untangle each other's hair from our infants' fists.

"I gotta change and get on the ice. You'll be okay?" RJ kisses Kody on top of the head and me on the lips.

Violet scoffs. Even though her husband doesn't play for the team anymore, she still likes to come to the games so she can hang out with the rest of the girls. "She'll be fine, Rookie—this is a bunny-free zone today, so we won't have to teach her how to take down a puck slu—"

One of the other women slaps her arm—I'm pretty sure her name is Charlene. "Vi, censor."

Violet cringes. "Right. Sorry. She's in good hands."

RJ kisses me one last time and disappears down the hall toward the locker room.

Violet slips her arm through mine. "We're so excited that you came today! I didn't really get much of a chance to talk to you when we came to Rook's, but your dad is great. Anyway, I wanted to tell you that we're all so glad you gave Rook a second chance, because this is pretty much the happiest he's been in over a year. You know, when he came back from Alaska last year, we were all worried about him. He's usually such a positive guy, but man, he was like Eeyore for a good six months, black cloud of doom hanging over his head."

"Really?"

"Oh yes, he was just so sad." Sunny pats her baby's bottom, and her three blond boys rush on ahead of us, along with Violet's and Poppy's sons. The three older boys are trying to keep control of the younger ones. "We all thought it was because of the anniversary of his father passing away."

"Because he used to go to Alaska with his dad and his brother, and he ended up having to go alone last summer."

"Exactly." Sunny nods. "So the guys thought it had to be that, but then he told them about you, and well, we all realized he was just heartbroken." She blinks a few times, like she's on the verge of tears. She waves a hand in front of her face. "Sorry, I'm in the first trimester, and I get more emotional than usual. I hate to see people hurting, and Rookie was down for such a long time."

Poppy gives her shoulder a squeeze. "He's really only been himself again the past couple of months."

"Since the birthday party, actually," Violet adds. "Last year he didn't date at all. He was like a monk. Worse than he was after that fake pregnancy."

"Fake pregnancy?" I remember seeing something about that in one of the many unpleasant articles I ran across when I looked him up after I found out he'd lied about his job.

"Oh yeah, like a couple years after he came to Chicago, he had this woman who was obsessed with him to the point that she faked a pregnancy. She even took plaster casts of her pregnant sister's belly and pretended she was expecting. She was all over social media with it until Rookie got his lawyer involved."

"Has anything like that happened since?" I can't imagine how I would deal with that.

"Nah. Rookie's been on the straight path for a long while, so no crazy bunny business since then. He was celibate for a good year after that went down."

"She was really crazy," Sunny adds.

"Crazier than me, even," Violet says. "Anyway, Rookie settled right down after that. And then when Alex retired, he stepped into the role of captain, and he's been pretty grounded ever since. It's hard to get in trouble when all your friends have kids and wives."

These are all the things I need to hear, I realize. It confirms again that the man I met in Alaska and the one who's come back into my life recently aren't different at all. It's just his job that's not what I thought it was. That one omission doesn't change who he is as a whole, and it doesn't diminish the connection we had before or what we're trying to build now. As I sit with these women and get to know him through them, I find myself growing more confident that I can handle this part of his life. The more I get to know him outside of our little cosmos, the more I want to make this work. And it will be a whole lot easier for both of us if I move in with him.

The transition from having my own apartment to moving into RJ's house takes place gradually, over the course of the next several weeks. I run into Walter again in the elevator, and he's sure to tell me, three times, that he's on his way over to his girlfriend's place.

Exhibition games start—those are *a lot* more crowded than practice—but I've discovered that I don't have to enter the arena the same way everyone else does. I have the option to sit behind the bench—or up in one of the private boxes.

The other wives, specifically Sunny, Poppy, Violet, Charlene, and Lily, take me under their wing and act almost like my personal bodyguards. I learn how to deal with the media—at first they're very interested in me and Kody.

RJ gives an exclusive interview explaining how we met, fell in love, and then, by the most unfortunate of circumstances, lost touch. It's all made to sound very romantic, and he paints a picture of me that I don't recognize but like all the same. He calls me brave and strong and brilliant, and I love him even more for it.

When the regular season begins, I discover how difficult it is to be without him. But at least when he's away I have Kody.

During his first series of away games we have a warm spell in Chicago, and with it comes a storm. I've come a long way in the past year with the help of regular therapy, but I doubt I'll ever be able to appreciate the beauty of a thunderstorm the way I once did as a child.

I pull all the curtains closed so I don't have to watch the lightning and thunder, change into one of RJ's flannel shirts so I'm surrounded by his smell, and check on Kody. He's sleeping peacefully.

I turn on his lullaby soundtrack and settle into the glider in his room, breathing through the anxiety, reminding myself that we're safe at home. After a few minutes my phone buzzes in my breast pocket. I slip out of Kody's room to answer the video call.

"Hey, baby, I just saw the weather—you all right?" Worry creases his forehead.

"I'm okay—congratulations on winning the game tonight." I try not to flinch at the rumble of thunder.

"Thanks. I wish I was there with you." He runs a hand through his wet hair. Based on the background, he's in his hotel room.

"Me too, but Kody's sleeping peacefully, and I'm wrapped in you, so I'll be fine," I assure him as I move the phone over my torso. When I return to my face, his expression has shifted from worry to hunger.

"Is that my shirt?"

"Mmm. It's almost like you're here with me when I can smell you." I sniff the collar, where his cologne is the strongest.

"I should start bringing something of yours to away games—maybe one of your nightshirts."

"Pretty sure that would raise a few questions with your roomie."

"Hmm. Good point."

"Speaking of, where is your roommate?"

"At the bar. I wanted to call you, maybe see if you need a sensory distraction." He settles on his bed, bare chest coming into view, a towel wrapped around his waist.

"That might be a bit tough considering we're in different states." I climb up onto our bed.

"Or it might be fun?" He cocks a brow.

"Are you suggesting phone sex?"

"Mmm. That sounds naughty, which I like, but we can also call it sensory exploration research." He tugs at the edge of the towel. "What do you think, Lainey, should we give it a shot? See if it's an effective calming strategy?"

I smile and pop the first button on the flannel shirt. "I don't see the harm in trying."

By the time we're done, the storm is long over, we're both relaxed, and I can definitely say it's an effective calming exercise.

Although Kody and I miss RJ when he's away, I have Eden and the new friends I've made to keep the anxiety at bay. I've never been much of one for social media, so I'm pretty safe from all the terrible things people post.

I've also been warned by the girls to avoid reading the comments like the plague. Well, Violet said I should avoid it like a herpes-covered dick, but I get what she means. It's rather disturbing how much people seem to love fabricating horrible stories and dragging up RJ's less-than-sunshiny past.

We persevere, though, and while I don't think I'll ever truly be comfortable in a hockey arena surrounded by thousands of RJ's adoring fans, I love watching him play and giving Kody experiences I never had when I was young.

Charlene tells me she has these great calming candies she'll be happy to share with me when we go to games, once I'm finished breastfeeding. For now I just drink copious quantities of chamomile tea and collect RJ's kisses like they're a protective and soothing balm for my ridiculous worries.

While there's lots of change, including Kody learning how to crawl before Christmas, one thing remains the same. I miss my family. They've been to visit twice more since the beginning of the season.

Kody and I flew to Seattle for Christmas, in part because RJ had games out west just before the holidays. His family flew up to Seattle to celebrate as well, so I was able to get to know them better. He's particularly close with his sister, Stevie. The two of them took Kody and

Max, his nephew, shopping one afternoon, which was super sweet. She made RJ wear a baseball cap—not Chicago inspired—and told him if he made a scene she'd leave him with both the kids.

I learned a lot about RJ in those few days. He's an incredible older brother to Stevie, and he takes the role quite seriously. And in a lot of ways he seems to want to fill the absence of his father for her. He and his brother Kyle have a great friendship. They share good-natured ribbing, and I get to hear all about what RJ was like as a teenager, so focused on hockey he didn't have time for girls—or anything, really.

He's also definitely a mama's boy in the most endearing way. It's clear in the way they accepted me so willingly and graciously into their family that they adore him, and I feel very much like I've gained another sister and brother—and a second mother.

He only had three days off before he had to leave for another away-game stretch, so his family went back to LA and I stayed put and enjoyed some time with my parents and siblings.

"I've been watching a lot more of this hockey," my dad says from his spot in the recliner. He has a sleeping Kody cradled in his arms—he's so big now, already wearing twelve-month clothing when his birthday is still months away. He's going to be like his dad, I think.

"It's exciting, isn't it?" RJ's team is playing in Colorado tonight, and he's already scored two goals and an assist. He's an incredible player, one of the best in the league, and that's not just bias talking—his stats prove it.

"Did you know there's going to be a hockey team in Seattle next year?" My dad adjusts Kody. I'm sure his arm is pins and needles, since he's been holding him like that for an hour. "They have something called an expansion draft."

I nod. "They take a player from every team in the league. Apparently the same thing happened a while back with Vegas." RJ hasn't made much mention of it, but the girls have been talking about it a lot, because they can only keep a certain number of players safe from the draft.

"It's too bad Rook has a no-trade clause—I'm pretty sure he'd be a top pick for any new team. There's also some talk that Alex Waters is looking at coaching, and those two are friends, aren't they?"

I give him a look. "How do you know all this?"

He lifts his shoulder in what's supposed to be a dismissive shrug. "Your boyfriend and I had some late-night chats while he was here. Besides, you're my baby, Lainey, and you're living with a big-shot hockey player, so sue me if I want to be in the know about everything."

"So you've become an internet stalker—is that it?"

"I think you call it research."

I laugh, and Kody stretches in his arms, smacking his lips. I check the time. I should probably put him to bed for the night, but I don't want to take him from my dad just yet.

"We miss you, Lainey, that's all. I know you've made friends out in Chicago, and that's wonderful. We don't want to stifle you, but any opportunity I see to have you closer rather than farther away and I'm going to make mention of it. Your mother is a worrier—and I'm sure that wasn't always the most helpful when you were growing up, especially after what happened in college. If you'd been in that classroom when that boy lost his sanity . . ." My dad clears his throat and smooths out Kody's hair, his voice just a whisper. "We might not have you—or this little miracle."

I push up out of the chair and hug him as best I can, considering he's stretched out in a recliner—which RJ bought for him since he loved the one at his place in Chicago so much—and holding a nearly twenty-pound baby in his arms.

"We just love you so much, Lainey, and maybe we loved you a little too hard, but we were just so scared of losing you." He sniffs into my shoulder.

I hug him like that, awkwardly, absorbing his love and his honesty, because in all the years since that tragedy happened, it's really the first time he's expressed how he felt about it. "I love you too, Dad. I know you were just trying to keep me safe, but I can't live my life being afraid of things that are outside of my control."

I release him so I can see his face. His eyes have that telltale shine to them, like he's fighting his emotions but losing. I sit on the side table next to his chair, and he grips my hand in his. "Rook is a good match for you. You're so much more . . . confident with him. Or maybe you always were, and he just brings that out in you better than we could."

"Dad—"

"I'm not being self-deprecating. I'm just reflective these days. I have ten grandchildren, and only one of my children doesn't live within a ten-minute drive. It gets a man to thinking, is all."

I laugh a little at that. "The youngest is always the wildest, or so I've heard. I'm just sowing my oats."

"If you're my wild one, I think we've done all right." He gives my hand a squeeze, and his expression turns serious. "That man worships the ground you walk on, and he feels an extraordinary amount of guilt for his mistakes—he'll do just about anything to make you happy."

"I know." I see it in everything he does for me and Kody. I feel it in his love.

"You might try to take advantage of that weakness, Lainey." He gives me a wink, and I laugh.

Kody squawks, so I take him from my dad and press my lips to his temple. "And your grandpa wonders where I get my sass."

CHAPTER 27
SHOTS, SH-SH-SH-SHOTS

Rook

I pick up Lainey and Kody at the airport in the afternoon on New Year's Eve. As soon as they're through the arrival gate, I'm all over her. "I missed you so fucking much." She doesn't even have time to give me trouble for swearing in front of Kody, because I cover her mouth with mine and kiss the hell out of her.

The flash and click of phone cameras reminds me that we're not in the privacy of our own home or bedroom, as does Kody's annoyed squawk at being ignored. I release Lainey and give her a sheepish grin. "To be continued. I'm so glad you're home."

I free Kody from his stroller and lift him into my arms. "How's my favorite little man? You take good care of Mommy for me while you were away?" I lay a noisy kiss on his cheek and tickle his tummy, making him laugh. Then I pull Lainey back in for another kiss, this time without all the tongue. "God, I love you. That was too long to be away from you."

"You've been gone longer with away games," Lainey points out.

"Yeah, but the house felt empty. It isn't home anymore without you two in it." It's the first time since she and Kody moved in that they haven't been home to greet me after an away series, and I finally understand why my teammates are always so antsy when we hit the landing strip in Chicago.

I strap Kody to my chest and take Lainey's bag so we can head to the valet, where a car is waiting to take us home. I didn't want the distraction of driving. Once we're all buckled in and on the freeway heading home, I stretch my arm across the back of the seat so I can play with the end of her braid. "Did you have a good visit with your parents?"

Lainey smiles softly. "It was great to be with them over the holidays. I think we all needed that, but it's good to be home. I'm more settled when we're all together."

I kiss her temple. "I get that. It's how I feel every time I step through the door after being away—like I'm whole again."

Once we're home and Lainey's suitcase is unpacked, we put Kody down for a nap and I spend the free time showing Lainey how much I missed every single inch of her. She's stretched out beside me, legs tangled with mine, head on my chest, following the dips and ridges on my stomach.

"This is our first New Year's Eve together."

She lifts her head and rests her chin on my pec. "I didn't even think to plan anything, with the flight home. I guess we'll be having a quiet night in, huh?"

"Well, actually, I have a proposition for you." I'm nervous, aware that what I'm about to propose might take some convincing. The team has been doing well this season, and we don't have a game until the second—which means we can go out tonight, if I can convince her it's a good idea.

"Oh? What kind of proposition?"

"So Randy thought it would be fun to go out tonight, and Alex has some connections at the Velvet Room, so he rented out one of the private rooms there for a party tonight."

"What's the Velvet Room?"

"It's a bar." I barrel on, hoping to erase the brief flash of panic on her face. "Most of my teammates are going, and all the girls will be there—Sunny, Poppy, Lily, Violet, and Charlene. Like I said, we'll have a private room once we're in there, so it'll be people you know and not a bunch of random strangers."

"What about Kody?" Lainey worries her bottom lip.

"I've already made arrangements for that. Miller's offered to have all the kids come over to his place. Kristen's agreed to help, and Lance and Miller's nannies are going to hang out and have a little celebration."

"They'll have all four of Miller's kids, Lance's son, and Kody?"

"And Robbie, Violet and Alex's son. Don't worry, they've got it covered. It'll be a fun night for everyone. What do you say?"

Lainey's fingers go to her mouth. "Will I need to dress up?"

"Yeah, but I've already got that covered. I picked up a couple of dresses in your size that you can try on. Vi and the girls have someone coming over to do hair and makeup, and they've already reserved you a space." I check the clock: she's supposed to be at Sunny's in a couple of hours if she agrees to go.

"All the girls will be there?"

"Yup, all of them."

"I've never gone out on New Year's Eve before."

"No time like the present to try something new, right?" I cross my fingers that it's something she's willing to give a shot.

"Okay." She nods, resolved at first, before she hits me with one of her heart-melting smiles. "We can go out."

"Yeah?"

"Yeah."

I kiss her—enthusiastically—and it looks like it's going to turn into a whole lot more until she realizes we're under time constraints. Parts of me are disappointed, but the rest of me is excited that she's excited, so I'm willing to delay the gratification.

An hour later Lainey is freshly showered, wearing a loose button-down shirt and jeans, and loaded down with a pile of dresses. I added them to her wardrobe this week with the help of Stevie's online shopping skills.

I drop her off at Sunny and Miller's place so she can get her hair and nails done with the girls. Violet greets us at the front door and holds up a hand when I try to come inside with Kody. "Babies and boyfriends are to head around the back. This is an adult-beaver-only zone. We'll see you in a few hours." And with that she closes the door in my face.

I drop Kody off around the back of the house where Miller's brood, Poppy and Lance's kid, and Violet and Alex's son are all hanging out with three nannies to support them. I hang out with the guys for an hour, have a beer, then go home and get ready myself.

At seven thirty all the babies are put to sleep in their various cribs and playpens, and the bigger kids are snuggled up in Sunny and Miller's little movie theater with popcorn and spill-proof cups of juice, so we head out for dinner.

We have a private room in an exclusive restaurant, so we don't have to worry about fans. Lainey looks fantastic in her slinky black dress, hair styled in a complicated series of braids that wrap around her head like a crown. I've seen her in plenty of dresses at this point but never quite this done up, and I can't take my eyes off her—or keep my hands off her either.

I'm relieved that she seems to be managing just fine, relaxed and comfortable around these women now that she's had a few months to get to know them. I've tried to ease her into my life slowly, giving her the opportunity to face some of her big fears in her own time.

After dinner we pile into the waiting limos and head to the bar. Lainey's cheeks are flushed from wine at dinner, and she snuggles into my side. "This is fun. I'm glad you convinced me to go out tonight."

I press my lips to her temple. "Me too."

A lot of the guys are probably at the club already, since Ballistic sent the invite to the entire team. Even so, we're a big group, and we draw attention. People recognize us as we're ushered past the line of people waiting to get in, and a low murmur of excitement follows us.

Lainey glues herself to my side, clutching my arm tightly as we enter the nightclub. Pounding bass greets us, and we walk down the dark, narrow hallway leading to the bar and the dance floor. There are several floors, and the room we've rented is up a level. Lainey says something I don't quite catch. I lean down as we keep moving, the bass growing louder.

We step out from the hallway into the main club, lights flashing to accompany the throbbing beat. Lainey's grip on my arm tightens even more, and I worry that this is just too much for her. That the hypothetical was much more reasonable than the reality of this situation. She's already had a long day, flying home with a baby, and now she's way outside her comfort zone with this. I don't think I should have pushed her into this. She can handle the pub just fine, but it took a few times before she was comfortable even there. When she comes to games they generally sit in the box rather than in the regular seats because it's not as overwhelming, and this . . . well, this is a million times worse than that.

It's loud, there are people packed into every inch of the dance floor, and it's slow moving through the throng of bodies toward the stairs that will get us to the second floor. I'm about to explain this to Lainey so she doesn't start to panic, when all of a sudden the music is eclipsed by the sound of screaming.

Between one breath and the next we're completely swarmed by Chicago fans. We've been having an amazing season so far this year, and publicity has been high, so going out can be an issue—but this is over the top, even for us. I'm assuming it has to do with the flowing alcohol and the celebratory atmosphere.

I attempt to put a protective arm around Lainey's shoulder to keep her safe, but she's not attached to my biceps anymore. Instead Violet, Charlene, and Lily form a protective semicircle around her and move her away from the screaming, clamoring fans.

Poppy and Sunny squeeze by me. "We've got her, don't worry."

As they move through the crowd I catch a glimpse of Lainey, craning to look over her shoulder as the girls usher her away. Her fingers are at her mouth, eyes wide with panic. She says something to one of the girls, face etched with concern, before she's swallowed by the sea of bodies.

Lance claps me on the shoulder. "It's okay, Rookie, they'll take care of her."

"But she hates crowds. I should've fucking known better. We haven't been in here for more than two minutes." My phone is in her purse, so I can't even message her to find out where she is.

"The girls have all been through this before—they'll manage. Now smile and take some selfies with yer fans."

Dressed-up women and sweaty guys surround us. Arms wrap around my waist and camera phones flash in my face as more and more people realize there's something going on that they want to be a part of. People push and shove each other out of the way. Two guys in the middle of the crowd bump chests like they're thinking about having a go at each other, while the rest of the drunken fans skirt around them.

Alex yells at everyone to calm down and take it easy as the horde of fans continues to grow. Security seems to have finally found their way to the fringe of the ever-expanding crowd, and they move people out of the way, trying to clear the congestion.

Four girls make that weird duck face and snap a million selfies with our group behind them and their flashes on, blinding us all collectively.

I blink through the dots in my vision in time to see paramedics rush by, heading in the same direction the girls went. I have no idea how long we've been stuck here, signing napkins and taking pictures.

"What the fuck is going on?" I ask Alex, who's standing right beside me.

"I dunno."

"What if something happened to Lainey? What if she's having a panic attack?" I can feel my own chest tighten at the thought of her having one without me there to help calm her.

"Let me check Violet's messages."

Security finally breaks through the crowd and makes a path for us, giving us an out. I try to head in the direction the paramedics went, but I'm too big to get through the crowd without hurting people.

"Shit, shit, shit." I run my hands through my hair, my own anxiety ratcheting up. I turn and grab Alex by the lapels of his suit jacket. "What if she's not okay? What if the goddamn paramedics are here for her? This was so fucking stupid. We should've stayed in tonight. Now she's going to be totally overwhelmed. What if she decides this is too much? What if she can't handle this part of my life? Shit. *I* can't even handle it right now!"

Time seems to move too quickly and too slowly. I have no idea how long it's been since the paramedics came through. They could've gone out a back way with her.

Alex claps me on the back of the neck. "Take a breath, man. It's not always gonna be like this. The girls are with her, and they're not going to let her go anywhere without you. Violet says they're not in the bathroom anymore."

"Where the hell are they?"

"It looks like they're in the private room now."

My throat feels tight as I follow the security detail—which we probably should've had right from the start—up to the second floor. The private room overlooks the dance floor and is full of my teammates. I frantically scan the room for Lainey, but it's dark, and everyone is freaking bigger than she is. I finally spot Violet in her red dress and beeline for her. "Where's Lainey? Is she okay?"

"She's right over—" Violet thumbs over her shoulder, and I don't even wait until she's finished speaking before I head in the direction she pointed.

I find Lainey in the corner over by the bar, flanked on either side by Sunny and Poppy. I grab her and pull her against my chest. "I'm so fucking sorry. We can go home. I didn't think it was going to be so intense. I'm so sorry."

She's rigid in my arms, and I'm terrified that I've fucked this all up, that it's too much too soon and that I've undone all the progress we've made with one stupid decision. She puts a hand on my chest and pushes, so I reluctantly release my hold on her and step back. My anxiety is through the roof, and I finally have some inkling as to how she must feel when things get totally out of control for her, because I feel like everything is out of control for me.

"Take a breath." Her warm, soft hand smooths up my chest.

"I'm so sorry. I didn't think. Let's go home. We'll use a back exit."

"RJ, I'm fine." She settles a palm on my cheek, and I cover it with my hand, keeping her connected to me.

"But we were swarmed." I run my free hand down her arm and search her face and any other exposed skin for marks or bruises or any other sign that she's been harmed in some way. "And then I couldn't see where you'd gone and you have my phone and there were so many fucking people and I didn't know where you were." Jesus. I think I'm losing it right now.

"Hey, hey." Lainey takes my face in both her hands. "Deep breath, baby. I'm here, and I'm fine." She wraps her arms around my neck. "Looks like my big teddy bear needs some safety cuddles."

I pull her against me, not really caring if I look weak or like an idiot, because she's right. I need her—to feel her and know she's safe and here. I bury my face against her neck and work on calming the hell down. "I thought this was going to be too much for you, and then you'd leave me."

She keeps her arms draped over my shoulders but leans back, forcing me to lift my head. "Why would I leave you over something like this?"

I keep my arms locked around her waist so she can't go anywhere, not that it seems like she's planning to. "I just . . . I thought it would be too much like what happened when you were in college, and then you'd decide you couldn't handle it, or me, or my life, and then you'd say forget it."

She fingers through the hair at the nape of my neck. "You do realize how completely irrational that is, right?"

I actually didn't realize that at all until she pointed it out just now. "I panicked," I say meekly.

"I panic all the time, and you still love me, don't you?"

"You're way more chill than you used to be."

"That's because I have you and your safety cuddles and Kody and all of these amazing people who love and support me. It's going to take a hell of a lot more than a swarm of fans to get rid of me, RJ." She tips her chin up, looking for a kiss.

I drop my head and steal a long one. "I love you," I tell her when I finally come back up for air.

"I love you too. Now, let's do some shots."

CHAPTER 28

QUESTIONS

Rook
Three months later

Every time I open my underwear drawer I break out in nervous sweats. It makes me respect my girlfriend, the mother of my child, and future wife even more, because a lot of things make her feel this way and she always powers through.

"So, are we planning a wedding or what?" my sister asks.

"I haven't asked y—"

A loud bang interrupts me, like something metal hitting the floor. "Did you finally propose?" my mother yells enthusiastically. I spot her as an indistinct blur moving around in the kitchen.

I give my sister a look—she could've warned me that our mom was listening in. She gives me her *I'm sorry* face, but it's not very convincing.

"He hasn't asked yet, Mom," Stevie supplies for me.

"Oh. And here I was getting all excited for nothing," she calls out.

"You two could try getting excited about the fact that playoffs are coming up soon and Chicago is currently number one."

Stevie rolls her eyes. "I've been shopping for my disguise just in case Mom and I end up needing to come visit for the finals this year."

There's noise in the background, and my mom asks something I don't catch.

Stevie smirks at whatever she said. "Mom wants to know what's the holdup on the marriage proposal—and frankly, so do I. You've had that ring for months now."

Awesome—now both of them are getting on my ass about this. "I'm waiting for the right time."

"And when will that be? When you knock her up again?" My mom's sass is second only to Violet's.

Stevie snickers. "Nice burn, Mom."

"I don't think the two of you living together out there in LA is good for you."

"Don't try to change the subject." My mom's face appears beside Stevie's, and she pins me with a look. "And Stevie is probably moving in with her boyfriend at the end of the summer, so I'm going to enjoy what's probably going to be the last time I have a fun roommate."

"Whoa. What? Moving in with your boyfriend? What the hell? Why don't I know about this?" Stevie usually tells me everything, even the stuff I probably don't want to know.

"Because I don't actually know if it's going to happen." Stevie pokes our mom in the shoulder. "I need to know what my summer plans are going to be, and you need to stop dragging your ass, because I'm banking on a short engagement so you and Lainey can get busy making more babies for me to love."

"You realize that this is a super uncomfortable conversation to have with my mom and sister, right?"

"You tried to have the sex talk with me two years ago, like I was still fifteen, so this is payback. Stop waffling and just ask her, dammit."

"I'm not waffling. I'm just trying to figure out the best way to ask her. And I want to make sure she's ready."

Stevie arches her brow. "You have a baby together, you live together, the last time we visited she was talking about how she thinks it would be best to have kids close together. I'm pretty damn sure she's ready."

"I'd like to have more grandchildren," Mom adds. "And it would be great if you could have a wedding before you give me another one. I'd also like to request a granddaughter if at all possible."

"First, let's get him to propose, Mom." Stevie grins evilly as Mom wanders back to the kitchen. "Look, Lainey doesn't need some big grand gesture. She just needs you to ask so she can say yes, and then we can start planning, and you two can have more babies or whatever. I say go with simple. Maybe do that thing where they put the ring in the bottom of a champagne glass or something."

"What if she chokes on it, though?" Mom asks.

"It was just a suggestion." Stevie slaps her thighs. "What's the thing that's most symbolic of your relationship?"

"Kody." That's a no-brainer.

"So include him somehow. He's the reason you're together, so make him part of it."

"That's actually a great idea." Simon and I have had similar conversations over the past few months. I asked him back at Christmas for permission to marry Lainey, and since then he's been on me about when I'm popping the question. He's also mentioned the expansion draft quite a few times, and often those two conversations happen at the same time.

Stevie smiles and bats her lashes. "See? Not just a pretty face."

"You've always been more than a pretty face, Stevie."

"So are you, RJ."

We all laugh, and I promise to call when I've popped the question, which hopefully will be tonight.

I end the call and exhale a long, slow breath. I've put off this conversation long enough. Lainey's contract with the aquarium is up in three weeks. It's already March, and playoffs are around the corner. And after that the expansion draft picks will happen.

One of our team members will go to Seattle. If Lainey agrees with my plan, it'll be me.

I've just finished getting dressed and styling my hair when I hear the alarm buzz downstairs, signaling Lainey is home. I find her in the front entryway, trying to get Kody out of his snowsuit before he takes off down the hall. He's definitely my son. He has two speeds: fast and faster. He was crawling by six months, standing by eight, and walking by nine. Now he's bumbling around like a drunken, miniature frat boy. He's also in the 99th percentile for height and weight, meaning he's going to be a big boy, just like me.

"Da!" he yells. He starts flailing, batting at Lainey's hands, when he sees me. I'm not sure if he's actually calling me *Dad* or if he's just making noise because he can, but I'm going to pretend it's the former.

Lainey raises her hands in defeat, and he rolls over, then pushes himself to a stand. He looks like an overstuffed marshmallow, his arms sticking straight out as he bumble-weaves over to me. I crouch down and put my arms out, ready to catch him. He makes it halfway before he falls, but he doesn't give up. He pushes back up unsteadily and stumbles the last few steps into my arms. "Good job, little man!"

I lift him into the air and make airplane sounds. He giggles and squeals. I tuck him under my arm like a snowsuit-covered football and close the distance between myself and Lainey.

She has one arm out of her jacket and one still in. I slide my fingers into her hair, tip her head back, and kiss her—with tongue—while Kody wriggles and laughs under my arm.

I release her and take a step back. "Hi."

"Hi, yourself." She arches a brow and shrugs the rest of the way out of her jacket. I set Kody down on the mat and help him out of his snowsuit. Once he's free, he plunks himself down on the floor and starts going through the contents of Lainey's purse, which would be fine if he didn't try to shove everything into his mouth like it's food.

"Give that to Mommy." Lainey plucks a lip balm from his chubby fingers. He yells his displeasure until she replaces it with a soft hockey puck. It immediately goes in his mouth.

"He must be teething again."

"He's chewing on everything these days—like a little beaver, aren't you?" Lainey picks him up and tickles his side, heading for the living room, which has slowly been overtaken by his toys.

We're in the process of trying to divide the space so the whole thing doesn't look like some kind of toddler amusement park.

Lainey sets him down in front of one of his educational toys that lights up and flashes . . . and plays annoying music, but he loves it and it keeps him entertained while we make dinner, so we deal with the noise.

"How was your afternoon at the spa?" Lainey went with some of the other wives. She deserves the break, because she moms it hard-core most of the time.

It's been baby steps all the way: getting her used to worrying less about finances, infusing her into my life and my world, acclimating to the media attention. I don't think that's something she'll ever be particularly comfortable with, but she seems to be handling it well, as long as I don't throw too much at her at once.

She holds her hands out and wiggles her fingers. They're painted Chicago colors.

I take her hand in mine and kiss her fingertips. "I like these."

"I bet you do." She steps into me, lowering her voice. "And I bet you can't wait to see what they look like when they're wrapped around your cock later."

I can feel my eyebrows trying to hit the ceiling. She's certainly not wrong, but Lainey generally isn't quite so boldly explicit. She bites her lip, and her cheeks flush pink. I smirk and say nothing, waiting.

"Violet told me to say that," she blurts.

"That sounds about right. You can tell Violet thanks for the hours of discomfort I face as a result, since I have to wait until Kody's in bed to have that experience."

She makes a face and looks over her shoulder to where Kody is happily playing, not getting into trouble. "We could put him in his room for ten minutes."

I laugh. "I think I'll take the prolonged anticipation, but I appreciate your thoughtfulness. Maybe we can get him into bed a little early tonight."

"I'd like that." She smooths her hands down my chest with a soft sigh, then steps back, aware if we keep touching and teasing each other we're setting ourselves up for quick and dirty later, and that's not part of my plan for tonight.

Lainey and I fall into our usual dinner routine, which means she tells me what to do and I do it while simultaneously getting all up in her personal space.

She stands in front of the fridge, bending to grab something from the crisper, so I take the opportunity for what it is and move in behind her. When she rights herself and steps back, she collides with my chest. I take the bag of carrots from her and kiss her neck. Lainey relaxes against me, tilting her head to the side, so I kiss all the way to her earlobe before I toss the carrots on the counter.

When she opens a cupboard to get a measuring cup, I step in and grab it for her. We move around each other, stealing kisses and furtive touches the entire time. Dinner prep is our foreplay.

"How was your meeting with your agent this afternoon?" Lainey asks as she sets the frying pan on the burner and brushes by me so she can get to the spice cupboard.

I pause in my carrot-chopping mission. "Good. I have something I want to discuss with you."

She sets the ground ginger on the counter and turns to face me. "That sounds serious."

I tug on her apron—team themed—and pull her closer. "It's not serious *bad*. I just have some options I want to run by you."

"Okay." She glances over at Kody. He's chewing on a book. It's meant to be chewed on, so she refocuses on me.

"So we've talked about the Seattle expansion draft . . ."

She nods. "A lot of the girls are speculating who they're going to keep safe. You have a no-trade clause, which makes you one of the nine."

"That's right, unless I opt to waive the no-trade clause for the expansion draft."

Lainey's eyebrows pull together. "But why would you do that? You're team captain, and you love it here."

"My contract expires in two years—I'll be traded eventually. I talked to my agent, and if I waive the clause, Seattle will pick me up."

Lainey chews her bottom lip. "Is that what you want?"

I pull her lip free from her teeth. "We would be closer to your family."

She flattens her palm against my chest. "But these guys are like your family. You have years with them."

I cover her hand with mine. "They're not my partner, though—you are."

She nods slowly. "I'm just getting used to everything here. If you're traded, we'd have to move at the end of the season, wouldn't we?"

"The timing would be good, though. Your contract with the aquarium is up soon. I'm sure they'd be happy to renew, but I also know you want to work on your PhD. And being in Seattle would make it a lot easier to see your family."

Understanding hits her, and she crosses her arms. It would be cute if she didn't look so irritated. "That can't be the reason you waive your no-trade clause. I won't take you away from your family so I can be closer to mine."

"You miss them."

"We can't jeopardize your career and everything you've worked this hard for just so it's easier for me to see my family until you get traded again."

I pick her up and set her on the counter. "First of all, going to Seattle won't jeopardize anything. And this isn't just about my career or me anymore, Lainey. This is about what's best for you and me and Kody, the three of us together. And if being closer to your family would be better for you, then it automatically makes it better for Kody and me."

"You'd have to leave all these people you care about."

"Not all of them." I curl my hands over her knees. "Alex and Violet are going to Seattle."

"They are?"

"This isn't public yet, but they're signing him as the head coach. He knows the general manager of the team personally. They want me. Players get traded all the time, Lainey—people come and go. A lot of contracts are up in the next year or so. If you say yes to this, my agent is ready to make a call. He's already been in talks with the owner in Seattle. They want to sign me for five years, and they're offering an extra million a year as incentive—but money aside, it would be a good move for us as a family."

"How long have you been thinking about this?"

I part her legs and step between them so I can get a little closer. "A while."

"It's a big change, RJ." She links her hands behind my neck, fingers sliding into the hair at my nape.

"Only for one of us. You're the one who's had to deal with the most change between us. Look, Lainey, those six weeks we had in Alaska were the best I'd had in my entire life, and the year that followed was dark without you. Having you back, falling in love with you all over again, and Kody for the first time, it's made me a better man." I clasp my hands behind her back so I can feel anchored.

"I want us to do this together. Make decisions together, figure out life and how to parent and how to get our kid to eat green things. I want to love you. I want to get razzed by your brothers at Christmas dinners. We'll be closer to both of our families, since mine is on the West Coast too. It makes the most sense, doesn't it? If you want to stay here, then the no-trade clause stays in effect—but if you want Seattle, then I lift the clause and we go."

"You're sure?" She bites her lip.

"Positive. Whadya say?"

"I say . . . let's go to Seattle and start a new team."

Lainey pulls me in for a kiss that lasts until Kody comes up behind me and hugs my leg, reminding me that we have a few hours before we can celebrate this decision privately.

I pick him up. "We're going on a new adventure, little man."

He pats both of my cheeks and grins, as if he understands. Lainey gets him a piece of frozen fruit stuffed inside a little mesh bag to chew on while I help get his dinner ready.

After we eat, I decide if we're celebrating one thing, we might as well celebrate two. Lainey's agreed to move to Seattle, so I'm pretty confident that means we're in it for the long haul.

"I'll take Kody up and get him ready for bed." I kiss the top of her head.

She drops a tea bag in her mug and looks up at me. "I can do that."

"I've got it. You enjoy your tea—we'll be down in a few to say good night."

She smiles up at me. "Thanks."

I take him upstairs, change him into his jammies, and make a stop in our bedroom. "I need your help tonight, little man, okay?"

"Da!" He shoves his fingers in his mouth.

I slip my hand under a pair of socks and find the box. Closing the drawer with my hip, I take a deep breath. I've practiced this a million times over the past couple of months, what I'm going to say, how I'm going to do this. But my family is right—I don't need a grand gesture, because that's not what Lainey likes.

She likes simple and thoughtful.

I flip the box over between my fingers and take Kody back downstairs. Lainey's tucked into the corner of the couch, reading a magazine.

I set Kody on the floor and hold up the small box, tied with a white ribbon. "Can you give this to Mommy?"

I pass it to him, not sure if handing something like this over to an eleven-month-old is actually a good idea or not. The first thing he tries to do is shove it in his mouth.

I pull it away from his mouth. "Take it to Mommy."

I point at Lainey, and he bumbles his way over to her, holding the box in one fist. "Ma!" I follow behind him and make sure he doesn't try to eat it again.

She sets the magazine on the table and uncrosses her legs. Sitting forward, she holds out her arms, ready to catch him if he falls. "Hi, baby, you look like you're ready for bed. Do you want Mommy to come up and tuck you in?"

He waves the box around in her face, and her gaze shifts from Kody to me. She tips her head in silent question.

"Give the box to Mommy." I drop down in front of her and help steady Kody's hand—sort of, since mine is shaking too.

"What's this? My birthday isn't for another two months."

"It's not a birthday present. Go ahead and open it." I set Kody on my knee.

There's a wet spot on the box and some teeth marks, but that's par for the course around here these days.

The ribbon unfurls as Lainey tugs the end. I kiss the top of Kody's head as she opens the lid, my stomach in knots, my palms sweaty. She withdraws the tiny velvet box inside.

"RJ?" Her eyes are wide and already hazy with the promise of tears. I love that about her, that I can see her emotions play out on her face as she experiences them.

Kody grabs for the pale-blue box, so I give him the pieces and set him on the floor. He plops down beside me—not the best wingman, but he isn't even a year, so I can cut him some slack. He slaps the two pieces together and squeals with delight.

"Let me." I turn the velvet box toward her and flip it open. The light on the side table hits the diamond, making it glint and throw prisms on the floor, which Kody tries to catch, giggling happily.

"Oh!" Lainey's hand flutters to her mouth, and she seems caught somewhere between laughter and tears.

"I love you, Lainey—both of you, so much. I thought those weeks in Alaska with you were the best of my life, but I was wrong. Every day with you beside me is better than the last, and I promise I'll spend the rest of my life loving you—all you have to do is say yes. Marry me?"

The sound that comes out of her is definitely half laugh and half sob. "Yes. A million times yes. I love you, and I can't imagine my life without you and Kody."

I slip the ring out of its cushioned home and slide it onto her finger. Lainey throws her arms around me and kisses my neck, my cheek, and then finally my lips, whispering *I love you* over and over.

Kody uses my knee to pull himself to a stand, shouting, "Ma!"

We both laugh, and I know that—despite the lack of romance— this is exactly the kind of proposal that works for us, because Kody is part of every single equation.

We take him up to bed. When he sees the ring on Lainey's finger, he tries to pry it off, and when that doesn't work, he tries to put her hand in his mouth.

Lainey holds his favorite teddy bear in front of him as a distraction. He grabs for it and cuddles it to his chest. We kiss him good night, put on his music, and turn on the night-light before we leave his room.

"This is beautiful. It's exactly what I would have picked for myself," Lainey says as we uncork a bottle of champagne so we can have our own private celebration.

I debate whether or not I should take the credit for it. "Remember when I took Stevie shopping over the holidays?"

"She needed something for some kind of event, but you came back empty handed."

"I may have lied about that."

"I figured it was just an excuse for the two of you to get some time together."

"Well, there was that too. But really I wanted her help picking out the ring. It was between that one and another one."

"You're so sneaky." She grabs the front of my shirt and pulls my mouth down to hers. "I can't believe you've been holding on to this for months!"

"I was just waiting for the right time to ask. I wanted to make sure you were ready."

"Still, that's a long time to hold on to that. And I can't believe Stevie never said anything."

I laugh. "She knows better."

Lainey bites her lip, a coy smile turning up the corner of her mouth. "You know, if we're being completely honest with each other, I have something I should probably tell you."

"Oh? What's that?"

"Remember that time you taught me to drive when we were in Alaska?"

"Of course." I had a hard-on the entire time. Lainey behind the wheel of a pickup is sexy as hell.

"So, I told you I didn't have a license, not that I didn't know how to drive."

"I don't understand."

"I used to drive my dad's pickup all the time. I just never bothered to get a license, because I didn't like freeway driving—and you were so excited about teaching me, so I didn't want to ruin it for you, or me, really."

I wrap an arm around her waist and pull her tight against me. "Now who's the sneaky one?"

"It was a little white lie."

"I guess that means we're even, doesn't it?" I drop a kiss at the edge of her jaw.

"Mmm. A lie for a lie. I think we're all done with those, aren't we?"

"Definitely. But this one served a purpose. Are you ready for a little private celebration, future Mrs. Bowman?"

"Very ready."

I spend the next hour showing Lainey with actions, and words, exactly how much I love her, and that I never want to be without her, ever again.

EPILOGUE

LIFE IN TRAINING

Rook
Four months later

Lainey's fingers are in my hair, tugging gently as her hips move in tandem with my tongue. Tomorrow I'm making her my wife in the same location I fell in love with her: Kodiak Island. So tonight we're having a little precelebration.

Well, actually, in about an hour Lainey's parents and my mom are coming over so Lainey can have a night with her girlfriends, and I'm going out with the guys. Bar options are limited out here, so we're going to have a campfire and drink some beers at one of the cabins down the road. It's the same place Lainey first stayed, except I bought it, demoed the cabin, and had a brand-new one built. It might be a little overkill, but I wasn't sure my family's four-bedroom cabin was going to be enough for us—and I'm planning to spend a good part of my summers here, so I might as well have room for my extended family and friends. The new cabin has eight bedrooms, eight baths, two kitchens, two great rooms, and a massive dining room. It also has a guesthouse with three bedrooms.

Lainey's family and my family both fit there. Our friends from Chicago and a few of the guys from Seattle that I'm already close with have rented out the majority of one of the lodges not too far down the road. The move to Seattle has been good for Lainey and me, and while I'll miss the guys in Chicago, having Alex as my coach and Lainey's family close by has been amazing. Even better, my sister is moving to Seattle for a job, so we'll each have family close by.

I'm already getting settled in with my new team, and most of the guys are great. Apart from a couple of pains in my ass, it's been a pretty smooth transition. Being captain of a brand-new team is daunting, but it's also inspiring. It was a position I almost didn't get, thanks to some hotshot named Bishop Winslow, but in the end it worked out for me. But more importantly, Lainey is happy in Seattle, and so is Kody.

And right now, based on the little whimpers and moans of encouragement, my almost wife is *definitely* happy.

One of Lainey's hands disappears from my hair to grab a pillow, which means she's about to come and she wants to muffle the sound because she's afraid she'll wake Kody. She's not particularly loud in bed, but I'd like to finish what we've started without interruptions, so I don't stop her.

Thirty seconds later her inner thighs clamp against my head, blocking out all sound apart from the rush of blood in my ears as she comes. As soon as her legs relax again, I kiss my way up her body and settle between her thighs, easing inside.

"The next time I make love to you, you'll be my wife."

"You're a sexy fiancé, but you're going to be an even sexier husband." She pulls my mouth down to hers, licking inside on a low moan— partly because I'm filling her up, but also because she loves kissing me after I've gone down on her. For as sweet and sheltered as Lainey once was, she's an adventure in and out of the bedroom, especially these days.

I move over her, matching the roll of her hips as I cradle the back of her head.

"I'm so glad you came back to me," I say against her lips.

"We came back to each other."

We kiss and cling and moan into each other's mouths. Lainey does that thing with her tongue that always amps me up, and I shift her right leg, tucking her knee against my ribs so I can hit the spot that makes her whimper my name and dig her nails into the back of my neck.

"I love you so much." I push up on my forearm, aware that she's close to coming again, and I want to watch it happen, because the next time it does she'll officially be mine forever.

She touches my cheek, eyes soft and full of need. "And I love you." Her soft gasp is followed by "Oh God" and my name. It isn't until the stiffness in her body eases and her hips stop jerking into mine that I change the tempo, moving faster, chasing my own orgasm.

She drags her nails down my back. "Let me finish you on top."

I love it when she says things like that. I don't know what it is about the phrasing, but it intimates a possessiveness that sets me off. I roll onto my back, taking her with me. She splays her hands out on my chest and rides me, hips moving in a figure eight, keeping me deep for several beats before she rises up and her ass settles on my thighs, breasts bouncing, long hair swaying down her back.

She leans down, back arching, nipples brushing my chest. "You're so beautiful." She bites my bottom lip. "And you're all mine." She grinds over me, hard and steady, squeezing me from the inside. "Every part of you is mine, just like every part of me is yours."

I grab her by the hips, sit up, and wrap her legs around my waist, lifting and lowering her, faster, harder, until her mouth drops open. "I'm right here," she whispers against my lips. "Come with me."

This time we fall through the clouds one right after the other.

We stay wrapped in each other, kissing, hands caressing, for long minutes. At least until both of our phones start going off. Now that we have Kody, I upgraded the service.

We grab them, clear our throats at the same time, and laugh against each other's shoulders as we answer our respective calls.

I can't hear the conversation on Lainey's end, but based on her responses I'm pretty sure the questions are the same.

"She's yours forever as of tomorrow—you can survive without her for one night."

My brother has a point—we're leaving for Hawaii in two days for a weeklong trip. The grandparents are going to take care of Kody and enjoy Alaska and the cabin.

"I'll be ready to go in fifteen minutes," I tell Kyle before I end the call.

Lainey lifts off, and I groan at the cold air that's nothing like her warm, wet softness.

She presses a kiss to my lips. "Less than twenty-four hours and you get to have me again."

"Forever."

"And ever."

We change into jeans and matching plaid shirts, because we are totally that couple. They also say *Groom to Be* and *Bride to Be* on the back. I open the window to let in a little fresh air and to help get rid of the freshly fucked scent in our bedroom.

Lainey absently runs a brush through her hair, grinning devilishly as the curtains flutter with a cool breeze. She's about to make a pithy comment, based on her expression. At least until something white skitters out from under the bed and across the floor. She yelps and clambers up onto the unmade bed. It's unnecessary, since it's just a piece of paper, not a mouse—which I've discovered she's fine with when they're outside, but not so much in the cabin. I bend to pick it up, recognizing Lainey's distinct handwriting. It's dated the day after I left Alaska, two years ago.

RJ,

    A storm took out the power and the phone lines were all down until this morning. I waited as long as I could

to hear from you. Even if you don't get this for another
year, know that this isn't where I want us to end, so if you
feel the same way please call me.
  Yours,
  Lainey

"It was here the entire time." It must've fallen on the floor and ended up under the bed.

"What was?"

I hold it out to her, and she takes it, her smile soft and sad as she realizes what it is.

She places a gentle hand on my cheek. "We made it back to each other—that's all that matters now."

I pull her into my arms, grateful that fate found a way to bring us back together. We stay that way for a long while, just holding each other, until static brings the baby monitor to life. We both look at it at the same time. Kody sleeps through the night most of the time, so we don't need it like we used to—but the little dots are jumping all over the place, signaling sound, so she turns it up.

"What's he doing?"

We can hear him babbling in his room—but there's another sound, a whoosh-clunk, like maybe he's hitting the side of his crib with something.

"I hope he hasn't managed to get out of his crib—I'm so not ready for that." Lainey turns on the video monitor.

He's only fifteen months old, but he's done everything early—and I mean everything. From his physical capabilities to words, this kid has hit the genetic jackpot. He's got his mother's incredible brain and determination and my size and athleticism. He's going to have the world in the palm of his hand, especially with a mom like Lainey to keep him in line.

"Oh my God, you need to see this." She motions me over and turns the video monitor so I can see.

Kody is still in his crib. At one end is his teddy bear with the Bowman jersey—it goes with him everywhere—and Kody is standing at the opposite end, holding the little hockey stick I bought him, playing with the puck, shooting it down to the teddy. We watch him shoot, toddle down to his bear and pick it up, then move back to the other end and do it all over again.

"He wouldn't let it go when I put him to bed, wanted to sleep with it. Now I guess we know why."

"Pretty sure this one is following in his daddy's footsteps." She tips her head back so she can aim her smile at me.

I slip my arm around her waist and splay my hand out over her flat belly. "Maybe he needs a little brother or sister to play with."

"I'll stop taking my pill so we can start filling up the bedrooms as soon as I'm Mrs. Rook James Bowman."

Lainey

I can't stop smiling, or crying, and we haven't even said our vows yet. Thank God for waterproof mascara.

Eden hands me yet another tissue, and RJ takes my hand in his, giving it a reassuring squeeze. His eyes are full of the same emotion as mine, but he manages not to let his leak out.

We watch as RJ's sister, Stevie, guides Kody, who is our ring bearer, down the aisle to us. It's a small wedding, just our immediate family and close friends. Well, as small as it can be with seven brothers and sisters on my side and a few of RJ's current teammates from Seattle, as well as the ones we've stayed close with from Chicago. Having people stare at me makes me anxious, but I've learned how to manage it this year.

Kody looks adorable in his tiny little black tux, bumbling happily toward us with a big grin on his face. Eden tries to take the pillow with the rings, but he clutches it to his chest and yells, "Mine!"

It takes some gentle coaxing from me and RJ to get Kody to let us claim the rings. Then, when our mothers try to lead him to the chairs in the front row, he calls out, "Mama! Dada!" and reaches for us.

"It's all right—all my vows today include Kody." RJ scoops him up, and I flank him, wrapping my arm around Kody as well.

He keeps playing with the flowers in my hair while the minister has us say our vows, and he pokes RJ in the nose more than once when he sniffles. And when the minister says, "You may kiss the bride," Kody presses a warm palm against each of our cheeks. We follow our own kiss with a big sloppy one on both of his cheeks. His giggles of pure joy set off a chain reaction in the guests.

Kody is the reason I ended up in Chicago; he's the reason I gave RJ a second chance. He showed me what real love looks like, the unconditional kind and the forgiving kind, and the kind that transcends time and distance and leads two hearts back to each other.

My heart is stronger for having been broken and healed by the man who gave me my greatest love. And from here, we get to watch it grow together.

ACKNOWLEDGMENTS

Sebastian and Kidlet, thank you for being such an amazing support system, for loving me, and for giving me the opportunity to follow my dreams. I'm so very lucky to have both of you.

Kimberly, you're far more than an agent. Thank you so much for the time, care, and energy you put into helping me make sure this was the best possible book and for helping find the perfect home for this story. It's an honor to work with you and call you my friend.

Lauren, Lindsey, and the entire Montlake crew, thank you for making this such an amazing, fulfilling experience from concept to publication. It has been an absolute joy to bring this project to fruition, and I can't wait for the next one.

Deb, there really aren't words for how much I love you. Thank you for always being there and for making my world a better place with your friendship.

Leigh, thank you for always having words of encouragement when I need them the most and for being such a fabulous, inspiring friend.

Huge love to my family for being my biggest fans and cheerleaders. Sometimes I'm mortified that you read my words, Mom, but thank you for being so proud. I'm so lucky to have your love.

Sarah P., everything is always so seamless with you. You're far more than a PA: you're a friend, and I couldn't do it without you. Hustlers, your positivity and excitement are so infectious—thank you so much for all your love and support.

Endless love to Nina for all the time and energy and insane organization it requires to help launch a book.

Jenn, Sarah, Brooke, and the team at SBPR, thank you for being so amazing and for making sure things run smoothly when I can't. I love that you're part of my tribe.

Gel and Sarah, you do such beautiful graphic work—thank you for sharing your talent with me.

Readers, bloggers, and bookstagrammers: thanks for being so passionate about the written word and about sharing your love of reading and stories, for getting excited with me, and for sharing that excitement with this amazing community.

Thank you to my author friends in this community who are always such cheerleaders for each other. I am so fortunate to be part of such an incredible group of entrepreneurs. Deb, Leigh, Tijan, Kellie, Ruth, Erika, Susi: You inspire me with your passion and dedication and your continued unwavering support. I adore all of you. To my real-life friends who know what I do and get it—Marine, Julie, Kathrine, Laurie, and Jo—thank you for reminding me that there's a world outside my head and making sure I come up for air every once in a while.

ABOUT THE AUTHOR

Photo © 2018 Sebastian Lohnghorn

New York Times and *USA Today* bestselling author Helena Hunting lives on the outskirts of Toronto with her incredibly tolerant family and two moderately intolerant cats. Helena writes everything from contemporary romance with all the feels to romantic comedies that will have you laughing until you cry.